Malpractice

Don Morse

PublishAmerica

Baltimore

ISBN: 1-59286-864-9
PUBLISHED BY PUBLISHAMERICA, LLLP
www.publishamerica.com
Baltimore

Printed in the United States of America

Dedication

This book is dedicated to William Morowitz, M.D., who planted the seed that sprouted into this multifaceted tale.

Acknowledgments

Special thanks to: my loving wife, Diane, for giving me the time and support to complete this book and for her excellent proofreading and advice; and my daughter, Caryn, for her input about dentist-dental staff interrelationships. Thanks also to: Flo Herring and Marvin E. Herring, M.D., for information about Japanese dolls; Dr. Herring and Charles Kastenberg, M.D., for medical advice; Attorney Joseph S. Caruso and Attorney Marshall Harris, for legal advice; Agent Harry Keogh, for malpractice insurance information; and Mike Bortnicker, for his helpful suggestions.

PROLOGUE

"Nitrogen is colorless and invisible. You can't smell it, and it definitely can't be tasted. Nitrogen is all around us. Almost eighty percent of the atmosphere is saturated with it. Nitrogen, in fertilizers, helps feed us. Nitrogen in explosives kills us. Nitrogen, in nitrites, gives us cancer. If we breathed pure nitrogen, we'd be dead. Yet we can't live without it. In one form or another, nitrogen infiltrates every tissue in our body."

It was a warm, humid Friday evening in June of 1963. Inside a small meeting room at the New York Sheraton, the air was delightfully cool. Dr. Stephen Carrol, one of the disciples of the renowned Dr. Harry Langa, was delivering the opening speech to a group of dentists. They were taking a three-day course on nitrous oxide/oxygen conscious sedation — putting patients into a state in which they are partially awake, deeply relaxed, euphoric and able to reduce or eliminate pain. After discussing the attributes of nitrogen, which is a component of the air the participants were breathing, he continued his lecture by talking about oxygen. "Oxygen, in some ways, is similar to nitrogen. Both are invisible, colorless, odorless and tasteless gases. But there's less oxygen around. There's only about twenty percent in air. From our first breath to our last dying gasp, we do everything we can to force that small amount into our lungs. Oxygen is found elsewhere as well. It's part of the water we drink and the carbon dioxide we breathe out. Oxygen also has its problems. Automobile exhaust fumes and cigarette smoke fills our lungs with deadly carbon monoxide, which is another oxygen compound. Even pure oxygen can be deadly. If we breathe too much of it, we get giddy.

If we take in too much oxygen over the years from smoking, overexercising, eating fatty foods and being in polluted environments, our body breaks it down to form an excessive amount of free radicals. Those free radicals can lead to cancer, initiate heart disease and make us old before our time. That's true, too much oxygen can reduce our life span."

Dr. Carrol took a sip of water and continued. "Life is a constant battle between good and evil. This is true for simple chemicals such as nitrogen and oxygen. In the 1770s, while the colonists were fighting for their independence from England, a chemist named Joseph Priestley was tinkering around, and he discovered oxygen. He was also fooling around with nitrogen. He found out that when nitrogen was mixed with oxygen in the proportion of one nitrogen to two oxygen molecules, a new gaseous compound was formed. He named it nitrous oxide. The medical authorities of the time attacked nitrous oxide with a vengeance. They claimed that it could cause diseases such as cancer, scurvy, leprosy, and plague. Not everyone believed those learned doctors. One adventurous researcher named Humphrey Davy decided to breathe in this 'deadly' gas. Instead of getting sick, he felt great. Warm, tingling sensations and feelings of lightness, giddiness and relaxation spread over his body. His hearing became sharper, and he felt as if he was floating. Davy started to laugh. In essence, he felt euphoric. Davy gave the supposedly lethal nitrous oxide a new name, calling it 'laughing gas.' Later, Davy tried the gas on volunteers. One of his volunteers was the famous poet, Samuel Taylor Coleridge. After inhaling nitrous oxide, Coleridge wrote, 'I experienced the most voluptuous sensations. The outer world grew dim and I had the most entrancing visions. For three and a half minutes I lived in a world of new sensations.'"

Dr. Carrol was having a new sensation, a dry throat. He took another sip of water, cleared his throat, and continued. "Soon, it became fashionable at dinner parties and other gatherings to inhale 'laughing gas.' Showmen began to travel throughout the country, stopping off at towns and villages to lecture on and demonstrate the joys of 'nitrous.' After awhile, they dispensed with the lectures and just had 'laughing gas' parties. Up to this time, it was only the pleasurable and unusual sensations of nitrous oxide that were noted. However, one day when Davy was suffering from a severe toothache and gum disease, he tried the nitrous oxide on himself. He wrote, 'On the day when the inflammation was the most troublesome, I breathed three large doses of nitrous oxide. The pain always diminished after the first four or five inspirations; the thrilling came on as usual, and uneasiness was for a few minutes swallowed up in pleasure.'"

Dr. Carrol paused for another sip of water, which was swallowed out of need, not pleasure. He then continued. "A few years later, a dentist named

Horace Wells attended a 'nitrous' party during which he saw a 'gassed' druggist jumping for joy. The druggist accidentally struck his leg on a wooden couch. His leg bled profusely, but he showed no indication of being in pain. That triggered a thought for Dr. Well's; *Why not have a tooth extracted under the influence of this gas?* Wells then had his own badly decayed tooth extracted by a colleague, Dr. John Riggs. Upon recovery, Dr. Well's remarked, 'It's the greatest discovery ever made! I didn't feel it so much as the prick of a pin!'"

The audience was silently attentive. Dr. Carrol continued. "Nitrous oxide, when combined with oxygen, then began to be used for general anesthesia. Yet nitrous oxide had its problems. Only a narrow margin exists between anesthesia and asphyxiation.

Without adequate oxygen, the patient can go into respiratory failure and die. Too much nitrous oxide can cause vomiting. In addition, an excess can cause the over-gassed patient to become violent."

Dr. Carrol reached for the glass of water and knocked it over. It smashed to the ground throwing shards of glass onto the stage. "Speaking of violence." He paused and laughed.

The audience responded with raucous laughter and applause.

Dr. Carrol continued. "In time, more predictable and potent anesthetics took the place of nitrous oxide and oxygen in the operating room. However, a pioneering New York dentist named Harry Langa discovered that nitrous oxide's relaxing, fear-reducing and euphoric properties, along with its ability to decrease pain, would be great for dental patients. It could also work without putting the patients completely out as occurs with general anesthesia. 'Nitrous' soon became popular with dentists and courses such as the present one began to spring up. With more general use, the public gave nitrous oxide/oxygen conscious sedation other nicknames aside from 'laughing gas.' They called it 'sweet air' and 'nap a minute.'"

A young, enthusiastic, New York University College of Dentistry graduate named Artie Rosner was in the audience that day. He had closed down his Mount Laurel, New Jersey practice for three days to attend the course.

On Saturday, the course participants observed demonstrations of nitrous oxide/oxygen conscious sedation. Sunday morning, they paired off in twos and used the "nitrous" on each other. After lunch, Dr. Carrol was demonstrating a chemical experiment in which nitrogen was mixed with oxygen to form nitrous oxide. The two gases had been combined, and the dentists were invited up to smell the "sweet air." As he approached, Artie Rosner lit a match for a cigarette. He tripped on the microphone wire, lost his balance, and fell into the experimental table.

"Aaaah!" he screamed as the flames engulfed his right hand.

The glowing match had fallen into the nitrous oxide-containing flask, which had just been unstoppered. Nitrous oxide supports combustion. That afternoon, it did so with a vengeance and the entire table went up in flames. So did Artie's right hand. Quick action by a couple of the dentists rescued Artie and doused the flames. Artie was taken to a nearby hospital Emergency Room, where he was treated for the severe burn. Fortunately, he did not lose function of his hand but subsequently was left with a large, ugly scar. Dr. Artie Rosner learned his lesson about the effectiveness and dangers of nitrous oxide. It was a Sunday Artie would always remember.

Stimulated by what he had learned during the "nitrous" course, Dr. Rosner ordered a unit. Ten days later, Artie watched with admiration as a worker from Atlantic Dental Supply and Manufacturing Company delivered a nitrous oxide/oxygen general anesthesia machine that had been converted for conscious sedation use. Because of the accident, Artie was unable to practice for over a week, but the burned hand motivated him to stop smoking and to stay alert at all times.

1

It was forty years later, and Dr. Artie Rosner had become one of New Jersey's dental pioneers in the use of nitrous oxide/oxygen conscious sedation. He became a disciple of Dr. Carrol's, and after the renowned practitioner died, Artie was one of three dentists who regularly gave nitrous oxide/oxygen conscious sedation courses. This allowed Artie to frequently get out of the stress from being a dentist and visit interesting places. He gave at least a dozen courses a year throughout the country. He also gave "nitrous" courses in Canada, Mexico, Bermuda, and a few European countries. The only downside for Artie was that whenever he was under stress, his right hand "remembered" with a sharp attack of excruciating pain. Fortunately, that didn't happen too often. Artie was a relatively calm person. He also stayed alert both inside and outside of practice and as a result had no other personal injuries or untoward results with patients.

Artie had found "nitrous" to be a great practice builder. It was especially effective with children. The kids were able to take all kinds of imaginary trips. They took rocket ship rides to the moon, Mars, outer space and even to other universes. Some accompanied Alice in Wonderland on her many adventures. Others went flying with Superman or soared with Batman.

In no time at all, Dr. Rosner was able to move out of his one-treatment room office into a separate building with a three-treatment room office along with two private offices, a lounge, a large laboratory, three lavatories and an expansive reception room. Dr. Rosner used the largest treatment room. He had a number of associates throughout the years that used the second treatment room. His current associate was Dr. Mark Procter. The third treatment room was used by Kathy Perrin — his present dental hygienist. The original converted "nitrous" unit was still in use, but Dr. Rosner had purchased an additional unit. It was a "fail-safe" nitrous oxide/oxygen conscious sedation machine that was used by his associates. Dr. Rosner was most familiar with the converted unit, so he was the only one to use it for conscious sedation cases.

It was 4:55 P.M. and the five o-clock patient, Dominic Hall, had just entered the reception room. Wednesday was a usual day off for most physicians, dentists and other healthcare practitioners. It was no exception at the offices of A.S. Rosner, D.D.S. at 100 Main Street in Marlton. The single-level, red brick building was part of a medical complex housing dental specialists, physicians of a variety of specialties, an optometrist, a podiatrist and a chiropractor. A well-established contracting firm that either sold or rented the individual professional buildings built the entire complex. Behind the buildings was a large parking lot.

Today, Dr. Procter had the day off. He spent it, as usual on rain-free days, at the Mt. Laurel Golf Course. Dental hygienist, Kathy Perrin, was also off. Her day was spent at the Cherry Hill Mall with Meredith Thomas, Dr. Procter's dental assistant. Artie Rosner, being a displaced New Yorker, followed the style of New York practitioners who took Friday as their day off. Nevertheless, Dr. Rosner didn't want to work too hard on Wednesdays. He kept the office open only for emergencies. So far, today had been a relatively easy day with only five patients showing up.

In five minutes, Dr. Rosner would be seeing his last patient of the day. Artie was now sixty-four years old and hoping to retire in a few years. He figured he deserved it. After all, he had worked hard all his life, married his childhood sweetheart, Marlene, and kept himself in reasonably good shape. Artie was about five foot-nine, weighed approximately one hundred sixty-five pounds, with just the start of a beer belly (although he rarely drank any alcoholic beverages). He had the typical middle-aged male bald spot, and his hair had more gray than black.

The Rosners couldn't have any children and weren't inclined to adopt. Fate struck Artie a cruel blow nine years before when Marlene died from uterine cancer. It had been a prolonged sickness that drained Artie physically, psychologically and financially. Artie had planned on purchasing his office building, but because of financial restraints he continued to rent. Marlene was all he had lived for and when she died, he suffered a severe depression.

For several months, he could only work one or two days a week. With the help of his psychiatrist and antidepressants, Artie got out of his depression.

He then purchased a medical insurance policy with a long-term rider. He didn't want a repetition of what happened with Marlene. He worked fewer hours, giving his associate more time. During the last few years, Artie changed his method of practice. As a result, he only performed the kind of dentistry that for him was not stressful. Most of the procedures he did were fillings on adults and full and partial dentures.

Dr. Rosner was fortunate that his newest associate, Mark Procter, took care of all the other procedures. Dr. Procter had a flair for surgery, root canals and bridgework and liked to treat children. Artie was pleased that his next patient, Dominic Hall, only needed an amalgam filling. Dominic, a middle-aged unmarried plumber, was a dental coward. He always got "nitrous" and with it, he was a reasonably good patient.

The receptionist, Phyllis Romaine, an attractive blonde in her early fifties, opened the movable window between her desk and the reception room, and said, "Hi, Mr. Hall. The doctor will be right with you."

At two-minutes to five, Julie Parsons, Dr. Rosner's dental assistant, entered the reception room and escorted the patient to Treatment Room No. 1.

Throughout the years, Dr. Rosner had made it a point to hire attractive dental employees. He had been brought up in the era when physical appearance was considered to be a major employment criterion. Although he was now aware that this was chauvinistic and discriminatory, he still liked to surround himself with beauty.

Even though he considered other factors such as intelligence and secretarial and clinical skills, he still hired relatively good-looking women. After all, he rationalized, attractive women often relax apprehensive patients. Dr. Rosner paid good salaries along with substantial health benefits. Hence, he had no trouble finding the type of staff he preferred. His current dental assistant, Julie Parsons, fit his requirements to a "t." She was twenty-five years old with a model's figure and looks.

As he was being seated in the dental chair, Dominic said to Dr. Rosner, "Yuh better get me good and numb. I got a big cavity and I know it's gonna hurt unless I'm really numb. But before yuh gimme that needle, I wanna get real deep with the 'happy gas.'"

"No problem, Dominic. We'll take real good care of you," Artie countered.

Julie placed the dental drape around Dominic's neck and then positioned the "nitrous" mask over his nose. Taking into consideration Mr. Hall's two hundred pounds on a five-foot nine-inch frame, Dr. Rosner set the indicated gas mixtures. He started off by giving fifty percent nitrous oxide and fifty percent oxygen with the goal to eventually get to an eighty percent nitrous oxide to twenty percent oxygen mixture. That setting supplies the twenty percent oxygen that is needed for proper breathing. The eighty-twenty mixture is usually effective to get a person into a deep state of relaxation, decrease the perception of pain and give a happy, if not euphoric, feeling. From previous experience with Dominic, the expectation was that in a few minutes, the nervous patient would be calm enough to get a painless block injection to numb the lower left second molar.

Dominic's eyes were closed, but he was still fidgety — kicking his feet out and crossing his arms over his barrel chest. Observing those movements, Dr. Rosner increased the gaseous mixture to sixty percent nitrous oxide to forty percent oxygen. A few minutes later, Dominic was motionless. The dentist then asked him to open his mouth.

The patient complied and said, "Hey, doc. I'm still not floatin.' Yuh, better up the gas before yuh gimme that needle."

"Sure, Dominic," Dr. Rosner replied as he increased the nitrous oxide to seventy percent. After a minute or two, Dominic Hall appeared calm. Dr. Rosner then examined the decayed tooth and took two x-rays: a bitewing — to determine the extent of the tooth decay; and a periapical film— to see if there was any bony infection present.

Using a rapid developing solution, in three minutes Julie was able to show Dr. Rosner the x-rays. Holding the films to the view box, Dr. Rosner observed from the periapical film that no bony infection was present. The bitewing x-ray showed him that the decay was deep, but it was not yet into the "nerve."

Dominic still appeared quite relaxed. "Julie," called out Dr. Rosner, "please give me a block injection. Mr. Hall's got no allergies or medical problems, so we'll use lidocaine with epi."

Julie Parsons handed Dr. Rosner a two-by-two sterile gauze pad and a cotton swab with topical anesthetic on it. With the gauze pad, he wiped the areas behind the last left molar tooth and the inside of the left cheek. With the cotton swab, he then applied the topical anesthetic to those two areas. Dominic moved slightly, but said nothing.

Taking no chances, Dr. Rosner left the topical anesthesia on the injection sites for a couple of minutes. He didn't want Dominic to feel the injection pinches.

Artie returned the used pad and swab to Julie. In turn, she gave him one carpule of the local anesthetic solution so that he could effectively numb the tooth completely. Dr. Rosner began to inject the solution.

Dominic screamed out, "Damn! That hurt. I'm not out enough. Get me deeper. Geez!"

Slightly shook-up, Dr. Rosner slowly removed the injection needle and increased the nitrous oxide to eighty percent, the maximum safe allowance. He waited about thirty seconds.

Dominick looked deeply relaxed.

Artie started the injection again.

Dominic didn't move.

That was good. It indicated to Artie that Dominic Hall was in a state of conscious sedation. Dr. Rosner injected deeper.

Julie was watching. Everything appeared to be going fine. In a few minutes, Dr. Rosner would begin drilling, and it wouldn't be too long before they'd be through for the day.

Suddenly, Dominic Hall ripped off the mask. "You bastard!" he screamed. He lunged for Artie and caught the dentist around the neck with his two powerful hands. Julie looked aghast at the patient. Dominic's pupils were huge. His eyeballs were rolling rapidly. He was breathing heavily.

Artie couldn't breathe. He felt as if he were dying. His face turned white.

Julie screamed. Phyllis ran into the room. The two woman jumped on Dominic Hall, trying to pry him loose.

Their repeated pounding had its effect. Dominic slightly loosened his grip on Artie and flailed away at the women. Julie fell on top of Phyllis, and they both landed on the hard floor.

By this time, Artie recovered somewhat. He turned toward Dominic and swung wildly with his right hand. It was a lucky punch that landed on his patient's jaw. Dominic staggered for a minute and hobbled out of the office. "I'll get you for this, you son of a bitch," he shouted as he exited the front door.

Everyone was bruised. Artie was in the worst condition. His throat was killing him, but at least he was alive.

"What was that all about?" Phyllis asked.

"Yeah, what happened?" Julie chimed in.

"Dominic Hall went into the excitement stage," Artie mumbled. "He got too deep; really strange. I mean, he got the standard dose. No one's supposed to get into excitement unless the 'nitrous' is increased above eighty percent."

"It wasn't. I was watching. You only gave him eighty percent," Julie added confidently.

"Who knows? Sometimes people react differently."

"What is the excitement stage?" Phyllis asked.

"I'm not in the mood to lecture," Artie answered.

"I'm sorry, doctor," Phyllis said apologetically.

Thinking it over, not wanting to upset his capable receptionist, and recovering somewhat by now, Artie said, "It's all right. Look, this is what happens. First comes conscious sedation — like twilight sleep. Then as the 'nitrous' is increased, the excitement stage comes and lastly general anesthesia. That's when the patient is unconscious."

"You mean," Julie asked, "that in order to get into general anesthesia with nitrous oxide and oxygen, a patient has to first get violent?"

"It doesn't happen often, but with some patients they pass through this excitement stage before they go out completely."

"Will he remember it?" Phyllis questioned.

"Some do, some don't" Artie answered.

"Thank, God, he was the last patient," Phyllis said. "I'll go back to the front desk and reconfirm tomorrow's patients."

"Do that, Phyllis." He paused a moment and then said, "First, I want to say something. I don't expect any repercussions from this, but would both of you please do me a favor?"

"Sure, doctor," they said simultaneously.

"I've been using 'nitrous' for about forty years and nothing like this has ever happened before. I wouldn't want people to become afraid of using it. Please don't tell anyone about this."

"You can count on me," Julie said.

"Me, too," Phyllis added.

"Thanks." Turning to Julie, he said, "Can you clean up the room?"

"Just give me a couple of minutes," she replied.

"Take your time. I'll be in my private office."

Dominic Hall staggered as he walked into the parking lot to find his car. His mind wasn't clear, but he knew that the dentist had hurt him real bad. "I'll kill that bastard," he muttered to himself as he entered his late model Buick Riviera. He opened the locked glove compartment and reached inside.

Five minutes after he left, Dominic Hall got out of his car, staggered through the parking lot and reentered Dr. Rosner's office. He was brandishing a pistol. "I'm gonna get you, you son of a bitch!" he screamed.

Seeing him enter and hearing his threat, Phyllis ducked under her desk. She had never been so frightened in her life.

Julie heard the loud screaming. She was petrified. *What am I going to do?* she thought. An answer came quickly. She hid in the darkroom.

Dominic kicked a reception room office chair and entered the hallway. "Where the hell are yuh, doc?" he screamed.

Dr. Rosner was in his private office. Hearing the ranting and raving patient, he locked the door. A few years before, Artie's office had been robbed. The robbers didn't take much except for drugs and a computer. After that happened, Artie purchased a Colt 45. He now unlocked the desk door and recovered the gun. He didn't know what was going to happen, but he was prepared.

Dominic passed by Dr. Rosner's private office. He saw the door was locked; he heard the movement inside. "Come out, you bastard!" he screamed.

That was the last thing Artie Rosner was going to do. He moved to the left side of the door in case Hall had a gun and was going to use it. Artie didn't want to be in the line of fire.

Dominic fired several shots at the door.

Phyllis heard the noisy patter, but didn't panic. She pulled the office phone down to her and called 911. After the response, she nervously said, "A patient has gone crazy. He's got a gun and is shooting."

"Where are you?" the officer inquired. After Phyllis responded, he added, "We'll be right over."

Phyllis hung up the phone and prayed.

Artie now knew Dominic Hall had gone overboard. The "nitrous" had triggered it, but the guy was now out of his mind. He loaded his pistol, cocked it and was ready for anything.

The door lock was broken. Dominic pushed it open. He was in a serious excitement state but was alert enough not to just barge in.

Artie was now partially hidden on the left side of the door. He had never fired a gun before, having missed both the Vietnam and Korean Wars. Artie was anxious but tried to calm himself.

Dominic looked to his left. He didn't see Dr. Rosner. As he turned toward his right, out of the corner of his eye, he caught a glimpse of the dentist. He didn't wait a second. He fired.

Artie felt the bullet enter his left thigh. Reflexively, he fired his gun just as Dominic turned toward him.

The bullet went straight into Dominic Hall's heart. He didn't know what hit him. He died immediately.

Seeing what happened and feeling the intense pain in his thigh, Artie fainted.

Once there was silence, the women ran into Dr. Rosner's office. Thinking that both men were dead, they screamed uncontrollably. The office reverberated with the intense sound.

The police arrived within minutes. Julie and Phyllis were sobbing, but now they realized that Dr. Rosner was not dead. The police questioned the three of them about what had occurred; the three versions were nearly identical. The patient received a normal dose of nitrous oxide and oxygen, but still he went into the excitement stage. He ripped off his mask and almost choked Dr. Rosner to death. He then pushed the women to the ground, and was hit in the jaw by the dentist. He hobbled out of the office cursing Dr. Rosner. A few minutes later, he came back with a loaded gun. He fired several shots at the dentist's private office door. Then he opened it up and fired at Dr. Rosner. The dentist returned the fire and killed the patient.

"Looks to me like it's a case of justifiable homicide," Lieutenant Marv Homer said to Sergeant Harvey Fox. "What do you think?"

"No doubt," the sergeant answered. He then called for an ambulance to take care of Artie and the deceased patient.

A few minutes after sworn statements were taken from the three, the ambulance arrived. It was later determined that Dr. Rosner's wound was not serious although he might be hobbling for quite a while.

A subsequent police investigation confirmed Lieutenant Homer's preliminary conclusion, and Dr. Rosner's killing of Dominic Hall was deemed justifiable homicide.

Dr. Mark Procter had to work extra hard for the next few weeks, taking the load of the entire practice, but within a month Artie was back in full swing. The only physical result for Artie was a slight limp of the left leg that lasted for a few months. Mentally, he relived that day for almost a year. Nevertheless, he continued to use his "nitrous" machine with many patients. Everything went as smooth as silk. Then something else happened to take his mind off the death of Dominic Hall.

2

Almost one year had passed since the tragic incident with Dominic Hall. The end of May was approaching and it had been a warm and rain-free month. On this Wednesday, the weather in South Jersey was typical. Consequently, Dr. Rosner was far from thrilled knowing that his first patient was that difficult ten-year old boy, Freddie Glaser. The young Glaser never took care of his mouth and only came in when he had a toothache. From last night's emergency call to his home, the dentist knew that Freddie had been up most of the night with a severe toothache. It was difficult enough for Artie Rosner to treat children of any kind, but an unmanageable kid was just what he didn't need. However, Freddie was the son of one of his best friends, Bernie Glaser.

Artie Rosner and Bernie Glaser had been childhood buddies. They had lived in the same neighborhood in the Bronx, both went to Dewitt Clinton High School and City College of New York, and both landed in the green pastures of southern New Jersey. However, their career paths diverged. While Artie was going to NYU dental school, Bernie went to the University of Pennsylvania, majored in business and later became an independent speculative investor.

Being aware that he had to work on Freddie, Dr. Rosner had a reliable ally, "nitrous." This morning, he was going to use "laughing gas" to control the difficult child. Although his associate, Dr. Procter, always used the fail-safe "nitrous" machine, Artie Rosner felt more at ease with the converted general anesthesia unit. He had no qualms about using the older machine because it had worked perfectly for him for so many years. The one problem case — that was last June — was no fault of the machine. Dominic Hall just had a bizarre reaction to a normal dose. Artie thought, *soon that Glaser kid will be off on an imaginary spaceship ride.*

Yesterday afternoon, Freddie Glaser got off the school bus. Fifth grade had been boring as usual. Freddie didn't care about the day's classroom lesson: the bones and the muscles of the human body. But he loved to skin small animals and look at their body parts. He figured he was doing mommy and daddy a favor. They were always complaining about how the rabbit ate the flowers and the squirrels ate the bird food. And that rat scared mom half to death. He was helping them out by getting rid of those horrible little beasts.

One thing Freddie learned at school was how to throw a baseball. That came in handy with his rock throwing. He became an expert at hurling missiles at fleeing animals. Once he incapacitated them, he performed his surgical work in the woods around the lake. Mommy and daddy never went there, and they were out of the house a lot. That gave him plenty of time to figure out killing and maiming strategies. Freddie also took great delight in pulling out limbs, antennae and wings of all kinds of insects.

Like everyone else, he hated cockroaches, but he believed that all bugs and insects were made to be destroyed.

He got his tools — pliers, scissors and hammers — from daddy's toolshed, which was near the lake. Freddie's greatest pleasure was in catching a butterfly and pulling out its wings. After he maimed the creatures, he would use daddy's hammer to smash the bugs to smithereens. Whether he destroyed a rabbit or a small army of cockroaches, Freddie gathered the remnants in one of daddy's discarded cigar boxes and then unceremoniously dumped the contents into the lake. He would laugh and think, *good food for the ducks.*

Freddy never told his parents about his actions, but he told his school chums. Most thought him weird, but a few occasionally joined him in his sadistic activities. A couple of the kids told their parents and through the adults, the Glasers found out about Freddie's cruel acts. The Glasers tried to stop him. Freddie acted repentant, but it was only a cover. He merely became more careful, and he ceased boasting to his friends. His parents thought he had stopped, but they considered that even if he hadn't, he was not harming other children. Freddie was their only child — for them, a late in life miracle — and even though he committed destructive acts, the Glasers believed that he would outgrow this phase. So they ignored his aggressive behavior and stopped harassing him.

Aside from the usual childhood diseases, the only untoward medical complication in Freddie's life was a fleeting epileptic-like seizure at the age of six months. It had occurred during a high-fever spike from a viral infection.

The pediatrician told them that although there was no evidence of brain damage, the child should be checked regularly and might require medication to prevent future seizures. Bernie Glaser did not go along with the pediatrician's advice believing the seizure was a once-in-a-lifetime event. The evidence seemed to bear out Bernie's contention because Freddie never had another seizure.

At 3:30 P.M., Freddie entered the family's magnificent ranch home with its beautifully manicured lawn and picturesque gardens. In the kitchen, his mother was ready with milk and cookies. She was aware of sugar and tooth decay, but she knew how much Freddie loved candy and cookies and felt she had to give in to his craving for sweets.

"Hi, Freddie. How was school today?"

"Great, Mommy," he replied while thinking, *it sucked.*

"That's wonderful. After you finish the milk and cookies, please put the glass and plate in the dishwasher. Try not to make any crumbs. I've got to go out for a little while. You'll stay here, won't you?"

"Sure, Mommy."

Pauline Glaser was a petite, middle-aged, attractive brunette with light brown eyes and pleasant features. As she was leaving, Pauline put on her coat and called out, "I'll be back by five. Be a good boy."

"So long, Mommy, I'll be fine." Freddie quickly devoured the milk and cookies. He had a "sweet tooth," but this time the chocolate chips got embedded in an open cavity. Freddie started to scream for Mommy, but she had already left.

"Damn, tooth!" He forgot about putting away the dishes and ran upstairs. He knew he wasn't permitted to take any medication by himself, but he was in a lot of pain. *Heck*, he thought, *they'll never know about it.* So he grabbed two aspirins and downed them with a little water. There would be no looking for little beasts today. Freddie went to his room and lay down in bed. At first, he had trouble resting. The darn toothache wouldn't go away. Finally, the aspirins started to work, and he was able to close his eyes. When he got up a while later, the pain was still there, but at least it was tolerable.

Freddie hated to go to the dentist. The sight of that balding dentist with his long needle and the drill was revolting. But the laughing gas was all right; too bad it was just a tease. Anyway, it looked like he would have no choice. He checked the clock on the wall. It was 4:45 PM. Since the pain was subsiding, Freddie decided to watch some TV until his mother returned.

Maybe, I'll be lucky and the toothache'll go away. If not, I'll let Mommy make the appointment.

Bernie Glaser was sixty-three years old but was in much worse shape physically than his friend, Artie Rosner. Bernie was taller and heavier. He had all his hair, but the stress of being a successful entrepreneur had turned his hair stark white. In order to consummate all the deals, he had to wine and dine his clients and that led to a large stomach and flabby backside. Some of his enterprises were quasi-legal, but that didn't faze Bernie. What was important to him was making money, and he had been very successful at that. After work, when Bernie got home, he was too tired to exercise and besides, exercise never appealed to him. Even though his weight had shifted and grew since his college days, Bernie still kept his good looks. His blue eyes and pleasant-sounding voice charmed secretaries and clients alike.

During the week, Bernie was at his office at 8:00 A.M. promptly. When he wasn't out of the office with a client, he worked through lunch — downing a sandwich and a soda while continuing to work. Unless he had an evening appointment, Bernie liked to get a head start on the rush-hour traffic. He made sure that he finished his work by a quarter-to-five. His office was only twenty minutes from his Medford Lakes, New Jersey home. If there were no traffic problems, he was generally home by a little after five.

One hour-and-twenty minutes after Freddie had turned on the TV in his bedroom, Bernie walked into the house. He entered the kitchen and saw the empty glass and plate.

He cleaned up the crumbs and deposited the dishes in the dishwasher. *Doesn't that kid ever clean up his mess?*

Bernie walked into Freddie's bedroom.

"Hi, Daddy," Freddie called out.

"Don't you have any homework?" Bernie questioned.

"I did it already," Freddie lied.

"Well, I'm sure you can do something more constructive than just watching crap on the tube. For a starter, you could have cleaned up your mess in the kitchen."

"Gee, Daddy. I'm sorry. I was gonna do that but I had a terrible toothache."

"If that's the case, I'll call Dr. Rosner. We might still be able to catch him in the office."

"That's all right, Daddy. The toothache's just about gone."

"I'm no doctor, Freddie, but something caused the pain. It'll come back."

"Could we just wait 'till Mommy comes home?"

"Okay, but I want you to at least do some reading. That's more important than watching TV."

"Gotcha, Daddy."

Pauline ran into a bit of traffic and didn't get home until 5:15. By that time, Freddie's tooth had calmed down, and he didn't bother telling Mommy about it. Since Freddie wasn't complaining, Bernie didn't say anything about it either.

Dinner was a roast beef meal with all the trimmings. The Glasers were still into eating fatty meat and didn't concern themselves with fat and cholesterol. Dessert was a rich chocolate cake. Sugar didn't faze them either.

Freddie loved chocolate cake, but he was afraid that some of it might get into that cavity and then the tooth would hurt terribly. With that in mind, when a piece was offered to him, he said, "None for me."

"How come?" Pauline asked, surprised.

"I've got a bellyache, Mommy. I ate too much. Don't worry, I'll eat it tomorrow." But when Freddie saw Mommy and Daddy devour the luscious-looking cake, he had second thoughts.

"Well, Mommy, maybe I can still squeeze in a little piece."

Pauline dished out a slim piece onto a small plate and handed it to Freddie.

At first, Freddie was able to keep the cake on the left side of his mouth. The cavity was in a lower right molar, and the rich succulent taste was melting in his mouth. Then it happened. A thin sliver got caught in the lower right molar. This time there was no holding back the scream.

As the sound reverberated throughout the house, Bernie Glaser called Artie Rosner.

"Artie, This is Bernie. I'm sorry to bother you at home but Freddie got a nasty toothache. Could you prescribe something for tonight? Can Pauline bring him in the first thing in the morning?"

Damn! Artie thought *I hate treating kids, and tomorrow is Wednesday and Mark's off*, but he said, "For a friend's kid, of course. I'll call Lambert's Pharmacy now for some pain pills and a small dose of a tranquilizer that he's had before. The prescriptions should be ready in about fifteen minutes."

"That's great."

"Good, Bernie, but you know Freddie's not the easiest patient. Make sure he takes the tranquilizer. Give him one pill before he goes to sleep and a second when he wakes up. One more thing. See that Freddie has a small breakfast. I don't want him to vomit from the gas."

"I'll take care of everything," Bernie responded.

"Fine. Tell Pauline to call the office at 7:30 tomorrow morning. My receptionist will be in. I try to fill the 8:00 A.M. time slot last. That way if it's not filled, I can sleep later. But don't worry, I don't want Freddie to suffer, and I don't think the eight o'clock's been taken yet."

"Thanks, Artie. I owe you one."

A half-hour later, Bernie Glaser picked up the prescriptions and made sure that Freddie took the pills as instructed.

The medications helped. During the night, Freddie's tooth still bothered him, but he didn't seem to mind the pain that much — the tranquilizer had kicked in. At 6:30 A.M., Freddie had a small bowl of Cheerios with milk. At 7:30, his mother gave him the second tranquilizer pill. Right after that, Pauline called Dr. Rosner's office and spoke to the receptionist, Phyllis Romaine. Freddie Glaser was given the 8:00 A.M. appointment.

At 7:50, Pauline Glaser brought Freddie into Dr. Rosner's reception room. Even after having taken the pain pills and tranquilizers, Freddie was moaning softly. He still was not happy going to the dentist.

Receptionist Phyllis Romaine left her seat behind the movable window and entered the reception room. It took a few minutes, but she was able to calm down the young boy.

At two-minutes-to-eight, dental assistant, Julie Parsons entered the reception room. Showing her perfect teeth, Julie smiled at Freddie and said, "Come on handsome, we'll take good care of you."

Freddie was still afraid, but her winning smile and gentle voice did the trick. Hand in hand, they walked into Treatment Room No. 1.

Pauline started to follow her son inside, but Phyllis asked her to remain in the reception room. She said, "Don't worry, Mrs. Glaser, he's in good hands. It's better for Freddie if you're not around."

Pauline returned to a cushioned chair and remarked, "I know. I've never gone inside with him before. Last night, he was in such a bad way. This morning, he was scared." She reflected a moment and added, "You're right, though, he's better off without me. I'm such a lousy patient myself."

The receptionist gave her a knowing smile, and Pauline picked up a recent issue of *National Geographic*. The piped-in music playing hits of the fifties and sixties was perfect. She didn't want to hear what was going on inside.

The moment Freddie was seated in the dental chair, he let out a muffled scream.

While Julie was placing the dental drape around Freddie's neck, she spoke quietly into his right ear, "Freddie, show me your bad tooth."

Freddie opened his mouth slightly and pointed to his lower right first molar. Julie looked inside and saw the large decayed lesion.

"Good, Dr. Rosner will be able to fix that in no time, but don't worry. We're going to give you the 'happy gas' now, and you'll be able to take a fabulous trip."

Freddie's mood lightened. He loved the "happy gas."

Julie continued, "While you're in the magic land, Dr. Rosner will take a picture of that bad tooth. Then, he'll put the tooth to sleep and get rid of that rotten tooth decay. After that, he'll put in a white filling. Remember, you won't feel anything. You'll be in never-never land."

That calmed Freddie even more. He closed his eyes while Julie placed the "nitrous" mask over his nose. Taking into consideration the child's age and size — five-foot and quite thin — Dr. Rosner set the indicated gas mixtures. He started off by giving fifty percent nitrous oxide and fifty percent oxygen with the goal to eventually get to an eighty percent nitrous oxide to twenty percent oxygen mixture. From previous experience with Freddie, the expectation was that in a few minutes, the youngster would be way out in imaginary space.

After a couple of minutes, the dentist increased the gaseous mixture to seventy percent nitrous oxide to thirty percent oxygen. He then asked Freddie to open his mouth. Even with the tranquilizer premedication along with the current mixture, Freddie was still not completely cooperative. He barely opened his mouth.

Dr. Rosner looked quizzically at Julie, as if to say, "What's going on?"

Julie responded with a shrug of her shoulders.

The dentist increased the nitrous oxide to eighty percent. The response was unusual. Freddie started to kick his feet and close his mouth.

Dr, Rosner appeared to be even more surprised. He whispered, "Julie, get me a mouth prop."

A few moments later, they were able to force the prop into Freddie's mouth. Dr. Rosner then examined the decayed tooth and took the usual two x-rays: a bitewing and a periapical film.

Freddie opened his eyes slightly.

Quietly, Dr. Rosner said, "Julie, I don't know why it's not working, but I can't increase the nitrous oxide any more; gotta keep the twenty percent oxygen; can't risk asphyxiation. Still, if I'm gonna clean out the decay and put in a temporary, I must work fast. Ask Phyllis to come here. Working together, the two of you should be able to restrain him."

Via the intercom, Julie called Phyllis at the front desk. "Phyllis, get here quickly, but smile as you leave the desk. We don't want Mrs. Glaser to get suspicious."

Phyllis came immediately and between the two of them, they were able to stabilize Freddie. This gave Dr. Rosner time to retrieve the x-rays and examine them on the view box. He observed from the peripapical film that no bony infection was present. The bitewing x-ray showed him that the decay was deep, but it was not yet into the "nerve."

Even with the previous tranquilizer and the 80/20 mixture, Freddie still didn't appear to be getting any deeper.

"Maybe we'll be lucky, Julie," Dr. Rosner whispered, "I'll remove the decay. I don't think it's into the 'nerve.' I'll put in a temporary filling. That should hold him over for about six weeks."

"Why six weeks, doctor?" receptionist Phyllis asked quietly.

She always asks dumb questions when I'm in a crisis situation, Dr. Rosner thought. *The heck with it. It'll only take me a few seconds to respond.* He whispered, "It looks like I'm going to have to get you away from that desk for a while and teach you a little more about dentistry. But to answer your question, it takes about that long for healing to begin. If the tooth stays painful or gets painful, that means the 'nerve' is dying. If the tooth remains calm, then a permanent filling is put in."

She nodded in reply.

He smiled, looked at his assistant, and said quietly, "Julie, please give me a block injection. Freddie's got no allergies or medical problems, so we'll use the lidocaine with epi."

Julie Parsons handed Dr. Rosner a two-by-two sterile gauze pad and a cotton swab with topical anesthetic on it. With the gauze pad, he wiped the areas behind the last right molar and the inside of the right cheek. With the cotton swab, he then applied the topical anesthetic to those two areas.

For some unknown reason, Freddie still did not appear to be deep with the "nitrous." In fact, he seemed to be even more alert. From his horrendous experience last year with Dominic Hall, Dr. Rosner realized only too well that some people who are given nitrous oxide have a weird reaction in which they get violent rather than relaxed. But in the past, "nitrous" always worked well for Freddie. He knew that Freddie wasn't deep, so Dr. Rosner left the topical anesthesia on the injection sites for a couple of minutes. He didn't want Freddie to feel the injection pinches.

Artie returned the used pad and swab to Julie. In turn, she gave him one carpule of the local anesthetic solution to effectively numb the tooth completely. Dr. Rosner injected the solution slowly to reduce the pressure as the anesthetic slowly went to the region of the inferior alveolar nerve. Once it reached the appropriate site, the numbness would gradually travel from the back of the right jaw until it reached the mid-point of the lower lip. The women still had to hold Freddie, but at least the injection went well.

After another couple of minutes, Dr. Rosner blew air into the cavity and probed it with a dental explorer. Freddie didn't react.

The dentist nodded to alert his female staff that he was about to start the work.

The drilling began. Freddie's eyes were wide open and he flinched, but he didn't cry out in pain.

Dr. Rosner spoke quietly to the women again, "For some reason, the nitrous oxide is not working. But he is numb. So I'm going to reduce the dose a lot and pretty soon give him pure oxygen. I'll get in and out of here fast."

Dr. Rosner lowered the dose to twenty percent nitrous oxide/eighty percent oxygen. It was difficult to discern, but Freddie seemed to be getting a little calmer.

Mark Procter and his best friend, Jim Auclair — another dentist — were about to tee up at the fourth hole. The green, fronted by a small pond, was one hundred sixty five yards away. It was 8:30 A.M and Mark was two strokes ahead. Mark was a twenty-eight-year-old bachelor who was the picture of health. He was tall and muscular with features resembling the movie star, Brad Pitt.

Mark was an all-Temple man, having graduated from both the Philadelphia undergraduate college and dental school. Jim Auclair, another Temple graduate, at age thirty two, looked more like the public's image of a dentist — medium height, average build, thinning hair, plain features and thick glasses. Nevertheless, he was Mark's equal in golf. Both shot in the high 80s, low 90s. Today, they were not having one of their better days. After two par four and one par three holes, Mark's score was 17 and Jim's was 19. The scores didn't concern them that much. The weather was fine, and they were happy to be away from their offices.

The decay had been removed. The "nerve" was not exposed. Dr. Rosner reduced the nitrous oxide dose even further. The dose was now ten percent nitrous oxide to ninety percent oxygen.

"Phyllis," Dr. Rosner whispered, "you can go back to the front desk. If Mrs. Glaser happens to ask, tell her you were in the back to look up some charts, but you peeked into the treatment room and everything looked fine."

The receptionist left and as she got up, her shoulder accidentally swung the arm of the overhead x-ray unit. The x-ray arm rebounded and hit Freddie on the back of the head. Being anxious to get back to the receptionist area, Phyllis was unaware of what she had done. Julie didn't see what happened either. She had been holding onto Freddie and felt him suddenly shudder. She thought it was just a nervous twitch.

Artie Glaser was the only one who saw the x-ray unit arm hit Freddie's head. He watched the child's head jerk back, but the child's eyes were closed. After the initial head reaction, Freddie stopped moving. Although Artie was concerned, he believed that no damage had occurred because the child seemed now to be stable. Since Freddie was no longer resisting, Julie let go of him.

Freddie Glaser was smiling on the inside. His mental world was awakening. It took a long time, but now he was on a spaceship that was moving at top speed. It was an exhilarating ride. He looked out of one porthole and saw the Earth fading away. Then, he turned his head and saw the moon approaching. In no time at all, the ship bypassed the moon and was heading for the planets. *Which one will we stop at?* he thought. That thought dissolved as he just sat back and enjoyed the ride.

While Julie was busy mixing up the zinc oxide eugenol temporary filling material, Artie examined the back of Freddie's head. There was no obvious bruise or swelling. Artie then returned to the front of the chair, and Julie handed him the temporary filling material on a plugger. After inserting the material into the cleaned-out cavity, Dr. Rosner raised the oxygen to ninety-five percent and reduced the nitrous oxide to five percent. Soon it would be over.

Freddie could see the red planet, Mars, in the distance. *Wow! It's really red.* Suddenly, the ship slowed down. It seemed that it was going to land on Mars. Freddie was ecstatic. He wondered what the Martians would look like. Soon he would find out.

The telephone rang at the front desk. Phyllis answered it and put the other party on hold. She buzzed the intercom for Treatment Room No. 1. Julie picked it up. Phyllis said, "Julie, tell Dr. Rosner that there's a man on the line from Acme Travel. Ask him if he wants to speak to him now or should I tell the man to call back later."

Julie relayed the message to her dentist.

Dr. Rosner looked at Freddie and answered Julie quietly, "The kid's stable now. The call's important. Tell Phyllis to switch it to my extension."

Dr. Rosner was not of the newer breed that makes travel reservations over the Internet; he still used travel agents. He picked up the phone and spoke quietly, "Yeah, Wally, no problem. Are the reservations all set?"

Julie noticed that Freddie appeared to be getter deeper into conscious sedation rather than coming out of it. She interrupted Dr. Rosner. "Doctor," she said, "shouldn't Freddie be waking up soon? He looks so relaxed. He's not even moving."

Dr. Rosner spoke into the phone, "Hold on for a minute, Wally." In response to Julie, he said, "I think he's enjoying the ride. He just doesn't want to come back to us. I'll give him one hundred percent oxygen now. Freddie'll be his old self in a minute." Dr. Rosner adjusted the setting to one hundred percent oxygen and zero percent nitrous oxide. He returned to his telephone call.

As the spaceship was about to land on Mars, out of nowhere there appeared a Black Hole. The ship changed course and went directly into it. Freddie was no longer happy. All was dark.

Julie took off the dental drape from Freddie's chest. Dr. Rosner wiped the child's chin and noticed that his face was just beginning to show tinges of a grayish blue color. He immediately ended the telephone call and screamed, "My God!" Artie grabbed the mask off of Freddie's nose and yelled to Julie, "Call 911; we've got a medical emergency." He paused for a second and then said, "Maybe, you can try one of the doctors next door." He thought about it; then shouted, "No! It's Wednesday. They're off. Just call 911."

As Julie was about to make the emergency call, Artie called after her, "After that, page Mark. When you get hold of him, tell him to get off that golf course and come here immediately." Artie was breathing heavily, his heart was racing and his right hand was "screaming" in agony.

The Black Hole was freezing. Freddie couldn't see, hear or feel anything except for the cold. Soon that disappeared. All around him was complete, silent darkness.

3

A few minutes after the 911 call, the medical emergency ambulance left Mt. Laurel General Hospital, and in the middle of a putt, Mark Procter heard his pager go off. The distraction caused him to flinch, and the ball missed the cup by six inches. Mark excused himself to Jim, got the number from the pager, grabbed his cell phone from his golf bag, and called the office. "Get in the golf cart," he yelled to Jim, "I have to quit. There's a medical emergency at my office."

Artie Rosner was a good dentist. He analyzed situations well and took appropriate actions. Although what had happened was puzzling, he knew that his patient required immediate oxygenation. Fortunately, the office had a separate oxygen unit. He ran to the equipment closet, rolled out the portable unit, turned on the unit to maximum pressure and placed the large mask over Freddie's nose and mouth. Julie quickly took Freddie's pulse. It was weak and thready, but at least he was alive. Gradually, the color returned to Freddie's face, and his pulse strengthened and became regular. His chest moved up and down in normal rhythmic inhalations and exhalations.

Artie Rosner let out a weak smile. "That was a close call," he uttered.

"It sure was," Julie added.

They gave Freddie pure oxygen for another three minutes. Dr. Rosner then removed the mask.

"You can rinse out now, Freddie," he said.

Freddie didn't respond. He appeared to be sleeping, but in reality he was still inside that Black Hole filled with absolute darkness.

The loud siren jolted Pauline Glaser out of her reverie. When she saw the two-man emergency team enter the office, she panicked. "What's happening?"

she screamed at Phyllis.

Phyllis shrugged.

Pauline frantically pushed past the receptionist. She had to find out what was going on.

Phyllis was also unaware of what took place, but she knew Dr. Rosner wouldn't want Mrs. Glaser interfering with any emergency measures. She quickly grabbed Freddie's mother, guided her back into the reception room, and said, "Please, Mrs. Glaser. I don't think it's serious," but she thought, *Why are you lying? It must be serious!* She added, "You can't interfere with them. They'll be out in a minute and tell you what's happening."

Pauline Glaser, crying hysterically, fell into Phyllis' arms.

Dr. Rosner met the two young men in the hallway in front of Treatment Room No. 1. He quickly explained the adverse reaction to the standard dose of nitrous oxide/oxygen and how they had resuscitated Freddie.

"The kid doesn't want to awaken," the dentist added. "Maybe, the small dose of Valium® he had last night and this morning kicked in with the 'nitrous' and he's just sleeping."

"We'll have to take him to the hospital for observation," the senior emergency specialist said.

"Do me a favor" the anxious-looking Dr. Rosner said, "reassure the hysterical woman in the waiting room that it's just precautionary. She's the mother. Her name is Mrs. Glaser."

"Sure," the senior specialist said.

"One more thing," Artie added. " On the kid's medical history form, there was no medical problems listed, but once she calms down, could you ask her if her son had any prior neurological problems? I'd do it myself, but this has gotten to me." Artie's right hand was still aching.

"Okay," answered the senior specialist, "but first let's get him out of here."

The two technicians quickly placed Freddie onto the stretcher. The junior one checked his vital signs, and all appeared to be normal.

At the same time they were entering the reception room, Pauline Glaser ran over to the stretcher. "What did they do to my son?" she screamed.

The senior specialist spoke to the terrified Mrs. Glaser, "At first, your son got a little deep into the 'nitrous' with just a normal dose. The dentist acted quickly, and your son now appears to be resting peacefully. To make sure everything is all right, we're taking him to the hospital for some tests."

Pauline was still worried but seemed a little less agitated.

The senior technician added, "By the way, do you think there is any reason he got so deep? Did he ever have any blow to the head or some brain condition?"

Pauline answered with a quivering voice, "He never got hit in the head, and I don't remember him ever falling." She thought for a moment and then said, "The only thing Freddie ever had was an epileptic-like seizure when he was six-months old, but that was it. He's been fine since then." She paused and added, "Are you sure he's okay?"

"It looks that way," the senior technician responded, "but you can come along with us in the ambulance, or you can follow us in your car."

"I'm too nervous to drive. I better go with you men."

Artie Rosner entered the room and said, "I'm so sorry this happened, Pauline, but give me your car keys. One of us will drive your car to the Emergency Room parking lot. We'll leave the keys at the front desk."

"Thank you," Pauline answered tearfully.

With its siren blasting loudly, the ambulance sped away heading for Mt. Laurel General Hospital.

Phyllis and Julie joined Dr. Rosner in Treatment Room No. 1. Appearing distraught, Artie Rosner spoke first, "I don't know what happened. I hope he's just asleep and not in a coma or something worse. I've never seen anything like this before."

"Could it have been the tranquilizer?" Julie asked.

"No way," the dentist responded, "I've given him that small dose of Valium® several times before, and he never reacted this way. Even if a tranquilizer would have an additive effect with the 'nitrous,' he should have been getting deeper when we increased the 'nitrous.' Freddie didn't get deeper. That's why the two of you had to restrain him. It makes no sense. It was only after the 'nitrous' was reduced and the oxygen was increased that he started to go under. I can't figure it out."

"I've been with you for two years now Dr. Rosner and never saw anything like this," Julie said. She paused for a few seconds and added, "I overheard the tech speak to Mrs. Glaser, and she admitted that Freddie had an epileptic-like seizure when he was six-months old. Could that have had something to do with what happened?"

"If it's not sleep, but God forbid, a coma, possibly Freddie did have some preexisting brain damage related to that seizure." He thought a moment and added, "Yeah, that might be a factor."

After momentarily staring into space, Dr. Rosner addressed his receptionist. "Phyllis, I'm in no mood to treat any more patients today. If any of them are emergencies, refer them to Dr. Cahn or Dr. Irving. If the patients can wait, reschedule them for the next available time slot. After that, let the answering service take the calls and you can go home. You'll be paid for the whole day."

He paused to collect his thoughts. "Julie, you can clean up the treatment room. Then leave. You'll also be paid for the full day."

Once Phyllis left, Artie Rosner held his head in his hands and closed his eyes. After a while, he opened his eyes and straight in his line of vision was the converted nitrous oxide/oxygen general anesthesia unit. Something wasn't quite right.

Dr. Mark Procter walked into the reception room. He greeted Phyllis who briefed him on what had occurred.

"Would you like to treat the patients Dr. Rosner asked me to cancel?" she asked.

"Hold off on that. Let me first speak to him."

Mark entered the hallway. He heard a deafening, "Ayeeee!!!" He paused momentarily and entered his treatment room, which backed up on the first treatment room, and listened to what ensued.

"I can't believe it!"

"What is it, doctor?" Julie questioned.

"Look at the nitrous oxide and oxygen tanks," Dr. Rosner stated emphatically.

Julie looked and exclaimed, "They're on backwards!"

"When I thought I was giving him one hundred percent oxygen, I was really giving him one hundred percent nitrous oxide. Can you believe it?"

"How could it have happened? I know your unit isn't the 'fail-safe' one, but still, how could the tanks be in backwards?"

"You're right, Julie, Dr. Procter's unit is the 'fail-safe' one. But, I've never had a problem with mine." He stopped in mid-speech and said, "Wait a minute. Weren't new tanks installed recently?"

"Oh yes, Doctor, you're right. The Mohlner Dental Equipment Service tech, Rudy Kennedy, installed them a few days ago. I don't think we used the unit since that time."

"That's it, Julie. Kennedy did it. He screwed me up. I can't imagine what's gonna happen now." Artie held his head in his hands and added, "I only hope Freddie Glaser is all right."

In the midst of a call, receptionist Phyllis Romaine heard the scream coming from Treatment Room No. 1. She was about to cut the patient off when quiet returned. Phyllis considered that it was minor and concluded the telephone conversation. She then walked into the treatment room.

"Is everything all right?" Phyllis asked the dentist.

Deciding on the spot not to get another person involved in the serious situation, Dr. Rosner said, "I just banged my head on the x-ray arm. I'm fine."

Satisfied, Phyllis returned to the reception room and continued with the calls. Hearing the alarm in his partner's voice, Mark Procter left his room and entered Artie's room. "It sounds like you've got a problem," he stated.

"Mark, you wouldn't believe it!" Artie exclaimed.

Dr. Rosner then gave his partner a step-by-step account of what had transpired. Julie contributed additional details.

Artie was near tears when he had finished. Mark, being sharp-witted and not personally involved, took charge.

"Let's think this through logically. If the kid is merely sleeping, this will all blow over. From what you said though, I don't think this is the case. Realistically, I believe that Freddie Glaser has brain damage. Until he's examined in the hospital, the extent of it cannot be determined."

"Do you think the brain damage was caused by asphyxiation?" Artie asked.

"That certainly is a possibility, but from what you said, even though you thought you were giving the kid eighty percent and then one hundred percent oxygen, you were giving him eighty percent and one hundred percent nitrous oxide. But you told me that he only received the eighty percent and one hundred percent nitrous oxide dosages for a short time period —maybe only for about a minute or so, right?"

"That's correct," Artie answered.

Mark reflected for a moment and then said, "There's another consideration."

"What's that?" Artie asked nervously.

"Freddie's only a small kid. What do you think he weighs?" Mark questioned.

"Probably only about eighty pounds," Julie responded.

"With that small size, cutting off the oxygen to the brain for even that short time period could cause brain damage. There's an excerpt I read in a recent issue of *Dentistry Today*. It quoted an article that appeared in *Nature Medicine*. Research was done on nitrous oxide/oxygen by Dr. Jevtovic-

Todorovic from Washington University's med school in St. Louis."

"I get *Dentistry Today*, but I skipped that article."

"You should have read it. The most important point the researcher found was that a thirty percent nitrous oxide mixture given for fifteen to twenty minutes probably causes no damaging effects. That wasn't everything, however. Some people are more sensitive to its effects than are others."

"Maybe, Freddie was one of the sensitive ones."

"Possibly, but there's more. Jevtovic-Todorovic said that nitrous oxide is toxic in higher concentrations. When given to rats, they developed brain lesions. He also said that people who breathe in nitrous oxide at levels that approach one hundred percent typically have a shorter life span than others."

"It looks like if the kid has brain damage, it could have been a combination of asphyxiation and the toxic effects of the 'nitrous.'"

"Possibly, Artie, but believe it or not, you did something that could have reduced the toxicity of the nitrous oxide."

"You're kidding," Dr. Rosner said.

"I'm serious. Jevtovic-Todorovic said that if you give nitrous oxide along with Valium®, or some other benzodiazepine antianxiety agent, you limit the neurotoxic side effects. In other words, the addition of the Valium® that you gave Freddie Glaser could have helped protect his brain cells."

"Mark, maybe there was some preexisting brain damage from Freddie's epileptic-like seizure that contributed to what happened."

"That's possible but we've got to consider the worst case scenario. If the kid has suffered permanent brain damage, there's undoubtedly gonna be a malpractice suit."

"Damn! You're right about that," Artie chimed in.

"Right. And it certainly is not going to look good if the other side finds out that the tanks were inserted backwards."

"If they find out about that I'll lose the suit without a second thought." Dr. Rosner then squeezed his hands and spoke. "You know, Mark. A couple of years ago I heard about all of those large verdicts in malpractice cases. Since, I was getting on in years I didn't want to take any chances. I found a New Jersey malpractice company, Healthcare Protective. It gives the highest coverage. I took out their six-million dollar maximum per occurrence malpractice policy."

"How much did it cost?" Mark asked.

"It was a little steep, but I had a Class A rating. That's their best. No intravenous or intramuscular sedation or general anesthesia is permitted, but they do allow the use of 'nitrous.' I also got a discount because in my many years of practice, I had never been sued."

"Great, but how much?"

"About ten thousand a year."

"That's high for dentistry, but considering the coverage, it's not too bad. Ob-Gyns and orthopods pay a hell of a lot more."

"It's good that I took out the policy. If permanent brain damage occurs, they can sue me for millions. If they win, the six million would help, but I'd be destroyed if they sue for more and win. What would I do if that happens?"

"Listen, Artie, it wasn't your fault that Rudy Kennedy messed up with the installation. Why does anyone have to know about the mix-up? There are only the three of us who know about the tank reversal. All that has to happen is for me to reinstall the tanks the correct way. Then if there is a malpractice suit, at least there's a fighting chance that there won't be a huge award."

Artie's eyes lit up. "That sounds interesting," he remarked.

Mark nodded and continued, "I mean it's not that you neglected anything. You called 911 right away. You gave the kid pure oxygen from another unit. No one can fault you for your emergency treatment."

Julie added, "That's right, Dr. Procter. I saw everything. The moment Dr. Rosner noticed Freddie was starting to get blue in the face, he immediately hung up the phone, ripped off the mask and gave Freddie oxygen."

"Hung up the phone!" Mark exclaimed. "What were you doing on the phone while you were working on a patient? — especially one like the Glaser kid."

"He was stable at that time, and it was an important call," Artie answered.

Mark considered the situation and said, "The main thing is that the kid was under that deep for only about a minute, and you did quick resuscitative measures."

"I just thought of something," Artie interjected, "It was Rudy Kennedy, the equipment tech at Mohlner Dental Equipment Service, who installed the tanks. Since he screwed up, why can't his company bear the brunt of the suit? That is, if there is a suit."

"That's all well and good," Mark replied, "but you brought the unit into the treatment room. You adjusted the dials. It is your responsibility and yours alone to have checked the tanks to see if they were installed correctly."

"I suppose you're right, but I've been using this unit for many years, and the tanks had always been installed correctly. It never dawned on me to check them on Wednesday."

"You know that and I know that, but under the definition of medical malpractice, you are liable to see that everything is installed correctly and working properly."

"So what should I do?" Artie asked.

"I told you before. Keep the equipment service company out of it. Let it be as if the tanks were installed correctly."

"All right."

"Artie, I know you can keep the secret about me reinstalling the tanks correctly. How about you, Julie? Are we gonna let Dr. Rosner hang for something he didn't do? What do you say? Can you keep the secret?"

Julie had always been an honest person, and she had worked for Dr. Rosner for two years and never saw him commit an unethical or immoral act. He did excellent dentistry and never cheated anyone. After all, he did save Freddie's life. Julie commented, "I can't let Dr. Rosner down. I know nothing about the tanks being inserted backwards. You can count on me."

"Thank you, Julie. I'll never forget this," Artie said.

"Good, Julie," Mark added, "you can clean up the room now. Then take off. It's still a nice day out there. I'll take care of the tanks. Artie, with any luck, you'll still be able to practice for a few more years until your retirement. Take off, now. Just leave everything to me."

Julie left the room and was out of earshot.

Artie started to leave by the employee exit. Mark quickly caught up with him and spoke. "If there is a lawsuit, the plaintiffs' attorneys will know nothing about the switching of the gas tanks. The first thing we've got to figure out is how a normal dose of nitrous oxide to oxygen could cause the possible brain damage that Freddie received." He thought for a moment and added, "Let's suppose the tanks were defective. They couldn't blame you, could they?"

"Mark, how could they be defective?"

"Let's say that the tank that was supposed to contain nitrous oxide actually contained oxygen and the oxygen tank really contained nitrous oxide."

"Could that actually happen?" Artie asked.

"I'm not sure, but it is a possibility. If it were true, then it would be difficult for them to fault you. At the start of the procedure, when you were getting no response with the nitrous oxide, it would have been because you were giving the kid oxygen. When you were trying to revive him with oxygen, you would have been giving him nitrous oxide."

"What you're telling me," Artie interjected, "is that all along I thought I was giving oxygen and nitrous oxide in proper proportions."

"Right," Mark added, "There would have been no way you could have known the tanks held the opposite gases."

"How could the gases be placed into the other tanks?" Artie asked.

"I'm not sure if it could be done. I majored in biochem in college and took a lot of chem courses. I know that nitrous oxide and oxygen have different densities, and I'm not certain if the gases could be removed from their original tanks without them dissipating into the room air. At least it might be worthwhile to try. First of all, I would need to borrow an empty oxygen tank. Can you get one without someone knowing?"

"I think so."

"Good. I think I can figure out how to unscrew the tank tops. Let's say I was able to empty the top half of the blue-painted nitrous oxide tank into the empty green-painted oxygen tank. Then I would re-screw the top. You'd now have an oxygen tank that only contains nitrous oxide. Next, I'd empty the rest of the nitrous oxide tank into the toilet. It would now be an empty nitrous oxide tank."

"What next?" Artie asked with great interest.

"I'd take your green-painted oxygen tank and hopefully empty the top half into the empty blue-painted nitrous oxide tank. Once I'd re-screw the top, you'd now have a nitrous oxide tank that only contains oxygen. I'd empty the rest of the oxygen tank into the toilet. All that would remain to be done is to bring back this new empty oxygen tank to the place where you got the other one. No one would know the difference. All oxygen tanks are painted green. I'd reinsert the green-painted oxygen tank that actually contains nitrous oxide into the correct slot in your anesthesia machine. Following that, I'd reinsert the blue-painted nitrous oxide tank that actually contains oxygen into its proper slot in the machine. If I could do all of this, then there would be a logical explanation for the kid getting so deep and you not knowing about it."

"We could then blame the equipment service company for installing defective tanks without me getting involved," Artie interjected.

"It could work because you would have done nothing wrong. As far as you would have known the tanks were installed correctly with the appropriate gases, and you did what you had to. The only thing is, for the time being, let me forget about mixing of the gases and simply switch these tanks to their rightful positions. We'll then wait to see what happens to Freddie and if there's a lawsuit."

"That sound's reasonable."

Dr. Mark Procter and Dr. Artie Rosner left the building. The bright sun stimulated Mark to consider other possibilities.

"If there is a suit, we'll find out what the plaintiffs' lawyers do and who they call in for depositions. Maybe the fact that the child had a prior epileptic-like seizure could have left some residual brain damage that allowed for the subsequent negative reaction with the nitrous oxide. There would then be no need for me to try and mix the gases and get the equipment service company involved."

Artie was amazed at Mark's ability to think through a stressful situation, but all he could say was, "Good."

"Right and who knows? Maybe my idea of remixing the gases into the opposite tanks is a bad idea because the gas tank company has some 'fail-safe' method that would not allow an oxygen tank to be filled with nitrous oxide and vice versa."

Mark leaned against the brick building, thought some more, and said, "We're still jumping the gun. We don't know whether or not Freddie has brain damage. For the time being, as I said before, I'll just reinstall the tanks into their correct position."

Artie, scratched his forehead, knocked his hand on the brick wall next to Mark and exclaimed, "I just thought of something else."

"What now?"

Before replying, Artie hesitated. He walked toward his car. Mark followed him. When Artie reached his car, he stopped and answered. "When Phyllis was leaving the dental chair after having helped Julie restrain Freddie, she accidentally bumped into the x-ray arm causing it to reverberate. On the rebound, it hit the kid in the back of the head."

"Did he react?" Mark asked.

"His head jerked for a second and then he was completely calm."

"Aside from you, did any one else see this happen?"

"I don't think so. No one mentioned it. Phyllis had her back to the equipment. She headed straight to her reception desk. Julie was busy holding Freddie."

"Did you examine the spot on his head?"

"Yeah. There was no sign of any injury or swelling."

"Did Julie see what you were doing?"

"I don't think so. She was busy mixing the temporary filling."

"Artie I don't believe you have anything to worry about on that score. I don't think the head blow had anything to do with Freddie's unconscious state. I've banged my head onto the x-ray arm many times and never had any side effects. I'm sure the same thing has happened to you."

"Many times."

"If you want my opinion, I think for the time being, we should keep this to ourselves. If the child is in a coma, undoubtedly the 'nitrous' is the cause of it. As I said before, maybe the possible preexistent brain damage could have had an additive effect."

Artie got into his car and started the ignition. "Thanks, Mark. I'm so pleased I hired you. You're an excellent dentist with an inquisitive mind. Most important, you're calm under pressure."

"Thanks. I try to keep under control. Let's hope that little Freddie comes out of this in good shape. You drive carefully; enough accidents for today."

Dr. Artie Rosner slowly pulled away.

4

It was 11:00 A.M., and Freddie Glaser was not in good shape. He was in a deep coma. Preliminary tests at Mt. Laurel General Hospital indicated that severe brain damage had occurred. The task of telling the distressing news to Bernie and Pauline Glaser fell in the hands of Dr. James Conover, the chief of neurology and the physician who had made the final diagnosis. He was tall, middle-aged and authoritarian looking, with dark-brown hair and a well-trimmed beard. It was decided that the findings would be presented in Dr. Conover's private office.

The prestigious neurologist hated this part of the practice of Medicine. As a result, he was in a somber mood while sitting in the contoured captain's chair located behind the walnut desk. Sitting opposite him were the Glasers.

Dr. Conover said, "I'm extremely sorry to tell you this news. So far, your son is completely unresponsive. By all indications, he has suffered brain damage."

Pauline Glaser cried hysterically.

Bernie Glaser, still in shock after receiving the telephone call from Pauline to come to the hospital a half-hour before, with tears in his eyes asked, "My God! Are you telling us the truth?"

"I wish I could give you better news."

"Is there any chance that he could recover?" Bernie asked.

"I have to be perfectly honest with you, folks. Right now, we don't know the complete extent of the brain damage, but it appears to be a permanent condition. We'll keep him in the hospital for another day or two to run some more tests. Once the diagnosis is confirmed, we'll discharge him."

Trying to control his emotions, Bernie asked, "What was the cause?"

Dr. Conover knew that he might have to testify later. He didn't want to condemn a fellow healthcare practitioner. Nevertheless, the obvious truth would come out. Reluctantly, he responded, "The brain damage appears to have occurred from asphyxiation — insufficient oxygen to the brain. There was one other thing we found. There is a slight bruise and swelling at the back of Freddie's head. Have you any idea how that might have happened?"

"Not that I know of," Pauline answered tearfully.

"It could have happened while he was being transported in the ambulance," the neurologist said. "His head might have accidentally hit any part of the stretcher, apparatus or inside of the vehicle. Regardless, I don't believe it means anything. We know the culprit was the nitrous oxide. How or why your child received excess nitrous oxide, I do not know."

Anger now overwhelmed Bernie's grief as he blurted out, "Artie Rosner was one of my best friends. How could he do this? Friendship is one thing, but if he's responsible, that son of a bitch is going to pay. I'll have him begging in the streets."

"I'm sorry you feel that way, Mr. Glaser. I am certain that there is some reasonable explanation."

Taking hold of his sobbing wife, Bernie left the neurologist's office screaming, "How could that bastard do this to us?"

Kenneth Hamilton was the senior partner in the law form of Hamilton, Burgess and Pettersen. Kenneth was sixty-four years old, of average height and weight, with a barrel-chest and stern face. He started the firm thirty-five years ago, and it grew into a thriving practice specializing in medical malpractice. Kenneth had been extremely successful in his practice against allegedly incompetent doctors and even against some who were excellent practitioners. He obtained several huge financial malpractice awards for both his clients and firm. In his private life, some might say he was not as successful, having never got married. However, Kenneth enjoyed the bachelor life. He thrived on being in complete control.

When Kenneth got off the phone with Bernie Glaser, he appeared distressed. He was caught squarely in the middle. Here was a case that he was reasonably sure could be won, and he could see big bucks coming out of the verdict. There was a catch, however. He was best friends with both Bernie Glaser and Artie Rosner. All three of them had the same background, and each wound up in Southern New Jersey, but in different careers. Artie was the dentist, Bernie was the speculative investor, and Kenneth went to Brooklyn Law School and specialized in medical malpractice. Because of his specialization, Kenneth never handled any cases for Bernie. Artie had never been sued for malpractice. This prevented their paths from ever crossing legally.

He was now faced with an apparent dilemma. Bernie specifically asked him to take the case, but Artie was a good friend. He could thwart Bernie's intentions and ask one of his partners to handle the case. He could forget about his friendship with Artie and listen to Bernie's wishes. He could refer the case to another law firm. He decided to speak to his partners about the case.

Mark Procter was still in the dental office. He had just hung up the phone. He had been speaking with Dr. Jake Daniels, a classmate of his at Temple undergraduate who later went to Temple Medical School and took graduate training in neurology. Jake was Mark's contact at Mt. Laurel Hospital, and he filled Mark in on Freddie Glaser's condition. Mark was distraught. The news was not good. *Well, now*, he thought, it's *imperative that he, Julie and Artie keep the secret of the changed gas tanks. I better break the latest news to Artie. I can tell Julie in private tomorrow at the office.* Mark decided that he would still hold off on changing the gas mixtures in each tank.

Inside his fourth floor condo apartment in Marlton, New Jersey, Dr. Artie Rosner was watching a TV talk show. He was seeing the picture and hearing the words, but looking at him, you would think that nothing on the screen was registering. His mind was engrossed on the morning's events. He mentally saw the kid having a severe reaction to the "nitrous." In his mind, he heard Mark's plans for switching the tanks and the gases, and Mark's viewpoints, especially the one on the possibility of a damaging lawsuit.

His reverie was interrupted by a phone call. Artie had Caller ID, and this let him know that the call was coming from his office. It didn't take too much deductive reasoning to figure out that it was Mark on the other end.

"Hello, Mark," he said.

"How did…? After the pause, Mark continued, "I know, Caller ID. At any rate, I'm afraid that the worst-case scenario has happened. Freddie Glaser is in a coma. He has brain damage."

"Damn!"

"Don't panic, yet. You still have a chance based on the kid having a preexisting neurological condition and me mixing the gases in the tanks, if I decide to do it. First though, you'll have to call your malpractice carrier.

What's their name again?'

"Healthcare Protective."

"Right. Tell them everything that happened. You know, the Valium®
. dosages, the initial unresponsiveness. What else? Yeah, the negative result
after giving the kid one hundred percent oxygen from the reconditioned unit,
and your use of the portable oxygen unit and reviving him at least to the
point of saving his life."

"Is that it?" Artie asked.

"In case that blow on Freddie Glaser's head resulted in a bruise or swelling,
the doctors would have found out about it in the hospital. So you better
mention the incident to your malpractice people. Whatever you do, don't tell
them about the switching of the gas tanks or my planned mixing of the gases."

"All right, Artie. I'll call them right now. Thanks again."

With that, Artie hung up and immediately called his agent, Arthur Fielding,
from the Healthcare Protective Company. He told him everything about the
event including the finding that Freddie had an epileptic-like seizure, which
the parents hadn't recorded on the medical history form. After detailing the
facts of the case, a meeting between the company's legal experts, and Artie,
Julie and Phyllis was scheduled for that Friday, their day off from the office.

Before he hung up, Fielding gave Artie a little encouragement saying,
"It's not a clear-cut case. I'm no doctor but I've heard that an epileptic-like
seizure could cause some brain damage. That might explain what happened
to the child. Don't worry, we'll get the best defense experts we can. We're
behind you all the way."

At the same time, inside one of the rooms of suite 405 of a five-storied
stone building located at 220 Lake Drive in Mt, Laurel, New Jersey, a heated
discussion was taking place. The walnut-paneled conference room was
spacious and bright. Large picture windows overlooked a lake with white
swans gliding leisurely over the water. Three lawyers and a recording secretary
sat in soft seats around a massive oak desk. The lawyers were drinking coffee
and eating muffins.

Kenneth Hamilton was speaking. "It is clearly evident that this is a
winnable case. A brain-damaged kid caused by a drug overdose. Direct cause
effect. Why and exactly how it occurred we don't know, but the damage
speaks for itself. This is just the kind of case that I built my reputation on. It
should be bread-and-butter for me, but Artie Rosner is a good friend. Should
I prosecute? Should I let one of you guys take over?"

He paused for a moment and then added, "We have another alternative. We could ask Bernie Glaser, the kid's father — who happens to be another good friend of mine — to give it to a different law firm."

Stan Burgess answered first. "In my opinion, it makes absolutely no sense to let a lucrative case like this get out of the firm. What do you think, Mike?"

Mike Pettersen then jumped in. "You're right; it belongs with us. With respect to who should prosecute, friendship is one thing, but we've got to think what would be the best thing for the kid and the firm as well. There's no doubt. Kenneth, you have to prosecute."

They agreed that Kenneth would be the lead attorney and the others would be there for support.

The next day, Thursday, the dental offices of Dr. Artie Rosner were in full swing. It was 4:00 P.M. and so far everything had gone well. Dental hygienist Kathy Perrin had two more cleanings on her schedule. Dr. Artie Rosner was about to begin his last patient for the day, Jerry Altschultz, a forty-five year old accountant. Mr. Altschultz was going to have two large amalgam fillings placed in his lower left first and second molars. Artie had had no cancellations or broken appointments for the day. That was just what the doctor ordered. The busy schedule allowed him to concentrate on the work at hand, leaving him less time to think about yesterday's horrendous occurrence.

Dr. Mark Procter also had a full schedule. He, too, was waiting to start on his last case for the day. So far, his patient, Gladys Atkinson, scheduled for a root canal, hadn't shown up. While waiting, he glanced at his dental assistant, twenty-three-year old, Ginny Walker. She was the newest member of the staff, having replaced Meredith Thomas three weeks ago. Meredith had been with Mark for two years but had to take a maternity leave. She wasn't planning on returning because she wanted to be with her child for at least the first three years.

Mark was intrigued by Ginny. The obvious reason was her striking beauty. She was tall with an exquisite figure. Ginny had auburn hair, blue eyes and the other features of a Cosmopolitan cover girl. Mark's mother had repeatedly told him, "beauty is only skin deep." It was apparent that there was much more to Ginny than good looks. She could carry on an intelligent conversation on most subjects. Her current interest was archaeology and anthropology. Those subjects also appealed to Mark. *Why would a girl with all that going for her choose to be a dental assistant? Heck,* he thought, *why don't I ask her now?*

For her part, Ginny was thinking about handsome Dr. Mark Procter. He seemed to have everything going for him. He had great looks, intelligence, was a good athlete and was single. She wondered why he was single. *Was he a confirmed bachelor? Did he fool around a lot? Was he not interested in getting married? Was he gay?* She quickly dismissed that last possibility. *Not the way he's been looking at me lately.*

Mark looked at his watch. The time was 4:07. He said, "What do you think, Ginny? Will Mrs. Atkinson show up?"

"If I remember from her last appointment, she was quite nervous. Maybe, the thought of having a root canal was too much for her. I hope she does show up, though. I really like the way you do endo."

"Thanks." The blush on his cheeks was evident.

"I mean it. It's too bad that so many people are afraid to have a root canal. I've worked with you on about a dozen already, and not a single patient had the least bit of pain."

"The truth is that unless the patient comes in with extreme pain or swelling, doing a root canal can be less painful than doing a filling." Mark paused momentarily. "We have some free time. Are you game to answer some personal questions?"

Smiling, Ginny showed her pearly whites and responded, "As long as they're not too personal."

"Oh, no!" Mark exclaimed. "Nothing like that."

"What are you waiting for?"

"I was wondering why is such a beautiful and intelligent young lady a dental assistant?"

Blushing, Ginny replied, "Thanks for the compliments, but don't knock dental assisting. It's a fine profession. You're right, though. Dental assisting is not my final career choice. Some day, I'd like to be like you, a dentist."

"You're joking."

"No, I mean it. I'm an only child. My parents had me late in life. My mother was forty-five and my dad was sixty. He was a dentist, and I planned on following in his footsteps. I went to Penn for two years, was pre-dent. Then my father had a heart attack and died."

"Sorry about that."

"Thanks. Anyway, between my father's retirement plan and the Social Security benefits, we had some money coming in. We needed more. I quit full time."

"That was too bad."

"It's all right. I'm going to school part-time in the evenings. When I have enough credits, I'll apply to dental school."

"Great."

"That's in the future. For now, I'm learning a lot by assisting you."

"You're making my head swell."

"I mean it." She paused a moment and added, " It's my turn to ask questions."

"Fire away."

"Why did you choose dentistry?"

"It was a whim. I had majored in biochem at Temple. I wasn't sure what I would do with it. My grades were good. They were good enough to get into med school, but I didn't like to deal with life-and-death situations. I was floundering around until one spring day in my senior year I had a terrible toothache. It was an upper second molar."

"I've never had a toothache."

"You're lucky. At any rate, I had been seeing the same dentist — Phil Golden — for the last five years. He was a great guy and an excellent dentist. He had a terrific chairside manner, too. Dr. Golden saw me as an emergency. He took care of the toothache painlessly. I saw him for three visits, and he did a great root canal. Later, he crowned the tooth. I still have it. My observation of Dr. Golden's technical ability peeked my interest. I asked him about dentistry as a career. He convinced me it was a great profession. That's it. Here I am."

"Great story."

At that precise moment, the intercom buzzer went off.

"Look's like our patient has arrived," Mark remarked.

Ginny thought, *I'll have to find out about his personal life another time.*

The time was 5:00 P.M. Kathy Perrin had dismissed her last dental hygiene patient and was cleaning her room. Jerry Altschultz was at the front desk sporting the two new fillings placed in his molars by Dr. Rosner. Gladys Atkinson was walking out the front door muttering to herself, "I can't believe it; the root canal didn't hurt a bit."

Five minutes later, the three patients had left the building. Phyllis Romaine walked to the front entrance about to lock the door. At that instant, a burly man with dark glasses entered.

"Can I please see Dr. Rosner?" he asked.

"The office is closed," Phyllis replied.

"It will only take a minute," the man answered.

"I'll check if the doctor can see you."

Phyllis went in to Treatment Room No. 1. Julie was cleaning up. Dr. Rosner had just put on his sport jacket and was walking out the door, about to leave from the rear staff entrance.

"Dr. Rosner, there's a gentleman out front who wants to see you. He said it would only take a moment."

"Did he say what he wanted to see me about?"

"No."

"I suppose I can spare a minute. Tell Dr. Procter to wait up for me."

"Yes, doctor."

Dr. Rosner walked into the reception room.

The burly man spoke, "Are you Dr. Rosner?"

"Yes, I am."

"Here's something for you."

The man handed Artie Rosner a large envelope, walked out, and slammed the door behind him.

"Wait a minute! What's this all about?"

Dr. Rosner ran to the door. By the time he got there, it was too late. The man had gone. A late model Volkswagen pulled out of the parking lot.

Hearing the commotion, Phyllis, Mark, Julie and Ginny entered the reception room.

Artie closed the door, shook his head and opened the envelope. He took a deep breath and began to read the enclosed letter. "You are hereby summoned to appear..." He couldn't finish the sentence.

There are many stressors in dentistry — finding a good location to practice, paying for expensive equipment, working on fearful patients, worrying about getting and transmitting AIDS, dealing with the mercury toxicity issue and fears about fluoride, fighting the managed care issue, getting an IRS audit, trying to keep up with the mounting cost of new equipment — but undoubtedly the worst dental stressor is receiving a malpractice summons. That is what Dr. Artie Rosner had the misfortune to have so ungraciously handed to him.

5

It was the following day, Friday. The law offices of Coniglia, Jameson and Carlisle were simple and unadorned in sharp contrast to those of Hamilton, Burgess and Pettersen, the plaintiffs' attorneys. Coniglia's firm was located at 66 Broad Street in downtown Marlton, New Jersey. The lawyers occupied the fifth and sixth floor of a high-rise professional building that overlooked nothing but traffic. Ernest Coniglia was the lead attorney for the firm that handled the bulk of the malpractice claims against doctors with policies from Healthcare Protective Company. He was a small, robust-looking man in his early sixties.

At 9:30 A.M., Dr. Rosner, dental assistant Julie Parsons and receptionist Phyllis Romaine were in a small conference room having intense discussions with Healthcare Protective's agent Arthur Fielding, and attorneys Ernest Coniglia, Herb Jameson and Laura Carlisle.

After listening to everything Dr. Rosner, Julie and Phyllis had to say about the unfortunate incident, the agent and the three attorneys went into Coniglia's private office to discuss the case among themselves. Fifteen minutes later, they returned to the conference room and sat down.

Speaking for the group, Ernest Coniglia said, "The consensus amongst us is that there is sufficient doubt about the circumstances of the case — especially with regard to the possible preexisting neurological condition — for the firm to fight the twelve million dollar lawsuit rather than have an out-of court settlement."

"That sounds like an incredible amount of money," Dr. Rosner said.

"It is," Coniglia replied, "but you have to realize that people sue for much more than they expect to get. Also four million of that is for punitive damages."

"Exactly what is meant by punitive damages?" Artie asked.

51

Coniglia replied, "Punitive damages are given when in addition to malpractice, the action is considered to be deliberate or malicious."

"That's ridiculous. I did everything I could to bring the kid back to normal."

"He certainly did," Julie confirmed.

Artie, Julie and Phyllis had previously said nothing to the attorneys about having forcefully restrained the child or the telephone call that Dr. Rosner received while working on Freddie.

Artie and Julie had no qualms about holding back that information. For Phyllis, it was a different matter. She was honest to the extreme and had to fight deep urges to keep quiet.

"That's all well and good," Coniglia said," "but lawyers usually ask for punitive damage, even if they don't expect it to hold. However, I must warn you that you can never tell with jurors, and some outlandish sums of money have been paid out."

"Incredible!" Artie remarked.

"Nevertheless, you realize that the limit on your malpractice policy is our maximum — six million dollars. That means you will have to get your own attorney to defend you against the excess amount of money. Of course, everything will be coordinated. Once we know who he is, our firm will work together with your attorney. The goal will be to give you the best possible defense."

Laura Carlisle chipped in. "You should realize Dr. Rosner that you were foolish to have continued to use an outdated 'nitrous' unit. Nevertheless, you should continue to use the machine provided that it is still safe. If you suddenly stop using the machine, the other side will rightfully conclude that there was something wrong with it."

"There's nothing wrong with my 'nitrous' unit," Artie said.

"Prove that!" Herb Jameson added. "Do a test run by using it on yourself. Be sure to get witnesses. You should even videotape the whole session including comments by everyone present."

"That's no problem. I'll do it."

The major decisions had been taken. The attorneys smiled as the shook hands with Julie, Phyllis and Artie. The members of the dental group were not smiling.

The Glasers lived in a splendid ranch house in an exclusive section of Medford Lakes, New Jersey. The backyard faced one of the larger Medford lakes. From the kitchen, dining room, den and master bedroom, the lake with its numerous ducks, swans and geese was in full view. The property had magnificent trees. There were stately oaks, graceful willows, pink and white dogwoods, majestic maples, flowering cherries and an assortment of evergreens. Flower beds were abundant and the rock-enclosed waterfall was flowing gracefully.

To this wondrous site, at 9:45 A.M., Bernie and Pauline Glaser brought in their unresponsive son, Freddie. Following them were a nurse, a physical therapist and a hospital attendant wheeling in medical equipment. They all ignored the external beauty. Pauline's mind was filled with thoughts of sadness and despondency. Bernie was sad as well, but the predominant emotion he felt was revenge. He was determined to make Artie Rosner crawl.

From the first day in the hospital, Freddie had to be helped in all his activities. He couldn't walk. There were only involuntary movements of his arms and legs. Simple acts such as eating and toothbrushing had to be performed by the aides. Freddie had to wear a diaper because urination and defecation had become involuntary acts. He had retained his other reflexes, but he had no knowledge of what he was doing or where he was located. Freddie's mind was still filled with emptiness, a dark void. There was absolute nothingness, not even a glimmer of light.

Inside Treatment Room No. 2 of the Rosner dental offices, at 9:55 A.M., Dr. Mark Procter had just completed the insertion of a three-unit porcelain-to-titanium alloy fixed bridge. The aesthetics and fit were excellent and the patient, Peter Kessler, was pleased. Once he walked out, Ginny Walker began to clean up the room.

Mark sauntered over to her and said, "While you're straightening up, I'd like to discuss this malpractice case with you. I can't get it out of my mind. I've never been sued, but being sued nowadays is part of the practice of dentistry. I know someday it'll happen to me, but I'm not looking forward to it."

"Seeing how it affected Dr. Rosner, I don't blame you."

"Yeah. I just hope we can do something to help him."

"I don't understand how it happened, doctor. Did he do something wrong?"

"It's somewhat of a mystery, but as far as I can tell, he didn't do anything out of the ordinary. One thing is that he used the old general anesthetic machine to deliver the gases. I'm glad that we use a 'fail-safe' unit."

"Can you explain what makes our 'nitrous' unit 'fail-safe'?"

"There are two main features. First, the connections for the nitrous oxide and oxygen are different. It's impossible to insert a nitrous oxide tank into an oxygen line and vice versa."

"Do you think there was a wrong hook-up with Dr. Rosner's general anesthetic 'nitrous' unit?"

Not wanting to get anyone else involved in the scenario of the switched tanks, Mark replied, "I don't think so. Dr. Rosner has been using that reconditioned anesthetic unit for many years, and he never had any problems. The important thing is that I checked the tanks afterwards, and they were properly positioned," Mark lied. The truth is that they were properly positioned now, but only because Mark had recently switched them as he promised Artie he would.

"I see."

"The other aspect of 'fail-safe.' is a shut-off switch that automatically cuts off the flow of nitrous oxide should the oxygen level go below twenty percent. This makes it impossible to asphyxiate a person."

"Does that mean if the child, Freddie Glaser, was receiving the gases from our unit, he wouldn't have developed brain damage?"

"Good insight, Ginny, but that's not all there is to it. There are complicating factors. Freddie Glaser had a history of an epileptic-like seizure, which could have resulted in brain damage. Even though he had received nitrous oxide before, he could have had a bad reaction this time."

"Sort of like 'the last straw that broke the camel's back,'" Ginny added.

"Something like that. The bottom line is that he could have had that bad reaction even if a 'fail-safe' unit had been used." Mark bit his tongue when he said this because he knew it wasn't true. In fact, he knew that he had been lying to Ginny all along about certain facts of the case. He rationalized that it was a necessary evil. It's difficult enough for three people to keep a secret.

Ginny had completed the clean-up and was setting up for the next patient. Mark decided to switch gears. "Ginny, there's something I've been meaning to ask you for quite a while."

I hope it's what I think it is, Ginny thought.

"I know it's a cardinal rule to never mix business with pleasure, but…" He paused and blushed.

"But what, Doctor?"

He calmed down and without hesitation said, "Would you like to go out to dinner tonight?"

With a coquettish smile on her face, she replied, "That depends. If it's a fast food restaurant…" She smiled while deliberately leaving the sentence incomplete.

"For you, only the best. All I need to know is, do you have any preferences? Do you like Italian, Chinese, Jewish, or Greek? Do you enjoy French, American, Mexican or what have you?"

"Anything but real spicy food will be fine."

"Great! Is 7:30 a good time to pick you up?"

"That's perfect. Do you know how to get to my house?"

"Not yet."

Ginny proceeded to give Mark directions. For the two of them, the rest of the day flew by.

It was 5:00 P.M. Artie Rosner was in his living room sitting in a lounge chair staring out the bay window at the cloudless twilight sky. A sudden thought interrupted his reverie. Artie went to the desk, picked up the phone and dialed a number in Delray Beach, Florida.

On the second ring, the telephone was answered. "Hello, Rosner speaking."

"Hi, Burt, it's Artie."

"You don't have to tell me. I'd recognized my own brother's voice in my sleep."

"How's retirement life treating you?" Artie asked.

"How should it be treating me? It's warm. I play golf. I go swimming. I go to the movies. I go to the races. I stuff myself." Burt was obviously having some fun at his brother's expense.

"Sounds really tough," Artie said sarcastically.

"Not only that, I got a girlfriend."

"You've got a girlfriend, Burt? Is she nice?"

"Who cares about nice? She's a companion. Enough small talk, Artie. What's the occasion for the yearly call?"

"I call you more often than once a year," Artie replied indignantly.

"Call me a liar. It's a twice a year. Anyway, what's up, Artie?"

"Listen, Burt. I'm in trouble."

"What kind of trouble?"

"I've been sued for twelve million dollars."

"Whew! When you screw up, you do it in a big way."

"No, Burt. It wasn't my fault."

Artie then described the details of the 'nitrous' scenario, leaving out the gas tank mix-up. He then added, "Burt, in case I'm wiped out financially as the result of a verdict against me, can I come down and stay with you?"

"What kind of a question is that? You're my kid brother. What are brothers for? Of course, you can stay. If you need some money, I'll be there for you. Don't panic. Things might turn out better than you think."

"I hope so, Burt. Thanks. I'll let you know what happens."

With that, the brothers hung up on each other. Artie was thankful for his brother's kindness. With that taken care of, Artie was looking forward to tomorrow when he would be able to demonstrate that his old "nitrous" unit was still functioning correctly.

It was the closest thing to Diana's Ristorante in Bologna, Italy. Mark had been there two years ago during a vacation in Italy. Dining at that exquisite restaurant was one of the highlights of his Italian vacation. He discovered the American replica two months ago when a patient of his handed him a card. The patient, Georgio Rosato, was the chef and owner of La Rosata, a recently opened Northern Italian restaurant in Voorhees, New Jersey.

Three weeks ago, Mark had taken his mother there for her birthday. She had told him, "Mark, this is too good for me. You should take a young lady here. It's so romantic. Which reminds me, when are you going to stop playing around and find a nice woman to marry?"

Tonight the first part of his mother's quest for him had been fulfilled. He had taken a young lady here. Concerning his mother's nuptial question, that remained a possibility.

Ginny never did get to ask her handsome dentist those personal questions, but now that wasn't necessary. He had invited her out to dinner and not to just an ordinary place, but to an enchanting restaurant. She knew that office romances could often be disastrous, but the present was all that existed. She was going to enjoy every minute of it.

La Rosata was off the beaten path, adjacent to a winding brook in a forested section of Voorhees. Mark called for reservations early that day asking for a window table. When they arrived for their 8:00 P.M. reservation, the picturesque restaurant was almost full. The waiter guided the well-dressed couple to their window table for two.

Mark and Ginny had simultaneous thoughts; *the candlelight setting with a perfect view of the lighted brook is idyllic.*

Mark had ordered a bottle of Connubio 1997 — a dry white wine from the well-known Gimignano wine region of Italy. The meal began with a flavorful minestrone soup followed by a house salad with a tasty light Italian dressing. Mark's main course was *Pasta Bolognese ala Ragu di Pollo*, a delectable chicken and pasta combination. Ginny had *Trancio di Troute con Risotto al Granchio,* a delicious filet of trout with all the embellishments. The wine flowed freely; the food was divine, and the conversation was effortless. Two members of a dental team, but not a word of dental talk was spoken.

"Ginny, being here with you is perfect, even magical."

"I know Dr. Procter, at times like this, life can be beautiful. It's so easy to ignore life's seamy side."

"You've echoed my thoughts. By the way, in the office it's Dr. Procter. Anywhere else..." He smiled and continued, "call me Mark."

"Great. If you don't mind, I'd like to find out about the real you."

" No problem. Fire away."

"Tell me, Mark, what do you do for fun and enjoyment?"

"I'm a bit of a sports nut. I love to play golf, tennis and ping-pong. I'm not too good at racquetball, and no more than an average swimmer. I'm a novice at skiing, not much better at bowling. I'm a great watcher, especially football, basketball and baseball."

"Aside from sports?"

"I'm a movieholic, dig the good foreign ones. I love all kinds of music but especially classic and jazz."

"How about books?"

"I read mysteries, thrillers, science fiction and science and health-related books."

"Do you have any other interests?"

"Lately, I've become interested in physics, stuff like cosmology and quantum mechanics. That's enough about me. How about you?"

"I have many of the same interests as you: tennis, swimming — at which I'm pretty good — but I'm not yet into golf. I love aerobic dancing, and I'm a pretty good skier."

"What do you like to read?"

"Like you, I read a lot of different subjects, but I also like woman's books. I don't go for science fiction or any of that physics stuff. That's way too deep for me."

"Is there more?"

"I also love movies and music. Not that much into classical, but smooth jazz is fine. I already told you about my current interest in anthropology and archaeology."

The small talk continued for the two hours. When they left the restaurant,

Mark and Ginny felt that a new page had opened in their lives — a page that could be part of a long book with them as the principal characters.

The next day was Saturday, which meant the Rosner dental offices were only open for a half day. It had been a busy morning. Dental hygienist Kathy Perrin completed six routine cleaning patients. Dr. Artie Rosner saw four patients. One had an impression taken for a partial denture. Another had a full denture insertion. A third had bleaching of the four upper front teeth, and a fourth had insertion of three composite fillings. Dr. Mark Procter also had a full schedule with three longer appointments. He prepared eight teeth for a complete lower fixed bridge. He inserted a lower implant, and he completed a root canal on an upper second molar.

It was twelve noon, and no more patients had been scheduled. Dr. Rosner called the entire staff into his private office and spoke.

"My malpractice attorneys told me that I have to receive a 'nitrous' administration on myself from my unit to show that it wasn't defective when I worked on Freddie Glaser. Witnesses are required, and it will all be videotaped. The whole thing should take no longer than a half-hour, but I'll pay everyone until one o'clock. Is that all right?"

Hesitatingly, Kathy answered, "I'm very sorry Dr. Rosner. It may sound vain, but I have a beauty parlor appointment. Could I possibly be excused?"

"That's all right. One less witness won't matter. Is everyone else okay for this?"

There were no dissents.

"Good. Let's get started."

"Dr. Rosner, before you begin can I speak to you in private for a moment?" Mark asked.

"Sure." To the others Artie said, "Please excuse us for a couple of minutes."

With that, the dentists went into Artie's private office. It was a large wood-paneled room with one entire wall lined with bookshelves containing medical and dental books and occasional novels and nonfiction books. Several diplomas were on the other walls. Artie sat in a swivel leather chair behind his broad oak desk. On the wall behind him was a blown-up photograph of Artie holding a prize-winning fish. Mark sat in one of the two smaller, leather swivel chairs.

After he was seated, Artie asked, "What's up?"

"Nothing major," Mark replied, "excerpt my idea of switching the gases is definitely out. If you have to now demonstrate the safety of using the gases on yourself, that precludes the possibility that the gas tanks were improperly filled with gases."

"You're right. It looks like I'll just have to go along with the premise that Freddie's epileptic-like seizure predisposed him to that unfortunate 'nitrous' incident. "

"It seems like you'll have to bank on that, Artie."

With that, the two dentists returned to Treatment Room No. 1 where the women were waiting.

Dr. Rosner was ready to have the "nitrous" used on himself in the presence of Dr. Procter, Julie, Ginny and Phyllis. Artie took off his dental jacket, loosened his tie and rested inclined on the contour dental chair. Dr. Procter began the administration. He started off with 50/50, then after one minute, moved to 75/25 nitrous oxide to oxygen.

Two minutes later, Mark adjusted the dials to eighty percent nitrous oxide/ twenty percent oxygen. He kept Artie at this level for five minutes. Mark then gradually reversed the percentages and ended up using one hundred percent oxygen. Julie videotaped the entire procedure and each individual's comments, including those of Dr. Rosner.

Everything went well. Within a few minutes, Artie went into a deep state of relaxation and in spite of everything, he even appeared euphoric. After receiving oxygen, Dr. Rosner came back to normal while feeling deeply relaxed. He commented on the feelings he had while under the "nitrous" and after receiving oxygen. The others mentioned how calm and relaxed he appeared.

The videotape was rewound and played back. Julie did a flawless job.

Dr. Rosner then thanked everyone and left for home.

While leaving, Phyllis commented to Julie, "Did you notice how Dr. Procter and Ginny were looking at each other?"

"Not really," Julie answered. "I was too busy videotaping, but I wouldn't doubt there's something going on. Look, they're still together."

Upon exiting, Mark remarked to Ginny, "At least he now has a chance." He paused. "I just thought of something. I'm not privy to Dr. Rosner's personal finances, but I would assume that if he loses the case and anything remotely close to that twelve million dollars is awarded, he'd be completely wiped out."

"That would be terrible." Ginny hesitated for a few seconds and then added, "If Dr. Rosner loses everything, what would happen to the practice?" She appeared worried.

"Dr. Rosner rents the office. He owns the equipment, furniture and supplies. He'd lose it all."

"That's terrible."

Mark took her hand in his and said, "He hasn't lost the case, yet."

Squeezing the young dentist's hand, Ginny asked, "If he did, what would happen to you?"

Once they reached the outside door, Mark said, "I'd be all right. I'm still an associate. It's ironical. At the end of this year, I was supposed to initiate payments to buy into the practice. If I had and he lost the suit, I'd be out the money I invested. Right now, I'm fine."

When Mark opened the door, Ginny asked him, "What about the patients?"

"I could take over the lease. If I took out a loan, I might be able to buy the equipment and the practice."

"How about me?" Ginny said with a laugh.

"Whatever happens, you'd still have a job."

"Is that all?"

"I hope not." He paused momentarily. "I know it's the last minute but would you care to go to a show tonight. I mean, if you're not busy."

Ginny looked around. Everyone had left the parking lot. "Mark, it is short notice. I do have a date for tonight, but I could always come down with a bout of the flu."

They walked outside with their hands remaining interlocked. Mark gave Ginny a kiss on her cheek, and they walked to their cars. At least two of the dental personnel at 100 Main Street in Marlton were happy that day.

It was a perfect Florida afternoon. The temperature was in the mid-eighties. The humidity was low, and not a cloud could be found in the sky. Burt Rosner was floating on his back in the condo's pool. It was a good time for reflection. *I always thought that I had the tough life. I was forced into early retirement at age sixty-two by that bastard Harvey Reynolds. I gave forty years of my life to Altro Electronics. I was the best electrical engineer they ever had. But youth had to be served. Reynolds had a young buddy that he was planning to put in my place. The S.O.B. couldn't wait three years for my regular retirement. He had to force me out.*

Burt came out of the pool, toweled himself off and sat in a lounge chair. He had been living in the first floor of a six-story condo in Delray Beach for the last five years. With all of his bickering, he enjoyed the leisure life. Altro Electronics gave Burt a good payout, and he had an excellent retirement plan. Financially, he had no complaints. He had more than enough money.

Burt's health was relatively good except for that one frightening experience. Two years ago, he had shooting pains down his left arm and into his jaw. The symptoms were from a minor heart attack. Burt recovered well. The major outcome was a slight lifestyle change. He had to be more careful with his diet, and he had to exercise. That wasn't bad. He met Goldie at the condo's gym.

A few weeks ago, Goldie was having trouble with the new abdominal machine. Burt also had problems with the same unit when he first started working out in the gym. The attendant was quick to help him out. He showed him how to fold his arms across his chest in order to begin pushing downwards. After that, using the machine was a snap.

When Burt saw an attractive middle-aged woman having difficulties, he rushed to her aid. She was thankful and pleasant. That morning, they worked out together. Goldie told him he had a good build. Burt figured she was pulling his leg. After all, five-foot six and weighing one hundred and eighty-five pounds wasn't exactly a good build. It wasn't bad, though. He had been losing some weight. Within the last month, he dropped five pounds. Working out regularly with Goldie since that first day helped him shed a few more.

"Hello, Burt."

The sun glare was in his eyes. "Who's there?"

"It's me, silly man. Goldie."

"My darling, Goldie. I was just thinking about you. Is it time for us to have a workout?"

"That can wait. I'll just sit down next to you. Let's chat."

Goldie Abrams was a bleached blonde with attractive features and prominent dimples on an otherwise wrinkle-free, roundish face. She moved her somewhat chunky frame into the lounge chair next to Burt.

He said, "Goldie, I've been meaning to talk to you. I've got a brother. His name is Artie, and he's a dentist in New Jersey. I've always been envious of him. Artie is a well-respected dentist with a successful practice. He even has a full time associate. The only misfortune in his life had been when his wife died."

"I'm sorry to hear about that."

"It was a terrible tragedy. Artie was depressed for a while, but he got over it. Since then, he had been doing quite well. By the way, he's two years younger than me, sixty-five to be exact."

"You're not sixty-seven. I never would have believed it. You look so much younger."

"Why are you always teasing me?

Goldie responded in a sincere tone of voice. "I mean it. You look great for your age."

After shrugging his shoulders, Burt continued, "At any rate, Artie told me of a horrendous occurrence that recently took place in his office. He was giving a ten-year old boy nitrous oxide. You know 'laughing gas.'"

"Yeah. I used to have that. It was great. In fact when I was a young child in New York, I went to the famous Dr. Harry Langa, the 'laughing gas ' pioneer. He was wonderful."

"My brother was also an expert with the gas. That was until last week when he had a disaster in the office. From a normal dose, a boy patient went into a coma."

"How terrible."

"I know, but the kid's father, who was one of Artie's best friends — I knew him, too — is suing him for twelve million dollars."

"That's unbelievable. It must have been a tough situation. I mean, to sue a friend."

"That's for sure. Artie was really upset. I can't blame him. He asked me if he could come down and live with me if he lost the case."

"Doesn't he have malpractice insurance?"

"Certainly, but he's insured for six million dollars. If he loses the case and the award is anywhere close to that twelve million, Artie will be bankrupt."

"Would you help him out?"

"Of course, I would. I'd also invite him down here to live."

"I hope Artie doesn't lose the case. If it does though, I'll get to meet him." Goldie had a flirtatious smile when she added, "What does Artie look like?"

"Cut it out, Goldie."

6

It was the following Saturday — more than a week since Dr. Artie Rosner had received the malpractice summons. The only ways he had been able to deal with the crisis were to lose himself in work and after dinner sit in his room and drink scotch. Excessive drinking was something new for Artie. When his wife Marlene had died, Artie had seen a psychiatrist and had taken Prozac® and Ativan® for several months. That worked. He now felt that he couldn't go back to his psychiatrist. The result was that he comforted himself with alcohol.

After finishing work at twelve noon, Artie stopped off at the Main Street Delicatessen in Marlton. He had a turkey club sandwich and a diet soda. Not having anything better to do, he went to the Marlton movie theater complex. Artie wanted to see something that was out of this world. So he chose, *Far From Heaven.* A couple of hours later, leaving the movie theater, he wondered if he would ever get to heaven.

Getting into his late model, dark green, Pontiac Grand Am, Artie drove to his condo apartment. He went to the bedroom and slept for three hours. Upon awakening, he felt hunger pangs. Although he had no date, Artie got dressed in a dark blue suit and wore his best black shoes. He went down to the garage, got into his car and drove to Main Street in Voorhees. He pulled into the popular Reilly's Bar and Grill. It was hardly a fancy place for someone so nattily dressed.

Artie sat at the bar and downed two scotch on the rocks. He then sat at a table for two and had another scotch. He ordered the house's steak special. The food was good, and the alcohol made it taste even better. Artie skipped coffee and dessert and left a generous tip. He was feeling a little woozy. He managed to get to the parking lot, took the Club® off the steering wheel and put on his seat belt. Artie was now going to head home and sleep it off. Tomorrow was Sunday, and he would have a whole day to recover from his alcoholic excess.

It was 9:00 P.M., and the traffic was light as Artie headed his car west on Route 70. He was feeling high as he gunned the gas pedal to seventy miles an hour.

Without warning, the car went out of control. Artie slowed the car down, but it still veered to the right and crashed head-on into a stanchion. Fortunately, there were no cars or pedestrians around, and no outsiders were injured or killed. The seat belt and air bag did their job, and Artie was not seriously injured. The front end of the car was partially wrecked, but the engine remained running. The stanchion had a dent in it. Nothing else was damaged. Artie was shocked. The burned area in his right hand ached severely, but he remained conscious. Artie had a few facial cuts and body bruises, but he didn't appear to be seriously injured. Artie put his head down on the steering wheel and relaxed for a few minutes.

A few cars drove by; two slowed down, looked at the scene and continued on. A maroon Mercedes then pulled up behind Artie's car. A tall, slim, African American man got out and peered inside Artie's car. He saw a man slumped over the wheel with his eyes closed.

"Are you all right, buddy?" he questioned loudly.

Artie immediately opened his eyes and said, "I think I am. I must've had too much to drink. It look's like I did a number on my car and the stanchion."

"Are you up to driving? If you feel unsure of yourself, I'll take you to the hospital."

Artie moved his limbs and said, "I think I can make it. The car's still running. Thanks for stopping by."

"To make sure, I'm going to drive to the Emergency Room of Mt. Laurel General Hospital. Do you know where it is?"

"Yeah, but I don't think there's anything seriously wrong with me."

"You could have had a concussion and not even know it. Follow me. I'll drive slowly."

"Okay. Thanks again." *There are some nice people in this world*, Artie thought.

It took about fifteen minutes to reach the hospital. They pulled into the Emergency Room parking lot. Once they got out of their respective cars, the gentleman walked next to Artie and helped him in. "By the way," he said, "My name is Philip, Philip Jones."

"I can't thank you enough, Philip. Stupid me is Artie, Artie Rosner."

They went inside, where there were several other patients in varying degrees of injury and distress. Artie was called to the counter. The receptionist asked to see his insurance cards.

Artie reached into his pocket for his wallet. He panicked loudly, "Damn! My wallet's gone!"

Hearing Artie's shout, Philip came over to the counter, "Did you drop it in the car?" he asked.

"It's possible," Artie answered. "I'll go out and look."

"No, you could still be injured. Give me the keys. I'll look for you."

"Are you sure?"

"Of course."

Artie handed the keys to Philip Jones. As he did so, he wondered, *Could I trust him? I've got a couple of hundred bucks in my wallet. He could leave and I'll lose my money and all the cards.*

Phillip went straight to Artie's car, turned on the inside light and searched for the wallet.

Artie didn't have to worry for long. Philip returned in five minutes. "There was no wallet there," he said.

"I must've left it at Reilly's. Someone probably would have stolen it by now."

"Don't jump to conclusions, Give them a call. Maybe, you'll be in luck."

"Thanks, Philip."

They went outside the hospital entrance so Artie could use his cell phone and call Reilly's. Soon after, he looked at Phillip with a broad smile and said, "I dropped the wallet on my seat, and a waitress picked it up. They said I could come and claim it any time I'd like to. I'll go there right away."

"Wait a minute, Artie. I drove down here with you to make sure that you would get here safely. I'm not going to let you drive back there by yourself. I know where Reilly's is. I'll go there, get your wallet and return it to you."

"Are you sure you want to do this for me? After all, we just met."

"No problem. All you have to do is call them back and tell them you are in the hospital and can't drive. Let them know that a tall black man will be coming to claim the wallet."

"Sure and thanks again," Artie said. He still had his doubts, thinking, *Of course, he could still take the wallet and run. Now that I think of it, why would he? There would be all those witnesses at the bar seeing him get the wallet. Anyway, I can tell he's a good man. I'm not going to worry.*

With that, Artie made the return call to Reilly's and explained the situation. Philip took off, and Artie reentered the waiting room. Most of the other patients were watching TV or reading. Arty was staring blankly at the wall. With all of his rationalizations, he still remained worried.

Forty-five minutes later, Philip Jones returned with the wallet. The money was intact, and all the cards were still in place.

"I don't know how to thank you, Philip."

"No need. I was just doing what any normal person would do."

"There's not too many of them around nowadays," Artie replied. He paused and added, "I'd still like to do something for you."

Artie took out his business card from his wallet and gave it to Philip. "Make an appointment, and you'll get free dental care. It could be a root canal, a crown or fillings, whatever."

Taking the card, Philip said, "I think I'll take you up on this. I haven't had a checkup in a year. Now go and fill out your paperwork."

After Artie had filled out the necessary forms, he sat down and waited. He expected he would be there for a while, but aside from embarrassment and a few aches, he was feeling fine.

Seeing that Artie was now in good hands, Philip shook hands with him and left.

A half-hour later, Artie was called inside and examined by a nurse and the ER resident. The physician verified that Artie had no broken bones, no concussion and only minor bruises and cuts.

After those wounds were taken care of, the resident said, "You are one lucky man. Your destination could have been the morgue. I hope you learned your lesson. Never mix alcohol and gasoline."

"I've learned it well, doctor."

Artie thanked him, left the building, got into his car and drove at about thirty-five miles an hour. When he got home, Artie made two telephone calls. First, he called his brother Burt in Delray Beach.

His brother berated him and reassured him that no matter what happened he would take care of him. "One final thing," Burt said, "Artie, don't get hung up with guilt over this. You're too hard on yourself. Bad things happen. Remember, you still saved the kid's life."

Reassured, Artie called his psychiatrist, Dr. Ralph Owen, and made an appointment for Monday evening. Dr. Owen was displeased that Artie hadn't spoken to him before he started his alcoholic binge, but considering medical confidentiality, he did not report the incident.

One positive aspect of the jolting car crash was that Artie stopped drinking alcohol.

At the moment Artie crashed into the stanchion, Mark and Ginny's lips met for the first time. It was a long, deep, sensuous kiss. Earlier, they had eaten dinner at La Pompadour, a French restaurant located on a picturesque lake in Haddonfield, New Jersey. The ambience, the delicious meal, the French wine and the feelings generating within the young couple were an overpowering combination.

Although in full control, Mark felt as if he were floating as he drove his aqua Corvette to Ginny's home. While Mark was driving, Ginny was also romanticizing. Mark brought Ginny to the door of her Cherry Hill, New Jersey garden apartment. He was about to give her a good night kiss and take off. After all, she was his dental assistant, and he didn't want to rush things.

Ginny was also aware of the inherent problems with an office romance. She still thought, *I couldn't let such a wonderful evening end like this.* She considered a way out saying, "Mark, you know I'm interested in anthropology. Part of my interest is a collection of native dolls that I've gathered from around the world. Most of them were sent to me from people on vacation. Would you like to see them?"

Always interested in different cultures, Mark quickly acquiesced. He said, "I'd love to," while thinking, *but I'm sure you're the prettiest doll of them all.*

The moment they entered the apartment, Mark closed the door and took Ginny into his arms. Mark was aware of the delectable perfume scent emanating from Ginny's neck. Ginny perceived Mark's barely perceptible cologne. As their lips blended into one, so did the mellifluous scents.

"Which way?" Mark asked as he paused from the deep kiss. Still wrapped in each other's arms, she guided him into her bedroom. That night, Mark never did get to see the exotic dolls.

It was three weeks since that catastrophic accident with Freddie Glaser and one-and a-half weeks since Dr. Artie Rosner's alcohol-induced mishap. On the Monday following the car crash, Artie was completely sober when he arrived at work. He confessed to his partner Mark about his recent alcoholic binge and the automobile accident. He also told him about the lost wallet and the Good Samaritan, Philip Jones. Mark understood and comforted Artie. He told him that worrying about the disaster with Freddie and being anxious about the upcoming malpractice case were counterproductive. Artie heeded Mark's advice and immersed himself in work.

Two days later — a Wednesday — Artie was once again the only dentist in his dental offices. His dental assistant, Julie, noticed that lately Dr. Rosner had appeared much calmer and for that she was pleased. The time was 8:55 A.M. The first patient scheduled was Mr. Herman Averill, a sixty-four-year old retired electrician. He was a regular patient but hadn't been into the office for over a year. The neglect resulted in an abscessed lower molar. Dr. Rosner no longer liked to do root canals or extractions, but today he was in a good frame of mind and was ready to deal with whatever was necessary.

Receptionist Phyllis Romaine announced to Julie that Mr. Averill had arrived. He walked in holding both hands on the upper left part of his face.

Cheerful Julie escorted Mr. Averill into Treatment Room No. 1. With an optimistic ring to her voice, she said, "Don't worry, Mr. Averill, in a couple of minutes the pain will be over. I'll take the x-ray, and Dr. Rosner will determine whether the tooth can be saved with a root canal or if it has to be extracted."

Mr. Averill moaned, "Thanks."

Julie escorted the patient into the dental chair and placed the dental towel over his chest. After finding out from the patient, the location of the tooth that was bothering him, she took a periapical x-ray. Five minutes later, Julie retrieved the x-ray from the automatic developer and handed it to Dr. Rosner.

Artie held the periapical x-ray up to the dental view box and determined that the decay of the upper left second molar was so extensive that it involved the furcation area between the three roots. There was also a large bony abscess around the ends of the roots. He brought the x-ray up to the dental light and pointed out the condition to his patient, saying, "As you can see, Mr. Averill, the decay has almost sectioned the tooth. In other words, there is not enough left for it to be restored. The tooth is also badly infected. That means root canal therapy is out of the question. The tooth will have to be extracted. The three roots come together. It should not be a difficult extraction."

Herman Averill still had a concerned look on his face.

Julie interceded, "Don't be afraid, Mr. Averill. Dr. Rosner will get you good and numb and before you know it, the tooth will be out."

Her gentle manner softened his concern, and he let out a weak smile.

Julie then retrieved the sterile tray containing the materials for an extraction of an upper molar. They included sterile gauze sponges, a plier-like upper molar forceps, and a subperiosteal elevator, which is used to move the tooth before extracting it. Another four items used in case the tooth had to be removed in sections were placed on the tray. These were a hemostat, a scalpel, sutures, and a needle holder.

While Julie was getting the tray, Artie examined the patient's chart, specifically, the medical history. There was no indication of heart disease, kidney disease, AIDS, allergies, or any other medical problems. *Good*, he told himself silently. "Julie," he announced, "please give me a short needle with one carpule of lidocaine with epi."

Julie handed Artie a cotton swab with topical anesthesia and a two-by-two gauze pad. Dr. Rosner wiped the alveolar mucosa region under the left lip that surrounded the roots of the upper left second molar. He then wiped the tissue on the palatal side of the tooth roots. Following this, he applied the topical anesthetic to the wiped areas.

Herman was fearful of dentists. He liked Dr. Rosner and his associate, Dr. Procter, but what they did frightened him. That's why he had waited so long before he came in with the abscessed tooth. Months ago, with his tongue, he had felt the hole in his tooth. At first it had hurt, but a few pain pills did the trick. The pain then stopped, and he thought he was home free. Last night, the pain returned with a vengeance, and he knew he had to come in this morning.

"Syringe," Artie requested.

Seeing the needle frightened Herman tremendously. He knew that Dr. Rosner used "laughing gas" for relaxation, but he was claustrophobic. He wouldn't let them put a mask over his nose.

Artie slowly injected the contents of the syringe under the left lip in the front part of the alveolar mucosa surrounding the roots of the upper left second molar.

Herman could hear his heart palpitating. It felt as if it were going to crash through his chest.

Having injected half of the solution, Artie withdrew the syringe and injected a few drops on the palatal side of the alveolar mucosa surrounding the tooth.

Herman felt pressure pounding in his head.

Artie handed the syringe to Julie. In less than a minute, the tooth should be out.

Herman saw the dentist approach with what looked like a large pliers. Fear overwhelmed him.

Dr. Rosner applied the dental forceps to Mr. Averill's upper left second molar.

Herman felt the crushing sound around his tooth.

Dr. Rosner pulled the tooth out with one swift motion. Julie handed him a sterile four-by-four gauze pad. "Bite down on this, Mr. Averill," the dentist requested. Herman now had tremendous pain that spread from his upper left jaw to his lower left jaw. The pain quickly spread to his left shoulder and chest. Instantaneously, Herman slumped forward in the chair.

Mr. Averill's face was blue. Artie noticed it immediately. He screamed out, "Julie get me the oxygen and the emergency kit. Phyllis, call 911." Artie felt his own sharp pain and muttered silently, *Damn that hand*!

The women responded to Artie's requests immediately.

Artie felt Mr. Averill's pulse. It was weak and thready, barely perceptible. He listened to his breathing. It appeared to have stopped. He thrust the oxygen mask on Herman's face and opened it up full force. "Julie," he exclaimed, "hold this down, I'll inject him with epinephrine."

Julie held the mask firmly. Artie retrieved a syringe with 1:1000 epinephrine. He injected it into Herman's right shoulder muscle. Artie knew that epinephrine was a stimulant to the heart. He hoped it would get from the muscle tissue to the heart fast enough to save his patient's life.

A few seconds later, Artie retook Herman Averill's pulse. It appeared to be a little stronger. "Thank God," Artie murmured quietly. The patient's chest moved up and down slightly. The color was returning to his cheeks.

"Mr. Averill, can you hear me?" Artie called out.

Herman Averill opened his eyes. He answered weakly, "Yes. What happened?"

Before Dr. Rosner could answer the two-man emergency squad entered the room and took over. While they were monitoring the patient, Artie explained what had occurred and the interventions that were done.

The technicians carried out Herman Averill on a stretcher. The senior member spoke to the patient, "Mister, you are the luckiest guy in the world. If Dr. Rosner hadn't acted immediately, we'd be bringing you to the morgue."

"Thank you so much, Dr. Rosner, I'll never forget you," Herman said.

"It's part of my emergency training," Artie responded proudly.

Artie suddenly remembering something and shouted, "Wait!" He ran back to the treatment room, reentered the reception room, handed the junior technician a four-by-four gauze pad, and said, "In a few minutes, take out the other gauze and have him bite down on this. After all that's happened, we don't want him to bleed to death."

The patient was taken to Mt. Laurel General Hospital. Phyllis and Julie applauded their doctor. Artie Rosner wore a great big smile.

The rest of the morning went smoothly and quickly. At 11:30, Phyllis called the hospital. The news was good. Mr. Averill had suffered a minor heart attack but was now stable. When it was time for lunch, Artie felt so good that he thought about first having a drink to celebrate. He quickly changed his mind.

That same morning Mark was contemplating an adventure. He loved to canoe and heard that New Jersey's Pine Barrens had canoeing in three of their rivers, the Mullica, the Wading and the Oswego. There were also historical sites in the region, the main one being Batsto Village. He thought it would be great to drive to the Pine Barrens, canoe, hike and visit the historical sites. When he told Ginny his plan, she agreed wholeheartedly.

Ginny packed a picnic lunch and was ready for Mark. The young dentist arrived at her Cherry Hill Garden apartment at 7:30 A.M. He carried his Nikon in one hand (he wasn't yet into digital cameras) and a dozen roses in the other. Ginny was dressed in a pale green polo shirt, gray shorts and a new pair of Nikes.

"They're beautiful," Ginny said as Mark handed her the roses. "I'll put these in a vase before I do anything else."

Mark couldn't help but admire her appearance. When she returned, he said, "It's a great improvement over a dental uniform."

"Thanks, but you're no slouch either." Mark smiled. His muscular build showed up well in a tight-fitting tan polo shirt, brown shorts and slightly worn-out tennis sneakers.

After a warm embrace, they took the camera, lunch, blankets and mosquito repellent and were on their way in Mark's new aqua Corvette. Ginny cuddled as close as she could to Mark while still wearing the seat belt. They headed east on Route 70. In about forty-five minutes, they would be in one of the most interesting natural areas in New Jersey. Even though New Jersey is small, the state's authorities left the Pine Barrens in its natural condition. It is the largest tract of open space between Boston and Washington D.C. The Pine Barrens comprises about two thousand square miles, which is one quarter of the area of New Jersey.

"You know, Ginny, we'll have to decide where to start and what to concentrate on. Should we start off by hiking or canoeing? Maybe we should begin at Batsto Village?"

"What's at Batsto Village?"

"I went to triple A and got an informative booklet about the Pine Barrens. Let's see how good my memory is."

"Yes, let's see," Ginny said with a touch of a sarcasm.

"Batsto Village is a rejuvenated ironworks community. I think it was originally founded in 1766 and was militarily important during the American Revolution. There are all sorts of colonial shops and small mills. They make candles, spin yarns, grind grain and make small equipment. The people are dressed in period costumes and act in character. Friends have told me it's well done, somewhat on the order of a Disney town."

"Your memory's excellent, and that sounds great. What is there to see with the hiking and canoeing?"

"Plenty. First of all, there are 'dwarf forests.' These are made up of thin and scraggly scrub oaks and pitch and short-leaf pines that grow only to about five feet in height."

"Why so short?"

"It's not known for sure, but it seems to be related to the fires that occur periodically."

"You digested that AAA booklet perfectly," Ginny said as she touched his right thigh with her left hand.

"Thanks," Mark said modestly. "The pines grow as they do for a couple of reasons. One is that the soil is sandy. The scrub pines also survive because they have a thick bark that insulates them against the high temperatures."

"That's sort of like your thick head that stops you from having a concussion every time you bang it on the x-ray machine."

"Hey, you're my assistant! You should look out for me."

"You move too fast for me."

"How's this for movement." Mark pulled off the road onto the shoulder and kissed Ginny fervently.

After a few passionate minutes, Ginny remarked, "We want to see the Pine Barrens, don't we?"

"You're right," he answered.

Mark and Ginny regained their composure and, rebuckled. Then Mark pulled the car back onto the road. He continued the talk. "Back to the pines. The pines that don't have a thick bark burn and are rapidly replaced."

"How come?"

"The scorched ground is a great environment for pine seedbeds. The pines have buds in their trunks and large limbs. After the pines burn, their buds fall out and sink into the ground. Once the fire dies down, the buds come out of their dormant state and develop. Soon, new pines start to grow."

"That's interesting, but we're not going to spend hours just looking at miserable-looking oaks and pines. What else is there to see?"

"There are many unpolluted streams and rivers. In fact, you're supposed to be able to drink the water."

"Only if we get real thirsty, Mark. Tell me more."

Mark held the steering wheel firmly with his left hand and gently placed his right hand into Ginny's left hand. After a few seconds, he let go and continued. "There are lakes where you can swim and fish and see dams and beavers at work. There are lots of birds and other small mammals. There's even an occasional fox."

"That sounds wonderful."

"It is. The barrens also have marshes, swamps, blueberry and cranberry bogs and several varieties of rare orchids."

"Orchids would be nice."

"I suppose those roses back home could use some embellishment."

Ginny inched over and kissed Mark on the neck.

"That was nice, but you do want me to pay attention to the road."

"Of course." Ginny moved back in her seat.

"The last two things to mention are the canoeing and hiking."

"I've rowed, but I've never gone canoeing," Ginny said.

"If you'd rather hike, the highlight is supposed to be the fifty-mile Batona Trail."

"Where does it go?"

"It runs from Ong's Hat in Lebanon State Forest through Batsto and Wharton State Forest and into Bass River State Forest."

"Mark, there's no way we can do even a small part of all this. Why don't we start hiking at the beginning of the Batona Trail and take it to Batsto Village? We can then spend a couple of hours at Batso. After that, we'll hike back to the car."

"Good idea. We'll save the canoeing for another day."

"Perfect."

In fifteen minutes, they pulled into the parking lot at Ong's Hat. Their memorable trip through the Pine Barrens had begun.

While Artie Rosner and Mark Procter were having a good day, nurse

Bobbie Wise and physical therapist Rhonda Fletcher were ministering to Freddie Glaser. Bobbie was a matronly fifty-five year old widow. She had been a practical nurse for thirty years and worked with comatose patients on several previous occasions. It was not a job she relished. She had just finished examining Freddie's vital signs. Everything checked out within normal limits. Rhonda, a younger and slimmer version of Bobby, was single and dedicated to her physical therapy career. She usually worked with stroke victims and felt it somewhat difficult to work with the unresponsive Freddie. Nevertheless, she exercised his limbs and massaged his neck and back. Freddie was still totally unaware of anything except for the complete void. It was his only existence.

Mark and Ginny were trekking through Lebanon State Forest. They had seen numerous pines and oaks, wild cranberries and blueberries, streams and swamps. They even got a glimpse of a beaver at work.

All of a sudden, they heard loud squawking. Ginny looked around and spotted two tree frogs. She saw their mouths opening and closing but the sounds were coming from the opposite trees. She called out, "Am I crazy, Mark or are they throwing their voices?"

"No, you're quite sane. I forgot to tell you, the Pine Barrens is loaded with..." After the pause, he continued, "ventriloquist tree frogs. They project their voice. Apparently, this is the only region in the world where they're found."

"That's cool."

Mark photographed the tree frogs. Then something new caught his eye. Looking down at a torturous-looking plant, he called out to Ginny, "Watch this, honey."

Ginny bent her head down to get a close up view. She said, "That weird plant has a mouth and it's eating all sorts of bugs."

"Another oversight on my part. I didn't tell you about that. It's an insectivorous plant."

"Whew. I'm glad it doesn't go for bigger forms of life, like us."

"No. We're safe on that score."

With his camera's fast shutter speed action, Mark caught the plant in action.

It was now 11:30, and they were approaching Batsto Village. Before they entered the village, Ginny was in for another surprise. A large crazy-looking winged insect headed right for her head. Seeing it, Mark screamed out, "Duck,

Ginny."

Responding quickly, Ginny moved her head but not before she had a good look at the weird-looking flying bug. "Something else you forgot to tell me, Mark. Am I right?"

"Sorry. You are correct. That's a well-known bizarre flying creature that's only found around here. It's known as the 'Jersey Devil.' There are no more surprises. We're here at Batsto."

They spent several hours at the unique village. They went to the general store and purchased two bottles of water and picked up a pamphlet describing a self-guided tour. They then went to the vicinity of the lake, spread out their blankets and relished the picnic lunch.

The tour was done at a leisurely pace. Mark was impressed with the restored ironmaster's mansion and the workers' small homes. Ginny watched with awe as the women spun intricate patterns with yarn and made stylish wax candles. They were both intrigued by the intricate objects the skilled technicians made out of glass and iron. The couple purchased post cards at the colonial post office — just in case Mark's pictures didn't turn out too well — and bought small gifts for each other at the general store.

In one small factory, they saw various pieces of equipment used in colonial times. They observed some early medical and dental equipment. Mark looked at a few frightening antique dental instruments. That brought his mind to Artie Rosner's upcoming malpractice suit. He remarked to Ginny, "If Dr. Rosner was smart, he would have donated his outdated anesthesia unit to a place like this. Had he done that, he wouldn't have had to contend with a malpractice suit."

Ginny's face momentarily expressed sadness. She didn't want this joyous day interrupted by a return to reality.

Before they began the return hike to the car, they walked to the lake, laid out the blankets and snuggled in each other's arms.

Mark had gone out with many attractive women, but none had the rare combination of looks and intellect that Ginny possessed. *Could I be falling in love*, he thought.

Ginny had had numerous dates with handsome and intelligent men. Mark was different. He was good-looking and bright. He also had a great sense of humor, but he had that ineffable quality of tuning into a woman's needs. Yes, he was something special. *How far will this go?* she wondered.

After about a half-hour of non-consummated but emotionally fulfilling closeness, the lovers got up and started back. During the return trip, the tired couple concentrated on walking and avoiding obstacles. They were too exhausted for observations of nature.

On the drive home, they stopped off at a local diner and had a satisfying but simple meal. Mark had Ginny back to her apartment by 8:00 P. M. They were both exhausted. At her front door, Mark and Ginny had an ardent kiss. Tomorrow was a workday.

7

It was another Wednesday — two weeks since Dr. Artie Rosner saved Herman Averill's life. Nevertheless, today, Artie was not working. He was home in bed with a stomach virus. His doctor told him that it appeared to be the twenty-four hour version, and he expected to be back in the office tomorrow. Mark and Ginny had agreed to switch with him and Julie. Artie and Julie would work on Friday and give Mark and Ginny that day off.

As usual, Phyllis was at the front desk. It was exactly 7:55 A.M when the phone rang. The caller was the patient who was scheduled for the eight o'clock time slot. She was calling to cancel her appointment. Phyllis buzzed on the intercom to Treatment Room No. 2. She spoke to Ginny. "You guys got a break. The first patient canceled. Why don't you get yourselves some coffee?"

Thanks, Phyllis." Ginny turned toward Mark and said, "Our first patient canceled."

"That means we've got some time on our hands. What should we do?"

"We could discuss pollution, terrorism, or maybe TV's latest craze; you know, the reality shows."

With a wink, Mark said, "We could do something else."

"Ginny laughed. "Uh, uh! No privacy, and not enough time."

"Only kidding. Let's get some coffee. I see Phyllis brought in some muffins. We'll have a real treat."

"Sounds good."

They went back to the staff room and Mark poured out two cups of coffee with sugar and milk. They were halfway through their muffins when the phone rang. Phyllis buzzed them on the staff room intercom. This time Mark picked up. Phyllis said, "There's a mister Wally Mann from Acme Travel. He had spoken to Dr. Rosner five weeks ago. You know, when that accident occurred with Freddie Glaser. I told him Dr. Rosner was home sick. Do you want to talk to him?"

Mark thought of something and said, "Yeah, put him on." Mark picked up the extension telephone. "Hi! I'm Dr. Mark Procter, Dr. Rosner's associate."

At the other end of the line, Wally Mann, from Acme Travel in Cherry Hill, spoke. "I expected to speak to Dr. Rosner. He told me he would be in the office on Wednesdays."

"He usually is," Mark replied, "but he's home with some kind of a virus. Is there anything I can help you with?"

"Not really. I had to firm up reservations for Dr. Rosner."

"I see. He'll be in tomorrow."

"Do you think it'll be all right for me to call him on a Thursday?" the travel agent asked.

"That should be fine."

"Dr. Rosner had told me to call only on Wednesday mornings between 8:15 and 8:30."

"I wonder why he said that?" Mark paused for a few seconds. He seemed to gain a sudden insight. "I think I can figure it out. Wednesdays we reserve only for emergencies, and the last time slot we schedule for is 8:00 A.M. Dr. Rosner probably figured he wouldn't have a patient at that time, making it a good time to call."

"That makes sense," Wally Mann said.

"Put it this way. If the reservation confirmation can wait 'til next week, call him next Wednesday. If it's urgent, call him tomorrow. The receptionist will let you know whether or not he's busy. Usually, we both have a five-minute leeway before the end of each hour. You can try him a couple of minutes before the hour."

"Thank you very much, Dr. Procter."

The two hung up.

Ginny took a sip of coffee and asked Mark, "What was that all about?"

"Something about reservations for a trip."

"Do you know where or when?"

"He didn't tell me anything, but Dr. Rosner's vacation time is the last three weeks in July. Maybe he was planning a trip for then."

Mark took a drink of coffee, reflected a moment and added, "I know these legal matters take a long time to develop. Even if he planned the trip before the problem with Freddie Glaser came up, he should still be able to get away in July."

"I hope he does. He needs to take his mind off the case."

They finished their coffee and muffins. The rest of the day was slow. They only saw five routine patients. The office was closed at 5:00 P.M. Mark and Ginny went to their separate homes, rested and got ready for the evening.

At 7:00, Mark picked up Ginny and they went out to dinner at LaFrere's, a new French restaurant in Moorestown, New Jersey. They each only had one glass of white wine, and a healthy fish dinner. At 9:00, Mark took Ginny home. They knew that Thursday the office had a full schedule of patients, but they weren't that tired. Their passionate lovemaking lasted several hours.

Mohlner Dental Equipment Service Company was located in a small store at 235 High Street in Voorhees, New Jersey. It was a low-key operation with Pat Mohlner, the owner taking care of most of the repair jobs and Rudy Kennedy handling the majority of the service operations. Two other employees, Joe Turner and Dave Nagle, were generalists who worked at both servicing and repairing dental equipment. All four of them were former employees of Rausch's Dental Supply and Equipment Service Company, a prestigious firm in the dental industry that had been in business for forty-five years. Two years ago, Pat, who had been an employee at that large company for twenty-five years, decided to go out on his own and took the other three men with him. Things worked out well. Everyone was making more money and getting better benefits than they did at Rausch's and the three employees got along well with each other and their boss, Pat.

At Mohlners, it had been a relatively slow day since most dentists were off on Wednesdays and those that were open usually maintained a skeleton staff for emergencies. Rudy finished servicing an ultrasonic scaling unit at Dr. Kaster's Voorhees office at 4:15 P.M. He was only five minutes from the company's store and when he got there — although he was supposed to work until five — Pat told him he could leave for the day.

Great, Rudy told himself, *now, I can get to Reilly's early*. He was thinking about the popular Reilly's Bar and Grill. Rudy Kennedy was one of its most frequent customers. Rudy was a forty-five year old, twice-divorced alcoholic. He was a short, thin man except for a large potbelly. Rudy was an excellent worker when he was sober, and he was usually sober during working hours.

Rudy was a friendly soul. He had been a good provider, but it was his drinking that led to the break-up of his two marriages. Rudy's alcoholic propensity was easily understood. His deceased father, who had died from liver cancer, had been an alcoholic. Rudy's parents split up when he was a teenager. That left Rudy with a formidable background in drinking and divorce.

Rudy walked into Reilly's and was greeted by two of his friends, Chubby and Bones.

"Hi, Rude," Chubby said, "you're early today."

"I finished my last job quick. I see you guys beat me to the punch."

It didn't take Rudy Kennedy long to catch up with his buddies. Soon, they were singing and humming songs from the old country. At 6:00 P.M, they took a momentary break from their liquid nourishment and ate burgers and fries. By eight, while Mark and Ginny were finishing off their dinner at LaFrere's, Rudy teetered out of the front door of Reilly's. Fortunately, his apartment was only a couple of blocks away.

The morning of July 12 — eleven days after Dr. Mark Procter spoke to the travel agent, Wally Mann — Dr. Artie Rosner left for a three-week trip to Costa Rica. The trip had been scheduled before the incident with Freddie Glaser. Since nothing substantial had happened with the malpractice suit except for back-and-forth activities between the opposing legal teams, Artie had decided to take the trip. Originally, he was scheduled to travel alone, but now he was in no mood to go by himself. His brother, Burt, was going to meet him in Florida. From there, they would travel together to San José, the capital of Costa Rica. Everyone in the office encouraged Artie to get away for the vacation. Even his malpractice attorneys urged him to leave considering the trial was still months away.

On a Tuesday — nine days after Artie Rosner had left for Costa Rica — at the Marlton dental office, Mark and Ginny were having their hands full. This was the eighth straight day that they had been working, and they only had three broken appointments in the eight days. It was 4:15 P.M. Mark had just completed the insertion of a single tooth implant in the region of an upper right central incisor that had been extracted two months before.

The patient was Mrs. Edith Boucher, an attractive 42-year old brunette. Her husband, Everett, had just returned from a European business trip and was away when the tooth had been extracted and the decision to make an implant had been made. Therefore, he had asked if Dr. Procter would explain the story behind this tooth. Mrs. Boucher agreed and so did Mark. He then looked at the patient's chart. From it, he was about to explain what had happened in the past and what he just finished doing. Wanting to know more about the reason for implants, Ginny also listened intently.

Mark looked at Edith Boucher and began. "You told me that when you were twenty years old you fell while ice skating and fractured the incisal edge of the tooth. The fracture went into the 'nerve,' and Dr. Rosner did root canal therapy. Afterwards, he made a post and core to give extra support to the tooth. The top of the tooth was then drilled down and a porcelain and metal crown was made. That's what most people call a cap. For twenty-two years, the tooth was fine. Two months ago, you said that you banged into the freezer door and fractured the entire tooth."

"That was terrible," Mrs. Boucher interjected.

"I'm sure it was. It was a longitudinal fracture, which is also known as a vertical fracture. The tooth was hopeless and was extracted. Since we couldn't leave you with an empty space, a flipper was made. That was a small plastic partial denture containing a life-like central incisor. When you left, no one would have known that you had a missing front tooth. However, a flipper is only a temporary measure. That's why we talked about the three alternatives, a fixed bridge, a partial denture and a single tooth implant with a porcelain-to-metal crown. The partial would entail a metal or plastic apparatus resting on your palate that would be removable. You didn't want that."

"Right. My friend, Gertrude, has one. She can't stand it."

"Some people do have trouble adjusting to a partial denture. The fixed bridge would replace the missing tooth but would entail drilling down and crowning the two adjacent teeth. The bridge wouldn't be removable, but two perfectly normal teeth would have to be cut down to make the three-unit bridge."

"I didn't want that."

"Right. That's why I told you about the single-tooth implant. Although it would be the most expensive, there would not be any cutting down of adjacent teeth. The implant would also be non-removable. The implant would go into the space where the extracted tooth had been."

"That's why I chose it, Doctor."

"Now that the implant has been inserted, we will cement in a new porcelain-metal crown that is a perfect color match for your other central incisor."

"Thank you, Dr. Procter. That was an excellent explanation. Although I'm a little poorer, at least I can understand why," Everett Boucher said.

"You may be poorer, but I'm a lot richer thanks to Dr. Procter," Edith

Boucher added.

In a few minutes, the patient and her husband left the office. Ginny smiled at Mark and said, "Good job."

"Thanks, Ginny."

At that moment, Rudy Kennedy entered Treatment Room No. 2.

"Hi, doc. Hi, Ginny. I'm here to service the high-speed unit."

"Good. Go right to it," Mark said. To Ginny, he remarked, "While he's working on the unit, you can clean the room, Ginny."

At 5:00 P.M, both Ginny and Rudy had finished their work. Mark called Ginny aside and said, "Why don't you go home. After all, you promised me home cooking tonight. I merely want to talk to Rudy for a few minutes about another piece of equipment. What time should I be over?"

"Seven-thirty should be fine. Don't forget to bring the wine. Tonight's chicken. Let's make it red wine for a change."

"Gotcha. See you later."

After Ginny left, Rudy approached Mark and said, "She's a real looker."

"Bright, too, Rudy. Listen, if you've got a minute, I want to ask you about something."

"Sure, doc."

"Do you remember the last time you installed the gas tanks on Dr. Rosner's converted general anesthesia unit?"

"I sure do. That's the only unit like that I've seen since I've been working. It's a real antique. I told old Doc Rosner several months ago to get rid of that dinosaur and get himself one of the new 'fail-safe' jobs. You know, like the kind you've got."

"You're probably right, but something came up after you installed the tanks. When was it?"

"Lemme think about that." He paused as if in deep reverie. "I dunno for sure, but I think it was around the end of May. I could go back to my place and find out exactly which day it was."

"No. That won't be necessary. I simply want to know if you could possibly have installed the tanks incorrectly by accident?'

Rudy stiffened up and glared at Mark. "What the hell are you asking me that for?"

"Calm down, Rudy. I'm not trying to blame you. What happened is that Dr. Rosner used the gases on a patient, and the tanks had been installed backwards. When he thought he was giving the kid oxygen, he was giving him nitrous oxide."

"No kidding'! What happened?"

"The kid went into a coma, and he's still in it."

"I feel real bad about that, but there's no way that I coulda switched the tanks."

"Why are you so certain?"

" 'Cause when I first started to work for Dr. Rosner and I saw that old unit, I figured there could be a problem with tanks being switched. So I got myself some green and blue paints. I made color-coded markings on that old anesthesia unit where the tanks attach. The nitrous oxide tank was colored blue. So I painted a blue mark where it attached to the unit. The oxygen tank was colored green, and I painted a green marking at the spot where it attached. There's no way I coulda switched them unless my eyes were closed. I don't work with my eyes closed!"

To prove his point, they went into Treatment room No. 1, and Rudy showed Mark the small color-coded marks. When Mark had previously re-switched the tanks to their normal positions, he hadn't noticed the small markings. He could now see that Rudy Kennedy was telling the truth.

"Thank you, Rudy. I don't know what happened, but be reassured no one will blame you. Dr. Rosner is being sued, but we will not mention anything about switched gas tanks. There's no way you or your company can be implicated."

"Fine, doc. Like I said, me switching those tanks was impossible."

"I believe you, Rudy. One other thing. Could you keep our conversation to yourself? I don't want the insurance companies knowing about the possibility of switched gas tanks."

"Heck, I've always liked you and old Doc Rosner. Mums the word. I swear it."

Rudy Kennedy left the office. Mark was now in a quandary. What really happened?

He sat in the dental chair, closed his eyes and pressed his hands to his forehead. After a few seconds, he had an insight. Artie had told him somewhat about Rudy Kennedy, especially the fact that he was an alcoholic. Rudy said the only way he could have switched those tanks was if he was blind. He didn't say anything about being drunk. If he were drunk when he installed the tanks, then blue and green might have looked similar. *Yes, that's it*, Mark thought. *Rudy Kennedy must've been drunk when he installed those gas tanks.*

Getting into his truck, Rudy was disturbed. *I know I put those tanks in right. I couldn't have been high. No way! I didn't drink anything that day. Or did I? Hell, no! I'm not gonna feel guilty about that kid. But if I didn't switch those tanks, who did?* He held his hands to his head and thought, *Could I have done it?*

8

Artie and Burt Rosner traveled to Costa Rica for a three-week holiday. Although originally Artie had planned it just to have an interesting and relaxing diversion, it now became a holiday to allow him to block out thoughts of the impending malpractice trial. Being a Florida resident, Burt was used to the warm climate, but he looked forward to the dramatic scenery and the native customs. To give them a permanent reminder of the trip, Burt took his Minolta camera with ten rolls of film, and Artie took his Panasonic camcorder with a half dozen videotapes.

The Rosners arrived in Costa Rica around 2:00 P.M. on July 12th. They took a cab from the airport to the bed-and-breakfast, known as Siete Hormingas Negras, which translates as Seven Black Ants. After unloading their luggage, the brothers had a light late lunch. Following that, they walked to the tourism center in San José, the capital city.

At 3:30 P.M., along with eight other American tourists, they sat down inside a small auditorium listening to an English-speaking guide enthusiastically describing the attributes of his native country.

"First, I would like to welcome you to our beautiful country. I will tell you most of the important facts, and when I'm finished you can see a short film showing the highlights. Costa Rica is one of the seven countries — all republics— in Central America. It is one of the smallest of the countries, slightly smaller than West Virginia. Costa Rica is sandwiched between Nicaragua on the north and Panama on the south. It is bounded by the Caribbean Sea on the east and the Pacific Ocean on the west." He pointed at the location on a wall map.

"Geographically, Costa Rica is a country of contrasts. Its large central section is an inter-mountain basin known as the Meseta. This is where you folks are now located. It is within this region that is our capital, San José, and the five other largest cities. Half our population lives in the Meseta. On the northern side, two volcanic mountain ranges, known as the Cordillera Central and the Corillera de Guanacaste, surround the Meseta. Within fifteen miles of San José is the active volcano, Irazu."

Sitting near the back of the room were Burt and Artie. "I hope it doesn't blow while we're here," Burt whispered to his brother.

The guide continued, "Southward from the Meseta is found the high and rugged Cordillera de Talamanca mountains. On the Pacific side, two peninsulas jut into the ocean. Closer to inland are tropical plains and further inward are mountain ranges. On the Caribbean side, the Nicaraguan lake plains extend into northeastern Costa Rica. Following the Caribbean shoreline southward is a narrow plain that extends southward into Panama. Costa Rica has a wonderful rain forest along the wet Caribbean slopes."

"It better not rain while we're in the forest," Artie said to Burt.

The tour guide paused and glared at the brothers. After they crawled back into their seats, he continued. "Ninety-six percent of the population is White, including Mestizo. Two percent is Black, one percent is Indian, and one percent is Chinese."

Unfazed by his brother's previous talking interruption, Burt raised his hand. After the guide reluctantly acknowledged him, Burt asked, "What's a Mestizo?"

"A Mestizo is a person born from White and Central American parents." The guide then took off where he had left off. "The religion of eighty percent of the population is Roman Catholic, and eleven percent are Protestants."

"We'd never fit in here," Burt whispered to Artie.

Artie merely smiled as the speaker continued.

"Nevertheless, because tourism is such a major industry, at any one time people of all races, religions and nationalities can be found in the country."

"At least, they won't kick us out," Artie whispered to his brother.

"Right on," Burt said in response.

Looking at the tourists in the first few rows, the guide said, "Most tourists remain in the Meseta Central, especially within San José and its suburbs. Education is stressed in Costa Rica, with ninety-three percent of the population able to read and write. As compared to the other Central American countries, wealth is more evenly divided. A lot of money is spent on education and freedom of expression is stressed. We have no military — only a police force. The official language is Spanish. Generally, English is spoken only around

Puerto Limon."

A tourist from the front of the room raised her hand.

"Yes?"

"Does that mean people in San José won't understand us?"

"No. Most shop owners and government workers speak English. Many of the cab drivers know basic words in English. Usually, you'll be able to find someone who can help you out."

The guide paused and then continued. "Aside from tourism, our country's major industries are farming, especially sugar cane, bananas, rice, coffee, plantains, corn, rice, beans, potatoes and oranges."

Another tourist from the front raised his hand. The guide acknowledged him.

"What are plantains?"

"A plantain is a tropical plant that grows as high as thirty feet. The same name is used for the fruit of that tree. So a plantain fruit is a greenish, starchy kind that resembles a banana. Unlike a banana, it can only be eaten if it is cooked."

The guide cleared his throat and continued. "Cattle are also important in our country. The principal manufactured goods are automobiles, trucks, buses and other forms of machinery. Goods such as processed foods, textiles and clothing, construction materials, fertilizer and plastic products are prominent."

He paused momentarily, took a sip of water and said. "There's something that I'm really not supposed to talk about, but because it's a fact of life, I'll mention it. Costa Rica is a transshipment country for the illicit transportation of drugs such as cocaine and heroin from South America and locally grown cannabis."

There was a hum in the audience. After quiet resumed, the guide went on. "Most of the foreign trade to countries such as the U.S., Guatemala, El Salvador, Germany, Italy, Netherlands, Great Britain and France pass through the port of Puntarenas, which leads into the Gulfo de Nicoya and out to the Pacific Ocean, and Puerto Limon, which leads into the Caribbean Sea."

The guide wiped his chin and continued. "Although our country is tropical, the climate varies within the three main regions. The coastal plains are hot throughout the year. The Meseta, where you are now, has a more moderate climate. In the mountains, especially at the highest elevations, the climate is cool. The coastal regions of southern Costa Rica get the most rain. The northwest and the Meseta Central have a more moderate rainfall that falls between May and October. Unfortunately, we are right in the middle of the rainy season. But I heard the extended weather report and it's not too bad."

Burt was about to say something, but Artie's look stopped him.

"Natural hazards are occasional earthquakes, hurricanes along the Caribbean coast, flooding of lowlands during the rainy season and active volcanoes."

There was a murmur from the audience.

After they quieted down, the guide reassured them. "Don't worry. We get adequate warnings. San José is an interesting city. It is modeled after a typical Spanish town. It has grid-plan streets lined with a mixture of mirrored high rises and elegant bungalows. San José has fine hotels, wonderful shopping with lots of bargains, excellent restaurants, exuberant night life and superb museums."

A hand went up from a woman in the middle of the auditorium.

"Yes?"

"That all sounds great, but is it safe here?"

"Compared to many other countries, Costa Rica, and especially San José, is safe. But there are crooks everywhere. Not only that, women should be extra cautious when going out alone, because of the machismo attitude of some of the men towards women. Don't walk out wearing expensive items, and women should never travel alone."

After drinking some more water, he said, "There is something I have to warn the men about. Sex for sale has become prevalent in Central America. Especially in the seedier sections of San José, young girls, and even some young boys, stand on street corners selling their wares. Some cab drivers pick up single men and ask them if they'd like cheap sex. Beware! The cops are cracking down, and no matter how young the children are, they can still carry the AIDS virus."

Unable to keep quiet any longer, Artie whispered to Burt, "That's not on our agenda."

"You bet," Burt replied.

The guide pointed to the front exit and said, "When you walk outside, you'll notice many buses and cabs. They are quite inexpensive. Are there any other questions?"

No one raised a hand.

He concluded, "Good. The fifteen-minute movie of Costa Rica's highlights will begin in five minutes. Thank you for your attention. Enjoy your stay."

Artie and Burt watched the film. They were tired and a bit overwhelmed from all the information. Regardless, they were stimulated. Both could use an exciting adventure. Burt wanted one because of the slow pace of life in Florida. Artie needed one to escape his problems back home in New Jersey.

They walked back to their B & B. Siete Hormingas Negras was to be their home for the next three weeks. It was a small B & B with seven rooms and three baths. Siete Hormingas Negras was located in the historic Barrco Otoya district. The owner, Paula Rodriguez, was an architect. She inherited the property from her grandaunt and converted it to a B & B. Paula lived here and was responsible for the entire interior of the B & B being exotically decorated right down to the toilet seats. All the walls were brightly colored, with numerous paintings. Paula had placed various tropical fruits in the garden to attract a large variety of birds.

At Siete Hormingas Negras, a hearty breakfast was included in the reasonable rates. Since Burt snored and the rates were cheap enough, Artie and Burt had separate rooms with a bathroom between them.

During the Rosners' first week, it rained for the first three days. Artie and Burt took buses to a different museum each day. On the first Monday, they visited the Museo de Jade, the Jade Museum. The stone facade of the exterior of the building was surrounded by a variety of unique trees, shrubs and flowers that were foreign to the Americans. Once they got inside, Burt and Artie were amazed at the largest collection of Jade in the Americas. The collection ranged in age from 300 B.C. to 700 A.D.

"If I had someone to love, I'd buy her a piece of jade," Artie remarked.

Burt countered, "If Goldie turns out to be more than a passing fancy, maybe I'll get her something in jade, but I think I'll wait on that."

They saw interesting jade vases, low tables for grinding corn, and ceramic fertility symbols. In one of them, the penis was quite large.

"Neither you nor I are in that ballpark," Burt quipped.

Tuesday was set-aside for the Museo de Oro, the Gold Museum. The building was a modern structure that dazzled even without sunshine. It housed the largest collection of pre-Columbian gold jewelry in Central America. There were sixteen hundred individual pieces containing a total of twenty thousand troy ounces of gold.

"If they melted down that gold, I bet there would be enough for all the gold fillings and crowns ever made in the U. S.," Artie stated.

"You've got a warped mind, brother. I'd like to have one or two of those pieces exactly as they are."

Wednesday, they headed for the Museo Nacional, the National Museum. It was housed in the Bellavista Fortress, an inspiring but frightening site.

The museum had a whitewashed colonial interior. It was filled with all aspects of Costa Rican culture. There were pre-Columbian artifacts, period costumes, colonial furniture and photographs of Costa Rican life throughout the ages. Artie and Burt learned that native Costa Ricans call themselves Ticos. The Rosners found this museum to be both enlightening and exciting.

They were blessed with warm and sunny weather for the next three days. Thursday, they took a cab to the Jardín Lankester, the Lankester Botanical Gardens. It was filled with lush gardens and greenhouses. There was a fantastic array of flowers including eight hundred species of orchids. This was one of the world's largest collections.

Glancing at several of the more exotic orchids, Artie remarked, "If I only had someone to whom I could give gorgeous flowers like these."

"Don't worry, when this malpractice thing passes over, you'll find someone."

Artie was upset that Burt brought up the malpractice suit. For a few days, he had completely forgotten it.

In addition to the orchids, the gardens were filled with native flowers such as bromeliads and aroids. There were also eighty species of trees including rare palms, bamboos, heliconias, torch gingers and other ornamentals. For Artie, the foliage was a new experience. Burt had seen some similar types in Florida, but these were more exotic. The Rosners' cameras were clicking feverishly at the gardens.

On Friday, they were treated to a novel experience. It was a visit to the Jardín de Mariposas Spipogyra, the so-called Butterfly Garden. There were thirty species of butterfly and as an added attraction; they saw several types of hummingbirds. The colors were magnificent. It got Artie to think that *all is well in the world.* Artie's camcorder was busy capturing the butterflies in flight.

All of a sudden, his mind went back to New Jersey and the stories he had heard about Freddie Glaser. He recalled the child's insect-destroying activities, pulling out butterfly wings and related destructive actions. Upon further reflection, he realized that as devastating as Freddie's activities had been, the kid was now in a coma and he was responsible. *Damn,* Artie thought, *I've gotta stop thinking about that lawsuit.*

On Saturday, Artie didn't think about the upcoming malpractice trial. He had something else to worry about. The day started off perfectly. They took a cab to the Orosi Valley. It was an area of breathtaking views of verdant landscapes. The tropical forest was filled with a variety of trees and all sorts of exotic birds and small mammals. Artie and Burt were walking slowly in the dark forest when suddenly they heard a loud rumble.

"What in the world was that?" Artie screamed.

"Beats me!" Burt answered.

No sooner did Burt reply than the ground beneath their feet started to move. The brothers crumbled down into the rumbling forest floor. Only a few moments after it started, the rumbling stopped.

"Would you believe it!"? Artie exclaimed. "It was an earthquake."

Artie and Burt got up and examined themselves and the shifted ground. They were unhurt but the ground wasn't so fortunate. By being careful, they were able to walk safely out of the forest. It would have made a great video, but Artie had been too shaken up to turn on his camcorder.

While leaving, Burt remarked, "I'm happy I moved to Florida instead of California. I don't know how they can take those earthquakes."

Sunday and Monday were cloudy with occasional showers. On Sunday, the Rosners went to the Mercado Central, the Central Market. It was a noisy and smelly place with a warren of dark, narrow passages where vendors in their stalls hawked all sorts of things. They were selling fruits, vegetables, fish, exotic spices and wood and leather handicrafts. Neither of the brothers was of the shopping breed. They passed through quickly, but left themselves enough time to make a few purchases. Burt bought himself an inexpensive watch and purchased a leather handbag for Goldie. Artie bought leather handbags for the female dental staff, Julie, Ginny, Kathy and Phyllis. He also purchased leather wallets for himself and Mark.

On Monday, they visited a few of the numerous small churches. They were quaint, interesting in their own right, but typical of the Latin America style.

On Tuesday and Wednesday, the sun returned. Tuesday, Artie and Burt took a cab to Tapantí National Park. The cab ride over the rough roads was bumpy. Once they arrived at the park, they found a bird-watcher's and photographer's paradise. The rugged terrain was also the home of a variety of insects, small mammals, amphibians and reptiles. The Rosners' cameras were going constantly.

Looking at one of the largest lizards, Artie remarked to Burt, "Maybe, we'll find some dinosaurs. I heard that Spielberg filmed 'Jurassic Park' in the forests of Costa Rica."

"No way! Just looking at dinosaurs in a museum frightens me."

On Wednesday, the Rosners walked to a large cement square known as

Plaza de la Cultura, Cultural Plaza. They spent the entire day here. The brothers walked around a lot, soaking up the sun while the sweat was pouring out. In between sitting on the benches and drinking cool tropical beverages, they bought cheap souvenirs and watched marimba bands. They also listened to Andean music and were fascinated by jugglers and clowns.

It rained all day Thursday. At night, they went to Teatro Nacional, the National Theater, to see a native show. The theater was housed in an enchanting-looking building with a sandstone facade decorated with marble columns with bronze capitals, Italianate arched windows and statues of two odd bedfellows: Ludwig von Beethoven and the seventeenth century playwright, Calderón de la Barca.

It continued to rain from Friday to Wednesday. Artie and Burt spent the time by either reading in the B & B's lounge or going to different museums and historical sights. All during the trip, they ate at a variety of restaurants.

Wednesday night, they had dinner at La Cocina de Léna in the charming El Pueblo Shopping Centre, which resembled a colonial village. The restaurant had white walls with old tools and straw bags hangings. While listening to folk music and watching native dancing, they ate Costa Rican fare. Both had black bean soup. Artie had tamales and Burt had ox tail with yucca.

Thursday, they both felt queasy, but the sun came out brightly. With such a day, they disregarded their physical ailments and decided to explore one of the best natural wonders in Costa Rica. They took a cab to Parque Nacional Volcán Poás, Poás Volcanic National Park. The banded, gray-brown crater was one mile wide and nine hundred feet deep. At its bottom was a hot water lake.

"Look, Burt, the volcano is alive."

"You're not kidding. It's belching up all kinds of lava."

"The red-color is from steaming hot sulfur. It's really incredible. I've never seen an active volcano before." Artie seemed to be extremely impressed.

"I hope it stays just the way it is," Burt remarked. "I wouldn't want it to be any more active."

Remembering the earthquake, Burt didn't want to take any chances.

Artie spent several minutes videotaping the active volcano. Burt contented himself with only a couple of shots. They then left and returned to their B & B. Since their stomachs had quieted down, they opted for a light American-style dinner at a nearby restaurant.

It was cloudy during the last three days of the Rosners' Costa Rican stay, and the brothers spent them resting and revisiting a few museums. On Sunday morning while sitting in the cab heading for the airport, Burt remarked to Artie, "Costa Rica is a great country, and they treat Americans very well. I wonder how expensive it is to buy a retirement condo."

"Aren't you happy in Delray Beach?" Artie asked.

"Delray Beach is fine. I was just thinking about you. If all goes well with the malpractice suit, this might be a nice place where you could retire."

"I'm a few years from retirement, and now that you've mentioned it, I'm still damn worried about that case.

9

It was the day after the Rosners had returned from Costa Rica. Dr. Mark Procter and Ginny Walker were thrilled to have Dr. Artie Rosner and Julie back on board. The gifts Dr. Rosner brought them were appreciated, but it had been a hectic three weeks in the office while the older dentist and his assistant were on vacation.

Julie had spent her three-week paid vacation with a boyfriend, Stuart Boyce, in Pompano Beach, Florida. During the lunch hour break, Julie told the other staff members of the fun she and Stuart had swimming, playing golf and tennis, going to the dog races, seeing shows, eating out in fabulous restaurants and simply basking in the sun. Mark, Ginny and Phyllis were somewhat, but not overly, jealous, because they knew their vacation time would start next week. Kathy, the dental hygienist, also had a vacation to look forward to; hers would begin in a few weeks.

Artie couldn't stop raving about Costa Rica. The rest of the staff was happy for him. He looked good with a slight tan and a calm appearance. Of course, they realized that couldn't last.

Mark and Artie went out to lunch together at Krebs, an informal restaurant in Marlton. The four women ate together at the Main Street Delicatessen.

While waiting for the main course plates to be removed, Mark spoke to Artie. "By the way, a couple of weeks ago, Rudy Kennedy, the tech from Mohlner Dental Equipment Service, was in the office to service the high speed unit."

"What about it?"

"After he finished working, about 5:00 P.M., I got him alone and casually asked him about the last installation of the gas tanks in your converted anesthesia unit."

"Why did you do that?"

"I wanted to see if there was any chance that he would admit that he might have unintentionally installed them backwards. Of course, I had to tell him that one of your child patients accidentally received an overdose and was now in a coma."

Artie appeared anxious as he said, "What did he say?"

"I forgot to mention this, but before I asked him about the switching, I asked if he remembered your converted general anesthesia unit. He told me he sure did. In fact, he said that it was a real antique and he told you several months ago to get rid of — what did he call it? — Oh, yes, a dinosaur. He said he told you to get one of the new 'fail-safe' jobs, like the kind I use."

"He might have said something like that, but there's no way he implied that my unit was unsafe. To get back to the important matter, what did he say about the switching and the kid being in a coma?"

"First he said that he was real sorry about the kid, but as far as the switching of the tanks was concerned, he vehemently denied it. He showed me a color-coded system he used to line up the green oxygen tank to a green marking he painted at the oxygen point of attachment on the unit and the blue nitrous oxide tank to a blue marking he made at the nitrous oxide attachment point."

"I never noticed any color-coded markings."

"Yeah, they were there. The markings are very small, but they definitely can be seen."

"The tanks were still installed backwards," Artie said emphatically.

"I know they were, Artie. Rudy said that only if he had been blind could he have installed the tanks backwards. He's definitely not blind."

"Wait a minute. He's not blind, but I know that Rudy Kennedy is a lush. I bet he was drunk when he installed those tanks. That's it. He couldn't tell blue from green."

"Artie, that's just what I thought. The guy must've been drunk and now he's lying through his teeth."

"What should I do about it, Mark?"

"I don't think you have to do anything. I told Rudy that I didn't understand how the tanks were switched, but that you wouldn't implicate him or Mohlner's in it. I asked him to forget about our discussion."

"What did he say to that?"

"He swore he wouldn't tell anyone. I think he can be trusted. You've known him much longer than I have. What do you think, Artie?"

"He'll keep his mouth shut. I don't think he'll want the whole world to know that he's an alcoholic. If that came out, his boss would have to fire him."

Mark stared at Artie momentarily and said, "I just thought of something. By telling Rudy about the possibility of the switched tanks, if he's subpoenaed and does talk, the lawyers on both sides will know about the switched tanks."

"You're right. I'll have to tell my malpractice attorneys about the switched tanks. After all, they'll be real pissed if I held out information like that from them."

"Look, Artie, I think you still shouldn't do anything now. First, you'll have to find out whom the plaintiffs' attorneys depose. If you find out they are going to depose Mohlner's Dental Equipment Service and Rudy Kennedy will be called, then before the actual deposition, you can tell your attorneys about the switch."

"Don't you think they'll be upset about finding out so late?"

"Yeah, Artie, they'll be upset, but they'll be a lot more disturbed if they find out after Rudy Kennedy is deposed. Meanwhile, wait and see. Make sure you keep in contact with your attorneys to find out whom the other side is going to depose."

"Thanks, Mark. You've come up with a good plan."

With respect to the malpractice case, nothing substantial occurred during the next six weeks. Artie Rosner continued to use his converted general anesthesia unit for nitrous oxide/oxygen conscious sedation with several patients, and no problems arose. The attorneys exchanged legal matters. The plaintiffs' attorneys deposed Phyllis, Julie, Ginny and Mark. In their depositions, they stated everything they knew with respect to what had occurred on that fateful day. In addition, they attested to the good character and excellent dental ability of Artie Rosner.

An officer of the Newhouser Medical Equipment Company was deposed after he had personally examined Artie Rosner's converted Newhouser general anesthesia unit.

In his deposition, he stated that the unit was functioning correctly for nitrous oxide/oxygen conscious sedation. The plaintiffs' attorneys deposed officers of the Southern Dental Society. They were looking for any evidence of unethical acts, complaints or previous malpractice suits filed against Dr. Artie Rosner. They found nothing.

The plaintiffs' attorneys had Artie answer interrogatories in which his background and the details of the incident were disclosed. Artie's malpractice attorneys had Bernie and Pauline Glaser reply to interrogatories with respect to the character and medical history of Freddie Glaser. The malpractice defense attorneys also obtained the child's medical records and found out that Freddie definitely had an epileptic-like seizure during the first year of his life.

On this Tuesday morning in mid-September, the Rosner dental offices had been busy. The time was 11:55 A.M. Artie had finished his last morning patient. He figured it would be enough time before lunch to call Warren Wilkins, his private attorney, who was sharing the load with Healthcare Protective's malpractice attorneys. Artie went to his private office and dialed Wilkins' office. Warren's secretary picked up and connected Artie with the attorney.

"Hi, Warren. It's Artie, Artie Rosner."

"Hello, Artie. What's up?"

"That's just what I was gonna ask you. What's new with the case?" Artie's voice quivered slightly as he added, "Do you have any idea when the trial might come up?"

"I'll answer your second question first. For now, we don't have any specific date for the trial. Either side hasn't yet completed the depositions. I would expect that we wouldn't go to trial for at least another two or three months. It could even take longer."

"Hell, it looks like I'll be on Prozac® and Ativan® for quite a while."

"You should be pleased that the medications are helping you. As for the first question, we've been evaluating the results of the depositions and interrogatories. From the way we look at the case, the best tactic we can use is to concentrate on Freddie Glaser's previous epileptic-like attack. We'll get the neurologist, Jake Daniels, to testify that there likely was neurological damage caused by that early episode that set up the untoward incident in your office."

"That's the only thing I can figure. I've used 'nitrous' with my machine for over forty years and never had anything more serious that a couple of excitement reactions and a half a dozen patients vomiting on me. I've had some people howl with laughter, and I've even had one woman who wept like a baby."

Feeling somewhat embarrassed, Artie paused, and then said, "There was one other incident. Some women get real sexy when they're under 'nitrous.' One attractive babe grabbed my testicles. It was a good thing that my assistant was right there or else the patient could've later claimed rape."

"I didn't know that nitrous oxide was a sexual stimulant," the attorney said.

"That only occurs with some patients."

"Your mention of the converted anesthesia unit reminds me that an officer of the Newhouser Medical Equipment Company, the company that made your unit, was deposed. He found that it was still working perfectly. That will be verified by the video tape that you made, and the depositions we took of several of your patients that had 'nitrous' after the calamity with the kid."

"Fine." Artie's voice showed a bit of hope. He added, "Anything else?"

"There's one other thing. Kenneth Hamilton, the plaintiffs' chief attorney." He paused a moment and added, "By the way, I heard he's a buddy of yours."

"He used to be. We grew up together in New York and moved here about the same time. The ironical thing is that Bernie Glaser, the father of Freddie Glaser, is also one of my best friends. All three of us were transplanted New Yorkers. Now one friend is suing me, and the other friend is his attorney."

"Life is full of strange things," Attorney Warren Wilkins said philosophically.

"You were starting to say something about Hamilton."

"Yes. Kenneth Hamilton told me that they are going to depose the technician at Mohlner Dental Equipment Service. I suppose they want to check out the installation procedure of the gas tanks on your unit."

"Uh, huh." His right hand sent out a sharp thrust of pain. *Damn hand with its memory. Is it gonna haunt me all my life?*

"Are you all right, Artie?" the concerned Wilkins asked.

"I'm okay. I just got a tickle in my throat. I think I'm catching a cold."

"Take care of yourself. I'll call you when I find out anything new."

"Thanks, Warren."

The two men hung up their phones. Warren Wilkins wondered why Artie was surprised at the mention of the technician at Mohlner's. *Maybe, it was my imagination*, he thought.

Artie Rosner knew he had to speak to Mark.

It was 12:05 P.M. Mark Procter had finished his morning patient and was leaving to go to lunch. Although he didn't hide his affair with Ginny, they didn't want it to be readily apparent. Consequently, he and Ginny went out to lunch separately. Ginny had already left for lunch with Phyllis, Julie and the dental hygienist, Kathy Perrin. Not seeing Artie, Mark considered he had a luncheon engagement with someone else.

When Mark reached the door of the employee exit, he heard his name called.

Mark turned around and said, "Artie! I thought you had left already."

"No. I was on the phone with my malpractice attorney, Warren Wilkins."

"Are you going out to lunch?" Mark asked.

Artie nodded.

Artie walked up to Mark, and they left the building together.

"We'll eat together," Mark said. He added, "What did Wilkins say?"

"He told me that Kenneth Hamilton, the plaintiffs' principal attorney, is going to depose Rudy Kennedy."

"Does that concern you?"

"Damn right, it does. What if that Kennedy lush doesn't keep his word and tells Hamilton about the switching of the tanks?"

"I think he'll keep quiet," Mark said, "but if you're really worried, tell Wilkins. He'll inform your other attorneys."

"Like I said to you before, they'll be real pissed that I didn't tell them before."

"It's better that they'd be annoyed than deceived. I still don't think it'll come to that. I told you before, I spoke to Rudy Kennedy and I trust him. I don't believe he'll spill the beans."

"You think I shouldn't do anything?" Artie asked.

"Yes, that's right. Do nothing."

"Okay, Mark. I'll go along with what you say."

It was three days later, and Rudy Kennedy was looking forward to getting home. For two months he had been living with Suzanne O'Brien, and after work he was going to give her an engagement ring. He realized he had struck out twice with his two previous marriages, but Suzanne was different. She didn't drink as much as him, but on occasion, she did go to the bar with him and have a couple of drinks for herself. All he could afford was a pearl ring, but he was sure that Suzanne would understand that it was the thought that counted.

He left Mohlner Dental Equipment Service Company at 4:55 P.M. Twenty-five minutes later, he opened the door to his apartment on the fourth floor at 26 Plaza Place in Voorhees. Unexpectedly, all the lights were out. The only light that was blinking was from the red message-waiting indicator on his answering machine. Sensing that it might be important, Rudy listened to the message. It was from his boss, Pat, at Mohlner Dental Equipment Service. "Hi, Rudy, this is Pat. As soon as you left, I got a call from an attorney's office. The firm is called Hamilton, Burgess and Pettersen. They want you to answer a deposition for a malpractice case against Dr. Artie Rosner. Do you know what it's all about? At any rate, they want you to call early Monday morning and make an appointment. I'll give you the number when you come in."

Rudy knew what that was about, but he was in no mood to think about depositions now. All he wanted to know was the whereabouts of Suzanne.

"Suzanne," he called out.

There was no response.

Rudy look around the two-bedroom apartment. Suzanne was nowhere in sight. Her clothes were no longer in the bedroom. Rudy looked in her closet. Her luggage was missing. He looked in the bathroom. Her makeup was gone.

"Why?" Rudy screamed. The walls had no answer. Rudy then saw a note under a glass on the kitchen table. Shaking, he picked it up and read:

Dear Rudy:

You're a swell guy and I liked being with you. We had a great two months together. I knew that you drank a lot, but I thought I might be able to tolerate your drinking. I really tried, but it didn't work out. I don't want to wind up like my mother — a widow at age 35 because my dad died of cirrhosis of the liver.

I think you should try AA if you ever want a lasting relationship.

God bless you.

Love,

Suzanne

"No! No! No!" he screamed and ripped up the note, threw it into the wastebasket and stormed out of the apartment.

It was 5:30 P.M. and Reilly's Bar and Grill in Voorhees was busy with the pre-dinner crowd. In a corner table sat Chubby O'Hare and Bones Wiley.

"I wonder what's keeping Rudy?" Chubby asked. "He's about fifteen minutes late."

"Don't you remember? Rudy got a new girlfriend. He probably went home to get her."

"Oh, that's right, Bones. What's her name? Wait! Don't tell me. It's…"

He fumbled for the right name. ". Suzie. No, Suzanne. She's a pretty good looker, too."

Chubby looked at the bar. He saw a greasy, wiry-looking man having a drink. He was by himself. He pointed the man out to Bones and remarked, "I never saw that guy here before. He looks like a gangster."

Bones said jokingly, "Man, it's a free country. Did you forget?"

At that moment, Rudy came in. His face was beet red.

"Having a problem?" Bones asked.

"You bet!" Rudy shouted. "My girl walked out on me."

"Quiet down," Chubby said.

"I don't give a damn!"

"Okay, Rude, what happened?" Bones asked.

"She left me a rotten note. She said she couldn't take my drinking."

"Any women who can't tolerate her man having a few drinks in the evening isn't worth the effort," Chubby said.

"Yeah, forget about her," Bones added. "Have a drink."

"Damn right I will," Rudy said. He called for the waiter. When the waiter arrived, he screamed, "I'll have a double bourbon on the rocks."

Chubby and Bones each had two drinks, but Rudy tripled the number of drinks they had, and each one was a double bourbon. After about an hour, Bones said, "Rudy, don't you think you've had enough?"

"I've just started," Rudy muttered.

"At least have something to eat," Chubby said.

"You guys eat. I'm doin' fine the way I am."

"Have it your own way," Bones said.

Bones and Chubby ordered grilled steaks with fries. Rudy kept drinking. His two friends tried to get him to eat something, but he continued to refuse.

"It's your funeral!" Bones exclaimed.

That became a self-fulfilled prophecy. Rudy Kennedy keeled over, spilling his last drink on Chubby. Chubby was temporarily shook up and wiped himself as well as he could. More alert to what was happening, Bones went over to Rudy. He lifted up Rudy's head and looked into his pupils. They were fixed.

Recovered by this time, Chubby took Rudy's pulse. He felt nothing. Rudy's chest was motionless. "Hell!" Chubby shouted. "Someone call 911."

The bartender responded immediately. Meanwhile two relatively sober young men came over and initiated resuscitative measures. Oblivious to everything, the greasy, wiry-looking man was still drinking at the bar.

After five minutes, Rudy had still shown no sign of life. The wail of the ambulance siren was heard. In another minute, the two-man crew was inside the bar. They initiated emergency procedures as they carried Rudy out on a stretcher. It was to no avail. Five minutes later, Rudy arrived at the Emergency Room of Mt. Laurel General Hospital. Despite desperate measures by the medical staff, Rudy Kennedy was pronounced dead.

The following Monday — three days after Kennedy's death — Mark came into the dental office carrying a folded newspaper. He placed it on the desk of his private office, a similar but smaller version of Artie's private office. He saw Artie in the hall about to enter his own private office. Mark called out, "Artie, come here!"

Artie was unaccustomed to being disturbed so early in the morning. *I hope it's nothing bad*, he thought. He quickly entered Mark's office and asked, "What's so urgent? Anything serious?"

"No, nothing like that, but did you happen to read the obituary section of the Sunday *Courier-Post*?"

"I make it a point not to look at the obits. After all, I might find my name in there."

"All joking aside, there was something interesting in the Sunday obituary section."

"Don't keep me in suspense. What did you find?"

He opened the page and pointed to the appropriate line. Mark then said, "Look for yourself."

Artie put on his close-up vision glasses and read, "Mr. Rudy Kennedy, an employee of Mohlner's Dental Equipment Service Company of Voorhees, collapsed and died in Reilly's Bar and Grill. He was forty-five years old. Preliminary indication of the cause of death is an alcohol-induced heart attack. No funeral arrangements have yet been made."

"I can't believe it! That's horrible. I really liked the guy."

"So did I," Mark remarked, "but do you realize what this means?"

"My God! He can't be deposed."

That's right, Artie. And if they call in one of the other servicemen from Mohlner's, neither would know anything about the switched gas tanks."

"That means I don't have to tell the attorneys from Healthcare Protective about the tanks."

"You got it. Now you don't have to worry about annoying them."

"You know, Mark I would rather that Rudy Kennedy was alive and that I took my chances on him keeping his mouth shut. I realize it's a lucky break, but why did it have to happen this way?"

"Nobody can predict what the fates have in store. For the present, you'll have to hope that your attorneys' consulting neurologist — my buddy, Jake Daniels — finds that Freddie Glaser had a preexisting neurological condition that predisposed him to that tragic accident."

"I hope so." Artie grasped his fingers together tightly and added, "I still can't get it out of my mind that Rudy Kennedy is dead. I wonder what stressed him out so much that he went on a drinking binge. Do you think he did it on purpose? Could he have been suicidal?"

"I don't know, Artie. He didn't seem to be the suicidal type. At any rate, we'll find out sooner or later. Now we better get to work. Both of us have a full schedule."

10

It was the beginning of December, over two and one-half months since the death of Rudy Kennedy. The time was 1:00 P. M., and it was the second day of the Glaser vs. Rosner trial. The jury had been chosen. They were four women and two men. The alternates were a man and a woman. Since this was a civil medical malpractice case, a decision for negligence would have to be decided in the affirmative by a vote of five out of the six jurors. The male sitting jurors were a middle-aged architect and a semi-retired accountant. The female sitting jurors were a middle-aged public school elementary education teacher, an elderly, widowed housewife, a young secretary, and a nurse in her mid-fifties. The alternates were a middle-aged female physical education teacher and a retired postman.

Joseph Warrington, who was in his early sixties, was the judge. He was an embittered, sickly, former prosecutor who wavered in his feelings towards doctors. Judge Warrington did not tolerate disobedience and humor in his courtroom. He also worked at a quick pace. The judge made it abundantly clear in his instructions to the jurors that he didn't want this to be a long trial. He had overseas plans for the Christmas holiday.

The trial was being held in Courtroom A at the Colonial Courthouse in the Burlington County Office Complex at 125 Queen Street in Marlton. The Colonial Courthouse was a two-storied red brick building that had served as a courthouse since Colonial times. Many attorneys believed that some of the ancient judges still haunted its presence. Courtroom A was the smallest courtroom in the building. For the audience, there were twelve rows with a long, hard-backed, wooden bench in each row. Today, only ten people were present including Dr. Rosner's assistant, Julie Parsons, his brother, Burt, — up from Florida — and eight curious on-lookers. The other members of

Rosner's dental team had to work today.

Viewed from the front of the courtroom, the jury box was on the left side. It consisted of two raised rows of seats in front of which was a wooden panel with an attached rail on the top. There were seven leather-backed wooden seats in each row. Eight were presently occupied with the six jurors and the two alternates.

Judge Warrington sat on a leather chair with a high, soft back and a headrest. The chair rested within a well-like enclosure on an elevated wooden floor. There was an inverted u-shaped wooden panel with a wide top surrounding the judge's enclosure. In a well in front of and beneath the judge sat the judge's clerk and the court reporter. The bailiff stood near the window to the right of the judge. One step down, to the left of the judge, and an aisle away from the jury box was the wooden witness stand with a leather seat.

In front of and to the left of the audience benches were the defense attorneys' leather seats in front of a small table. Sitting there was the defense team that consisted of the Healthcare Protective attorneys, Ernest Coniglia, Herb Jameson and Laura Carlye, and Artie Rosner's private attorney, Warren Wilkins, and Dr. Artie Rosner. On the opposite aisle was the plaintiffs' attorneys' leather seats and table. Sitting there were Attorney's Kenneth Hamilton, Jim Burgess and Mike Pettersen and Bernie and Pauline Glaser.

The walls were paneled with paintings of colonial jurisprudence scenes. A hanging chandelier descended from the ten-foot ceiling partially illuminating the room with diffuse light. There were standing lamps on both sides at the front and back of the courtroom.

The plaintiffs' attorney, Kenneth Hamilton, dressed in a dark blue suit, leaned over the jury box and addressed the members in a loud and clear voice. "Ladies and gentlemen, I know for a fact that Dr. Artie Rosner is an excellent dentist and a caring individual." He stood up, turned toward the defendant and pointed him out to the jury. He turned back to the jurors. "Dr. Rosner has engaged in the general practice of dentistry for over forty years. However, I cannot let the fact of his competence, experience and longevity in dental practice interfere with the deliverance of justice. Unfortunately, Dr. Rosner's alertness is not what it used to be."

Hamilton paused for effect and continued. "On Wednesday, May 27th of this year at 8:15 A.M, he was treating a ten-year old boy, Freddie Glaser, with nitrous oxide/oxygen conscious sedation. This is what we know as 'laughing gas.' Little Freddie had a toothache. It would have been a simple matter to numb the tooth, clean out the decay and put in a temporary filling.

Dr. Rosner did all that."

The attorney looked at Dr. Rosner, turned back to the jury, and continued. "Dr. Rosner took care of the cavity, but he did not pay attention to the child that bore that cavity. The child was given an overdose of nitrous oxide, but before that, he ordered his assistants to do something despicable. We will show that because of malfunctioning of his conscious sedation unit, Dr. Rosner had his assistants physically restrain Freddie Glaser in order to get Freddie numb, remove the decay and put in the temporary filling."

The jurors appeared stunned at this accusation.

Attorney Ernest Coniglia whispered into Artie Rosner's ear, "Is that true?" Artie whispered back, "Yeah."

"Then why in hell didn't you tell us?" Coniglia whispered.

"I'm sorry. I had no idea that Julie or Phyllis would have mentioned that in their depositions," Artie said quietly.

"You should know that you're sworn to tell the truth in a deposition," Coniglia countered quietly.

Hearing the murmuring, Kenneth Hamilton glared at Coniglia and Dr. Rosner. He then turned toward the jurors and continued. "Why did his conscious sedation unit malfunction? I'll tell you why. Dr. Rosner is set in his ways. Over forty years ago, he purchased a general anesthesia unit that was converted so that it could be used for nitrous oxide/oxygen conscious sedation. Dr. Rosner used that machine on Freddie Rosner even though in his own office he had a 'fail-safe' nitrous oxide/oxygen conscious sedation unit. Had he used the 'fail-safe' unit it would have been impossible to have placed Freddie Rosner into his present condition. What, you may ask, is the poor child's present condition?"

Hamilton paused, walked away from the jury box and moved toward the plaintiffs' box. He retraced his steps and continued. "Freddie Glaser is in a deep coma that from all indications will be permanent." He then pointed to Kenneth and Pauline Glaser. "Mr. and Mrs. Glaser have lost the love and companionship of their darling child. Why? Because that dentist..." After the pause, he again pointed at Artie Rosner. "That dentist was not vigilant."

The jury appeared shocked.

Hamilton leaned on the railing, stood up erect, and continued. "We will show that it was not only bad enough that Dr. Rosner failed to observe the fact that his patient was getting too deep with the gas mixture, he also had the audacity to take a telephone call while he was working on the poor child."

Slight stirring could be seen in the jury box.

Again Ernest Coniglia turned toward Artie Rosner and asked incredulously in a low voice, "You did that?"

Artie answered quietly, "I answered the phone because the kid was quiet by then. From all I could tell at that time, he seemed to just be in a normal conscious sedation state. Like I told you before, once I saw him turn blue, I immediately began resuscitative measures. I'm sorry but I never thought one of my staff would let that telephone thing out."

"I hate to say this, Dr. Rosner, but you are screwing yourself. I hope we can bail you out, but I have my doubts," the attorney whispered.

The plaintiffs' lawyer continued. "Let us not think that Dr. Rosner is evil. The moment he found out that Freddie Rosner was turning blue from lack of oxygen, he ripped off the mask of his out-dated unit and gave the child forced oxygen from a portable emergency unit. Dr. Rosner's quick action saved Freddie's life."

He paused for emphasis and said, "Yes, but what kind of life did he leave Freddie? A life in which his every move has to be monitored. A life of which he has no conscious knowledge. Freddie Glaser is in a permanent vegetative state and all because of that man." Kenneth Hamilton then pointed an accusatorial finger at Artie Rosner.

"This is not merely a case of medical malpractice. Punitive damages must be assessed here. Dr. Rosner used an outdated, malfunctioning, converted general anesthesia machine for conscious sedation in spite of the fact that in his own office he had a perfectly functioning 'fail-safe' unit. He also had his assistants forcibly restrain the poor child to perform his dental procedures. If he were alert, he would have immediately removed the mask and used the 'fail-safe' machine. Dr. Rosner couldn't do that. He was too stubborn."

"Why didn't you use the 'fail-safe" machine?" Attorney Coniglia whispered to Artie.

"I didn't see any reason to change. My machine had been working well for over forty years. I just thought the kid was taking a little longer to get deep. I guess I was wrong," Artie said quietly and meekly.

"You sure were," Coniglia said with quiet emphasis.

"In addition," continued Hamilton, "Dr. Rosner took a telephone call while he was working on the child. A dentist should never take a telephone call while a patient is being administered anesthetic gases. You can never tell when an untoward reaction might occur. Can you imagine going to a doctor for a medical procedure, and the doctor answers the phone while administering gas — even if you are partly awake? It is inexcusable to talk on the phone while using a gas mixture on a patient."

Kenneth Hamilton paused and walked back and forth in front of the jury. Then he turned toward them and added, "You might say to yourself; 'what if the call were urgent and important?' Let's say that if the child was normal appearing and the telephone call involved a serious or emergency problem, and it would be a very short-lived call, we might consider it all right for the doctor to answer the call. Do you know what that important call was that Dr. Rosner received? Do you know what was so urgent that it couldn't wait?"

Hamilton paused. The jurors looked up with great anticipation. Hamilton spoke. "The telephone call was from Dr. Rosner's travel agent. Yes, that's what I said. His travel agent."

A loud moan came from the audience.

Ernest Coniglia spoke in a loud whisper to Artie Rosner, "How could you?"

Artie answered, "He looked so relaxed. I thought it was all right."

Judge Warrington pounded his gavel and screamed, "Silence in this court!"

After quiet had been restored in the courtroom, Kenneth Hamilton stepped down and said, "That's all I have to say."

Judge Warrington gently rapped his gavel and said, "We'll have a fifteen-minute recess before we hear the defense attorney's opening remarks."

While leaving the courtroom, Artie spotted Julie walking toward the rear exit. He waved to her. Artie took Julie by the elbow and led her to the back of the hallway. He made certain that no one else was around. He then said in a bitter tone, "Julie, how could you?"

"What are you talking about, Dr. Rosner?"

"You know what I mean. How could you tell Hamilton and his group of vultures about you holding the kid and the telephone call?"

"Dr. Rosner, I had no choice."

Artie looked her straight in the eyes and said, "What do you mean?"

"Phyllis gave her deposition first. When she returned, I asked her about the questions and her answers. Everything sounded fine until she told me about the restraining and the telephone call."

"My God! Why couldn't she keep her mouth shut?"

"Dr. Rosner, don't you know Phyllis? She is the most honest person I've ever met. Phyllis couldn't tell a lie if her life depended upon it."

"I should've remembered that."

"I believe you should have. When I was deposed, I had to tell the truth. I didn't want to have to face perjury charges."

"I'm glad about one thing."

"What's that, Doctor?"

"Mark made certain that Phyllis wasn't within hearing distance when the three of us talked about the switched gas tanks."

"That's right. Phyllis could never keep a secret."

At that moment, Artie saw his private attorney, Warren Wilkins, waving at him.

"Thanks, Julie," he said, "my attorney wants me. He's about to give me hell."

The recess was over. The jurors returned to their seats. The bailiff announced the entrance of the judge. Everyone stood. Judge Joseph Warrington entered and spoke, "Sit down everyone. We will now commence with the defense's opening statement."

Diminutive, Attorney Ernest Coniglia, dressed in a pale gray suit, approached the jury box. In contrast to Kenneth Hamilton's brash and loud tone, Ernest Coniglia spoke in a quiet, dulcet manner.

"Good afternoon, ladies and gentlemen of the jury. I agree with my esteemed colleague that Dr. Artie Rosner is an excellent dentist and a caring individual. We will show you that on the morning of May 27th of this year, Dr. Rosner did not deviate from those qualities."

Coniglia looked at Artie Rosner for a moment, then faced the jurors and continued. "Dr. Rosner did use a converted general anesthesia machine for nitrous oxide/oxygen conscious sedation. However, this was not an aberration. For many years, this type of conversion was done successfully with general anesthesia machines. Dr. Rosner has used his particular machine continually for over forty years. With it, he has given many thousand administrations of nitrous oxide and oxygen without a single serious side effect. That is, until the unfortunate accident occurred with Freddie Glaser. I will return to that unavoidable tragedy in a moment."

Artie thought, *It's a good thing I never told Coniglia about the bizarre excitement reaction with Dominic Hall.* He had another thought. *I'm glad no one asked Phyllis about that or she would have spilled the beans about that as well.*

"First, let me continue with the converted unit. To prove that nothing is wrong with his machine, since the accident with Freddie Glaser, Dr. Rosner had his converted unit used on himself for the administration of nitrous oxide/

oxygen conscious sedation. It was used without incident. Several people witnessed the procedure, and the entire procedure was videotaped. This tape will be shown to you."

Coniglia pointed to a desk where videotape sat. He continued. "Since then, Dr. Rosner has continued to use his converted general anesthesia machine for another forty patients with perfect results. It is true that there are now available 'fail-safe' units, but should one throw out an old and reliable dog because a new pup has arrived in the house? The problem ladies and gentlemen did not lie in the machine. The problem was with that poor unfortunate child, Freddie Glaser."

The jurors listened attentively.

Ernest Coniglia rubbed his hands together, walked back and forth in front of the jury box, stopped in the center, and continued. "You see, ladies and gentlemen, every patient in the office of Dr. Artie Rosner and his associate, Dr. Mark Procter, is given a medical history form to fill out. At each recall appointment, the form is updated. The answers to the medical questions are filled out and signed by the patient. In the case of a minor, the form is filled out and signed by one of the parents or a guardian. Concerning Freddie Glaser, the child's mother filled out and signed the medical history form on six separate occasions. The last time was the morning of this May 27th. In every case, the answers to specific medical diseases and conditions were checked as not being present. The child's medical condition was listed as being in perfect health."

He let that remark sink in and continued. "Subsequently, we have determined that Freddie Glaser was not in perfect health. The medical records indicate that at the age of six-months, Freddie Glaser had a viral infection and during a period of high fever, the child had an epileptic-like seizure. I will return to that in a few minutes."

The jurors buzzed slightly upon hearing about the deceit on Pauline Glaser's part.

Once the jury box was quiet, Coniglia said, "There is a dental component to the medical history form. Mrs. Glaser filled out that section and indicated that Freddie loved sweets, didn't take good care of his teeth, and was afraid of the dentist. The dental record shows that Freddie was only brought in for treatment when he was in extreme pain or had a swollen jaw. His dental care was limited to emergency treatments."

Artie whispered to his attorney Warren Wilkins, "The kid was an impossible brat."

Wilkins answered quietly, "Yes, but that's no excuse for not taking the utmost care."

Coniglia continued, "Therefore, when Dr. Rosner found out that Freddie was in extreme pain, he agreed to see the child as the first patient in the morning. Knowing how apprehensive Freddie was, he prescribed a mild dose of a tranquilizer for the child to be taken the night before and the morning of the appointment."

Coniglia turned toward Bernie Glaser and said, "Bernie Glaser, the father of Freddie, was, and still is, a lifelong friend of Dr. Artie Rosner. That is why that in spite of the child not having taken care of his teeth and only coming in for emergency treatments, Dr. Rosner bent over backwards to alleviate the child's extreme pain."

He turned back toward the jurors and continued. "When the normal dosage of nitrous oxide/oxygen was reached, as shown on the dials as eighty percent nitrous oxide and twenty percent oxygen, for some reason Freddie was not getting into a relaxed and calm state. Since twenty percent oxygen is needed for normal breathing, Dr. Rosner did not raise the percentage of nitrous oxide and lower the percentage of oxygen to less than twenty percent even for a few seconds. There were two witnesses to swear to that fact. However, Dr. Rosner knew that the child was in agony from his tooth and the only way for that agony to be relieved was for the tooth to be numbed, the decay to be removed and a sedative filling placed. To do this, Dr. Rosner had to ask his dental assistant, Julie Parsons, and his dental receptionist, Phyllis Romaine, to restrain the child just long enough to give a local anesthetic injection and get the child's jaw numb. Although it sounds unusual, Pedodontic, that is, Children Dentistry books describe the need to occasionally physically restrain difficult children during dental procedures."

That sounds reasonable, thought the elementary school teacher juror. "Once Freddie's jaw was numb, Dr. Rosner was able to clean out the decay and place a temporary sedative restoration. Having accomplished that, he gradually lowered the dose of nitrous oxide until it was only five percent. Dr. Rosner then noticed that even with that very low dose of nitrous oxide, Freddie appeared to be getting calmer and more relaxed. He assumed that this particular time, the child was relaxed because he was now pain-free, and that it had just taken longer for the combined tranquilizer and conscious sedation to work. Therefore, when a telephone call came in from his travel agent, for which he only had to verify certain reservations, Dr. Rosner had no qualms about answering it. Dr. Rosner had been observing his patient at all times, and the child now showed signs of deep relaxation."

The accountant juror thought, *That could be possible.*

Coniglia then raised his voice for emphasis. "In addition, as I had just mentioned, Dr. Rosner had greatly lowered the percentage of nitrous oxide and was giving the child ninety-five percent oxygen. Hence, while still keeping an eye on the child, he answered the phone call. For no reason he could understand at the time, Dr. Rosner noticed that the child was beginning to appear cyanotic, which means, blue in the face. He immediately hung up the phone, ripped off the mask and had the receptionist call 911. Dr. Rosner then brought his emergency oxygen unit to the site, and he immediately administered one hundred percent oxygen under force."

Sounds like he acted quickly, the widowed housewife juror thought.

Looking directly at the housewife and nurse jurors, Coniglia said, "This was enough to save Freddie's life. Unfortunately, Freddie remained unconscious and unresponsive. At the time, Dr. Rosner did not know that Freddie would be in a sustained coma. All he knew was that he had saved Freddie's life."

The women and the accountant jurors seemed to be "buying" Coniglia's explanations. The architect male juror looked somewhat skeptical.

Ernest Coniglia was ready for his coup de grace. He again paced back and forth in front of the jurors. He stopped suddenly, put one hand on the rail, and stated,

"Remember when I told you that Freddie Glaser had an epileptic-like seizure that occurred at the age of six months. Even though he has had no seizures since that time, there has been evidence from his behavior that he had suffered brain damage. We have witnesses to attest that little Freddie Glaser was far from an angel. He loved to skin small animals and examine their body parts."

Immediately, Kenneth Hamilton stood up and shouted, "Objection! This is completely unrelated. It is only to disparage the victim."

"What is your purpose in bringing out this material?" the judge asked.

"It is directly relevant as I will show in a minute," Coniglia answered.

"It better be. Objection overruled."

Appearing greatly perturbed, Kenneth Hamilton sat down.

Looking at the judge, Coniglia said, "Thank you, your honor. He then faced the jurors and resumed his defense. "Once Freddie incapacitated the small animals, he performed his surgical work in the woods around the family home lake. Freddie also took great delight in pulling out limbs, antennae and wings of all kinds of insects. He told his friends that all bugs and insects were made to be destroyed. Freddie told them that his greatest pleasure was in catching a butterfly and pulling out its wings. After he maimed the creatures, he would use his father's hammer to smash the bugs to smithereens. Whether he destroyed a rabbit or a small army of cockroaches, Freddie gathered the remnants in one of his father's discarded cigar boxes and then unceremoniously dumped the contents into the lake."

Ernest Coniglia gave the jurors time to digest this latest information. Both the men and women appeared taken aback at this latest revelation.

He continued. "I do not want you to think that these actions were completely under Freddie Glaser's control. We will bring forth a neurologist who will testify that sadistic behavior, as evidenced by Freddie Glaser, could be the result of brain damage. He will show that brain damage can occur from prior epileptic-like seizures. The neurologist will testify that even in the case of a single seizure, brain damage could occur. He will also testify that the type of hidden brain damage that Freddie Glaser might have had would make him prone to damaging and severe reactions from a normal child's dose of a tranquilizer and a normal conscious sedation mixture of nitrous oxide and oxygen."

A slight moan came out of the audience, and the jurors appeared to be holding their collective breath.

Wringing his hands again, Ernest Coniglia continued. "As I mentioned before, in answering and signing the medical history form, Pauline Glaser never stated that Freddie Glaser had an epileptic-like seizure as an infant. Therefore, Dr. Rosner had no knowledge that Freddie had any previous neurological complications. Not knowing of any prior medical disturbance, Dr. Rosner did nothing wrong. In fact, once he found out that the child was getting blue, he did everything he could to save his life. After all, he did save Freddie Glaser's life."

The attorney cleared his throat and continued. "I understand the terrible pain and suffering Mr. and Mrs. Glaser are going through as the result of their son's coma. It is true that even though Freddie Glaser exhibited sadistic behavior with small animals and insects, he never harmed a child or adult. Dr. Rosner is extremely sorry for Freddie's condition. He only wishes it could have been avoided."

Ernest Coniglia walked toward the defendant and pointed to Dr. Rosner. He then turned and spoke to the jurors. "Ladies and gentlemen, look at Dr. Rosner. Is this a non-vigilant man? No! Not in the least! He was completely vigilant at every stage of the event. He acted in the most prudent manner. Dr. Rosner is not guilty of malpractice and certainly not deserving of punitive damages. Thank you for your kind attention."

With that, Ernest Coniglia stepped down. Judge Warrington dismissed the jurors. He spoke to the attorneys. "This afternoon's session is over. We will resume tomorrow morning promptly at 9:00 A.M. Good afternoon everyone."

Still sitting in the plaintiff box, Kenneth Hamilton spoke to Pauline Glaser. "For God's sake, why did you never write on the medical record that Freddie had an epileptic-like attack when he was an infant?"

Pauline answered, "Bernie and I didn't think it was important. It was a one-time occurrence, and Freddie never had another seizure. I certainly don't believe that his little pranks with bugs and stuff are due to brain damage."

"Yeah, I think the whole thing is a hoax," Bernie Glaser added.

"We'll see," the attorney retorted. "See you folks, tomorrow," he concluded.

That evening, Artie Rosner rehashed the day's events with his brother, Burt, who was staying with him. Artie then called Mark Procter and filled him in on the details of the opposing attorneys' opening arguments.

"It looks like the crux of the defense is going to be the possibility of Freddie Glaser having a preexisting neurological condition," Mark remarked.

"I hope your neurologist friend, Jake Daniels, can make a convincing argument."

"I don't want to get your hopes up too high, Artie, but I spoke to Jake just before you called. He told me that everything Coniglia said in the opening statement is possible, but...?

Impatient with Mark's pause, Artie cried out, "What?"

"Jake said that with only one epileptic-like seizure at the age of six months and no repeat episodes, it won't be easy to prove the relationship between the seizure, subsequent brain damage and the reaction to the 'nitrous.' He also said that it would take strong, persuasive speaking on your attorney's part to convince a jury that Freddie had preexisting brain damage that led to his aberrant behavior with bugs and small animals."

"Is that it?"

"There's more. Jake told me that it would be even more difficult to prove that the brain damage caused the kid to become comatose from a normal dose of nitrous oxide and oxygen. Another thing that's bound to come out is that you used 'nitrous' on Freddie several times before and nothing unusual occurred. Jake said that's going to be a tough nut to crack."

"Could it be done?"

"Jake only mentioned that it is possible."

"Mark, maybe I should have told my attorneys about the switched tanks?"

"It's too late for that now. You'll just have to hope for the best. Praying to God wouldn't hurt either."

"I've never been too religious."

"Maybe, you ought to start now."

When Artie got off the phone, he spoke to his brother. "Burt, do you pray to God?"

"All the time," Burt answered.

"I think you'll have to show me how."

11

During the remainder of that week and the first three days of the following week, many witnesses were called. Representatives from Newhouser Equipment and Mohlner Dental Equipment Service, and a chemist and a biochemist took the stand. It was determined that the converted general anesthesia unit was functioning correctly. Nevertheless, it was emphatically stated that Dr. Rosner's unit had no safety features and had he used a "fail-safe" nitrous oxide/oxygen conscious sedation unit, Freddie Glaser would have always received the proper amount of oxygen.

Joe Turner, one of the technicians at Mohlner Dental Equipment Service, testified that the nitrous oxide and oxygen tanks on Dr. Rosner's converted unit had been connected correctly. The chemistry and mode of action of nitrous oxide and oxygen were revealed. The video of Dr. Rosner's "nitrous" test was shown.

Julie, Phyllis, Ginny, Kathy and Dr. Mark Procter took the stand. They attested to the integrity and clinical skills of Dr. Rosner. Phyllis did admit that force was used to restrain Freddie Glaser, and that Dr. Rosner received a telephone call from his travel agent while working on Freddie Glaser.

Several of Dr. Rosner's patients attested to his dental skills and caring chairside manner. Herman Averill, the patient whose life was saved after suffering a heart attack in the office, gave a glowing account of Dr. Rosner's management of a medical emergency. Philip Jones, the Good Samaritan who had helped Artie when he crashed into the stanchion, later came to Artie's office for several gratuitous fillings. Since he had been treated with the utmost care and respect, Philip had nothing but praise to say about Artie's clinical ability and care. Two of the officers of the Southern Dental Society attested to Dr. Rosner's clinical skills and moral character.

Two of Freddie Glaser's friends testified to his sadistic behavior with small animals and insects. Mr. and Mrs. Glaser testified that Freddie did have an epileptic-like seizure at the age of six months and that he had no subsequent seizures. They did admit that he showed sadistic tendencies toward insects and small animals but that he never harmed a human. The Glasers considered these actions to be merely the pranks of an active child. They had been certain he would outgrow that behavior.

Pauline Glaser stated that Freddie loved candy, cake and all kinds of sweets, and that he didn't brush or floss his teeth frequently enough. She also stated that Freddie was extremely fearful of dental treatment and only went to the office when he was either in extreme pain or had a swollen jaw. Pauline Glaser admitted that she lied in filling out the medical history form in Dr. Rosner's office. She stated that she failed to indicate the one epileptic-like seizure because it had never reappeared, and she was told there was no indication of brain damage. Pauline reaffirmed that she and her husband did not believe that Freddie's behavior with insects and small animals was related to brain damage.

A dramatic video of Freddie Glaser in his present comatose state was shown. The demonstration vividly revealed that Freddie could do nothing without the help of his nurse and physical therapist. The video ended with a close-up of Freddie's blank stare.

This morning, the tenth day of the trial, Chief of Neurology at Mt. Laurel General Hospital, Dr. James Conover, testified that Freddie Glaser was in an intractable coma and likely would not recover. Dr. Alex Boomer, a pedodontist (children's dentistry specialist), testified that on occasion, small children might have to be temporarily restrained in order for emergency dental work to be carried out.

He also testified that with normal but extremely apprehensive children, a small dose of a minor tranquilizer, such as Valium,® could be given the night before and the morning of the procedure. In addition, for those normal, apprehensive children, nitrous oxide/oxygen conscious sedation can safely be combined with a small dose of Valium.® Dr. Boomer also affirmed the recent scientific report that Valium® and similar drugs can reduce the possibility of brain damage coming from nitrous oxide.

The final witness of the morning was clinical psychologist and stress management expert, Dr. Melvin Kamfer. He testified that stress could impede the immune system, reduce the body's defenses to drugs, and sometimes cause a normal dose of a drug to cause an exaggerated or abnormal response in the body.

This afternoon was devoted to the testimony of Dr. Jacob Daniels, a neurologist from Mt. Laurel General Hospital. After being sworn in, Dr. Daniels qualifications as an expert were accepted by both sides and Judge Warrington. Defense attorney Ernest Coniglia then questioned Jake.

"Is it true Dr. Daniels that your examination of Freddie Glaser's medical records showed that he had an epileptic-like seizure at the age of six months?"

"Yes."

"Do you have an opinion on whether that one seizure could have caused brain damage?"

Kenneth Hamilton immediately stood up, raised his hand and shouted, "Objection! That is pure conjecture."

Judge Warrington asked Ernest Coniglia, "Is that question relevant to your defense?"

"Absolutely," Coniglia answered.

"Objection overruled. Continue, counsel."

Looking perturbed, Kenneth Hamilton sat down.

"Thank you, your honor." Turning to the neurologist, Hamilton continued, "Can you answer the question, Dr. Daniels?"

"Yes, I have an opinion. It is that one seizure could have caused brain damage."

"Do you have an opinion on whether it is possible for the brain damage to be undetectable by the use of current medical instrumentation?"

"I do, and my opinion is that certain areas of brain damage are undetectable."

"What is your evidence for that?"

"I wrote an article on that subject in the latest issue of the medical journal, *Neurology*."

"Is this the article?"

Coniglia handed a journal reprint article to Dr. Daniels. He looked at it and said, "Yes, that is the article."

Kenneth Hamilton raised his hand and called out, "Have we seen that article?"

"Yes," Coniglia replied. He handed the article to Hamilton, who looked at it, acknowledged that their side had previously seen it, and returned it to Coniglia.

Coniglia marked it as Exhibit No. 25 and moved that it be admitted in evidence.

Judge Warrington received and checked the article and handed it to his clerk for admittance. The clerk then placed it with the other court exhibits.

Ernest Coniglia then asked, "Are there other ways to determine brain damage?"

"Yes," neurologist Jake Daniels answered.

"Can you elaborate?"

"The behavior of the person can be examined."

"Did Freddie Glaser show any behavioral evidence of brain damage?" the attorney questioned.

Dr. Daniels replied, "Brain damage can cause aberrant behavior. That would include things such as destroying small animals and insects."

Again Kenneth Hamilton bolted out of his chair and shouted, "Objection! With all due respect to his qualifications, Dr. Daniels is not a psychologist, psychiatrist or sociologist and therefore cannot attest to behavioral changes."

"What do you have to say, counsel?" Judge Warrington asked Ernest Coniglia.

Coniglia looked at him and answered, "It is true that Dr. Daniels is not a psychologist, psychiatrist or sociologist, but as a neurologist he is knowledgeable of the behavioral effects of brain damage."

"Objection overruled. Continue."

Sitting down Kenneth Hamilton, appeared grim.

Coniglia said, "Thank you, your honor." Returning to his line of reasoning, he faced the neurologist and said, "Dr. Daniels, if Freddie Rosner had preexisting brain damage when he had nitrous oxide/oxygen conscious sedation administered to him by Dr. Artie Rosner, do you have an opinion about whether the brain damage could have made him more responsive to a smaller amount of nitrous oxide than would be the case for a normal individual?"

"Yes, I do."

"What is your opinion?"

"A person with brain damage could have an accelerated response to a drug such as nitrous oxide, especially when it had been combined with Valium.®"

"The records, which you read, show that Freddie Glaser never went into a coma in the four previous times he was treated by Dr. Rosner. There were also no indications of an epileptic-like seizure in the medical history forms on Freddie Glaser's dental chart. Therefore, do you have an opinion on whether Dr. Rosner acted within standard medical procedures when he used

nitrous oxide/oxygen conscious sedation in combination with Valium®
premedication during the treatment of Freddie Glaser?"

"I do have an opinion. From reading the dental records of Freddie Glaser
and listening to the depositions of Dr. Rosner's assistant and receptionist
and those of Mr. and Mrs. Glaser, it seemed within reasonable medical
probability for Dr. Rosner to treat Freddie as he did."

"Can you then account for the fact that at this visit, Freddie Glaser went
into an intractable coma?"

"In my opinion, the previous administrations of nitrous oxide might have
caused some minor additional brain damage that was enough for him to react
in a dangerous manner this time. In addition, Freddie Glaser could have been
under considerable stress from pain and fear that further reduced his resistance
to a normal dosage of nitrous oxide.

"The coma then could have occurred from a reaction of the nitrous oxide
with the preexisting region of brain damage causing a reduction of oxygen
supply to that area of the brain. With the reduced oxygen supply, a coma
resulted."

"Thank you, Dr. Daniels. I have no further questions." Ernest Coniglia
then left the front of the witness stand.

Judge Warrington turned toward the plaintiffs' attorneys and asked them,
"Do you wish to cross-examine?"

"Yes I do, your Honor," Attorney Hamilton answered.

Kenneth Hamilton smiled broadly as he approached the witness. He spoke
more quietly than his usual style.

"What you have said so far is very interesting, Doctor. I would merely
like a clarification of certain issues."

Dr. Jacob Daniels expected the worst. He quivered ever so slightly in his
seat.

"Dr. Daniels, in your opinion, is it usual for a child to have one incident
of a viral-infection spiked fever causing an epileptic-like seizure that would
lead to lasting brain damage?"

"It is not usual, but it could happen."

"In your opinion, if a child had a seizure when he was six-months old and
lived for another nine-and-one half years without another seizure, would
you be inclined to believe that the child did not have brain damage?"

"Given those circumstances, it would be unlikely that the child had brain
damage, but as I said before, brain damage would still be possible without
any subsequent seizures."

"Dr. Daniels, previously you stated that although brain damage from a single epileptic-like seizure might not be detectable from medical instrumentation, it could be assumed by certain behaviors."

"That is true."

"You also stated that Freddie Glaser's sadistic activities with small animals and insects could be the result of brain damage that might have been initiated by an epileptic-like seizure when he was six-months old."

"I did say that."

"Nevertheless, in your opinion, is it not probable that the type of sadistic behavior that Freddie exhibited could have absolutely no relationship to brain damage but could be merely a personality characteristic that developed because of occurrences in the child's life?"

"I suppose it is possible."

"Not possible, but probable." With a dramatic flair, Kenneth Hamilton went back to his box and picked up a medical journal. He returned, holding a journal in his hand and continued. "According to a study written up in an article in this recent issue of *Child Behavior*, more than ninety percent of sadistic animal-and insect-destroying behavior of children is caused by environmental factors such as parental abuse, peer pressure and unrestricted free time."

Back at the plaintiff's table, the Glasers flinched when they heard the words "parental abuse."

"Can we see that journal?" Ernest Coniglia asked.

"Of course," Kenneth Hamilton answered as he handed the journal to Coniglia.

"Had we seen this journal before?" Coniglia asked.

"Yes, it was part of the exhibitions. It is exhibit No. 34," Hamilton replied.

"Let me see that," Judge Warrington said. After receiving the journal, he glanced at it , quickly reviewed the article in question, and said, "Yes, this is fine. Admit it into evidence." The judge then handed the journal to his clerk who placed it with the other exhibits. The judge added, "Continue counsel."

Hamilton smiled at the judge and said, "Thank you, your honor." He then paused a moment, glanced at the jury, returned to the witness and spoke to him. "What do you answer to the findings of this study?"

"They could be true, but Freddie Glaser might have been one of the ten percent in which brain damage elicits sadistic behavior."

"Let us leave sadistic behavior for now because we will never know for sure. Freddie cannot be here to tell us why he acted as he did. In fact, he can't tell us anything. Let's now turn to the treatments by Dr. Rosner. Was the morning of May 27th of this year the first time that Dr. Rosner used his converted general anesthesia machine to administer nitrous oxide/oxygen conscious sedation to Freddie Glaser?"

"No. Nitrous oxide/oxygen was used by Dr. Rosner for Freddie on four previous occasions."

"Were there any untoward effects from those previous administrations?"

"Nothing on the chart indicates so."

"You're correct, Dr. Daniels. The depositions by dental assistant Julie Parsons and the interrogatories by Mr. and Mrs. Glaser and Dr. Rosner indicated that Freddie was fine after having 'nitrous' on those previous administrations. Now comes the most important question. Although you stated this before, in your opinion, why on the morning of May 27th did Freddie Glaser become comatose following the administration of nitrous oxide/oxygen from the converted general anesthesia unit?"

"As I said before, the previous 'nitrous' administrations might have caused some additional brain damage, and the stress of that morning could have made the child more susceptible to the damaging effects of nitrous oxide that culminated in a coma from the administration of May 27th. It's sort of like, the last straw breaking the camel's back.'"

"That sounds all well and good, but there is absolutely no proof that something like that could happen. Is there?"

By now, Jake Daniels was getting flustered. "No, sir there is no proof, but…" Jake stammered slightly and concluded, "it could have happened."

"Is it not probable that contrary to what he said, Dr. Rosner was so busy in trying to numb the resistant child and then clean out the tooth decay and fill the tooth that he didn't take the time to check that he was giving the correct dosage of nitrous oxide?"

Ernest Coniglia raised his hand and shouted, "Objection! This is pure conjecture. Dr. Daniels was not there to see what happened."

"Objection sustained!" the judge said emphatically. To the jury, he said, "Please ignore that last question from Attorney Hamilton." To the recording secretary, he said, "Please remove the section from 'Is it not' down to 'nitrous oxide.'" To Attorney Hamilton, he said, "Continue, counsel."

Hamilton looked at the judge and said, "I'm sorry, your honor." He turned, faced Jake Daniels, and said, "Let me ask you this. We know that Dr. Rosner took a telephone call while working on Freddie. Could that have added to his distraction and prevented him from checking both the dials of gas administration and the reactions of the patient? Is that not probable?"

Again, but even more vehemently, Ernest Coniglia shouted, "Objection! Pure conjecture. Dr. Daniels cannot give an opinion because he wasn't there."

"Objection sustained," Judge Warrington stated. "I must warn you counsel. Discontinue this line of reasoning. Jurors, please ignore that last question. Ms. Secretary, delete that last section. Now continue, counsel."

Hamilton again faced the judge and said, "I will discontinue this line of questioning, your honor." He returned to the neurologist and said, "Let me rephrase that last question. Would taking a telephone call while administering conscious sedation gases be considered a deviation from standard medical or dental practice?"

Jake Daniels appeared concerned as he answered. "I don't know if it is a deviation from standard medical or dental practice, but it certainly couldn't be recommended."

"Thank you, Doctor. I have no further questions."

Judge Warrington looked at the harried Jake Daniels and said, "You may step down now, Doctor."

After Jake Daniels sat down, the judge spoke again. "Mr. Hamilton, do you have any further witnesses?"

"No, your Honor," the plaintiffs' attorney replied.

"How about you, Mr. Coniglia?"

"We have no further witnesses," the defense attorney answered.

"Good. Tomorrow, gentlemen you'll give your closing arguments, and we'll wrap up this affair."

Judge Warrington looked at the jurors, attorneys, plaintiffs, defendants and visitors and stated in a loud voice, "Court is adjourned until tomorrow at 9:00 A.M. promptly."

When Artie Rosner got home at 5:30 P.M., he left his brother Burt watching TV and flopped down on his bed. It had been a rough day. Artie rested for a half-hour, went to his desk and called Mark. After the third ring, Mark picked up the phone.

"Mark, it's Artie."

"Hi, Artie. How did it go?"

"Not too well. Your buddy, Jake Daniels, was doing fine with the questions from my side's attorney, Ernest Coniglia. The tide turned when Hamilton lashed into him."

"How did that happen?"

Artie then gave Mark the details of Dr. Jacob Daniel's afternoon on the witness stand. He then added, "After listening to Hamilton, I'm sure the jury won't buy the story that the kid went into a coma because of preexisting brain damage. Damn it! I should've told the truth about the switched tanks. Especially now that Rudy Kennedy is dead and is not around to deny the fact that he switched the tanks. I know I'm gonna lose the case, and with or without punitive damages, I'm sunk."

"Don't worry, Artie. Things may not be as bad as you think. You never know what jurors are thinking."

"That's the point. That's what I'm worried about."

"Try to keep your cool. You have your health and from what you told me, if worse comes to worse, your brother, Burt, will take care of you down in Florida. After all, things could be a lot more tragic than retiring in sunny Florida."

"Thanks, Mark. You're right as usual."

Artie hung up the phone and walked over to Burt, who was watching the TV news. "Burt," he said, "When you get home, prepare that extra room for me. It looks like I may be needing it soon."

"It's been ready ever since you called me at the end of May."

12

At 9:15 A.M. the following day, Kenneth Hamilton got out of his seat and walked slowly toward the jury box. He was dressed in a new dark gray suit and was wearing expensive black shoes. Facing the jurors, he spoke loud and clear. "Good morning, ladies and gentlemen. I know this has been a difficult two weeks for all of you. Therefore, I will not burden you with a long speech. As I emphatically stated in my opening remarks, Dr. Artie Rosner is a good and moral individual. He had been an excellent dentist, but the past is not always a predictor of the future. Dr. Rosner, for reasons we may never know, was not vigilant on the morning of May 27th of this year. Nevertheless, the terrible occurrence that surfaced on that fateful day started many years before. Dr. Rosner was set in his ways."

Hamilton cleared his throat and continued. "In the matter of dealing with the health and lives of a doctor's patients, it is absolutely essential to keep up with the times. Medical advances in drugs and equipment occur rapidly in this era of scientific achievement. Did Dr. Rosner heed these advances? In some areas, he did, but with one major piece of equipment, he did not. Dr. Rosner used the same machine for delivering nitrous oxide and oxygen to his patients that he purchased over forty years ago. Think of that. Would you want to fly in a forty-year old airplane without any current safety equipment? Would you drive a forty-year old car without seat belts, air bags, signal lights, power brakes and other modern safety features? Yet, Dr. Rosner, who is an admitted expert in the field of nitrous oxide/oxygen conscious sedation, used the same converted general anesthesia unit that he purchased many years ago. He was perfectly aware of the fact that for over twenty-five years, 'fail-safe' equipment was available. I am certain that it was not for monetary reasons that he did not purchase a 'fail-safe' unit for himself. It was nothing more than stubbornness. After all, he did purchase a 'fail-safe' unit for his associate, Dr. Mark Procter."

Coniglia whispered to Artie, "That wasn't too bright buying only a new unit for your associate."

Artie replied quietly, "I suppose in hindsight, you're right."

With a stern face, Hamilton continued. "Ladies and gentlemen, as the representative from Newhouser discussed, with a 'fail-safe' unit, it is impossible for an individual to receive less than twenty percent oxygen. If twenty percent oxygen is unavailable, the nitrous oxide automatically shuts off. That means that the brain receives sufficient oxygen for it to function. Had a 'fail-safe' unit been used on Freddie Glaser, this trial would not be taking place. Freddie Glaser would not be in an intractable coma. Freddie Glaser would be in school, playing with his friends or interacting lovingly with his parents. Pride and stubbornness on the part of Dr. Rosner are the reasons for Freddie Glaser's coma."

Kenneth Hamilton paused to let his remarks sink in. He turned and glanced at the defense section. Dr. Artie Rosner had his head in his hands.

Hamilton turned back toward the jurors and continued. "Even with that outdated unit, had Dr. Rosner paid attention to what he was doing, Freddie Glaser would not be comatose today. We admit that Freddie Glaser ate a lot of sweets, did not properly take care of his mouth and only went to the dentist when he was in pain or had a swollen jaw. We also admit that Freddie Glaser was extremely apprehensive about going to the dentist. Still, he had gone to see Dr. Rosner on four previous occasions and each time, he received the correct mixture of nitrous oxide and oxygen. From what he told his mother, he got into a pleasantly relaxed and happy state."

Hamilton raised his voice as he said, "Not only that, the dental work was done correctly, and Freddie had no further problems with the treated teeth as was indicated on his dental record and from the testimony of his parents. Therefore, even with the use of the outdated unit, Dr. Rosner had been vigilant on those four previous occasions, and everything went well for Freddie."

Staring at the center of the jury box, Hamilton continued. "What was different on the morning of May 27th? Something must have been on Dr. Rosner's mind to have distracted him and prevented him from giving the child the correct mixture. Why was it only in that instance that Freddie Glaser had to be physically restrained in order for Dr. Rosner to take x-rays, give an injection, clean out the decay and fill the tooth? Although physical restraint has to be used occasionally when no other means are available to treat them, this was not the situation with Freddie Glaser."

Hamilton walked toward the judge and back toward the jurors. He stopped, leaned on the rail, and slowly said, "Was there something wrong with the gas mixtures? Obviously not, because we saw the subsequent video of Dr. Rosner being administered nitrous oxide/oxygen conscious sedation from his converted unit. He reacted well. We also heard the testimony of several of his patients who subsequently received the same gases from the same unit without a problem. Nothing was wrong with the unit and nothing was wrong with the gases. The fault lies with Dr. Rosner not giving the correct administration of nitrous oxide and oxygen."

The jurors appeared to be listening attentively to every word spoken by Kenneth Hamilton.

The attorney stood up and continued. "At first, Dr. Rosner gave too little nitrous oxide and Freddie had to be restrained. Dr. Rosner then gave too much nitrous oxide and Freddie became comatose. Even that could have still been prevented if Dr. Rosner had not been on the telephone talking to his travel agent. Had his eyes been peeled on his patient, he would have seen that the child was non-responsive, and that his pink color was changing to blue. He was too busy making arrangements for a vacation in July. It is true that once he saw that his patient became cyanotic, that is, blue in the face, from lack of oxygen, Dr. Rosner did take immediate action. He did save Freddie's life, as empty as it is. Nevertheless, he was more concerned with an upcoming holiday than the safety of his patient."

Kenneth Hamilton paused and looked at the faces of the jurors. They appeared to react favorably to his message. He then resumed his speech. "The other side brought in a neurologist, Dr. Jacob Daniels, to purportedly show that Freddie Glaser's epileptic-like seizure at the age of six months caused brain damage that led to sadistic animal-and insect-destroying behavior, and subsequently predisposed the child to go into a coma from a normal dose of nitrous oxide/oxygen. Concerning the likelihood that a onetime epileptic-like seizure would cause long-lasting brain damage, even Dr. Daniels admitted that, although it was possible, it was not probable. As I showed you in the *Child Behavior* article, the odds are greatly against Freddie Glaser having his sadistic-like behaviors with animals and insects being the result of brain damage. The final evidence that preexistent brain damage could not have set Freddie up for that horrible outcome on May 27th is that on four previous occasions, Freddie Glaser had received nitrous oxide/oxygen conscious sedation from Dr. Rosner's converted unit without any dangerous side effects. In fact, the child had found the experiences to be decidedly pleasant. The argument that the administration on May 27th was 'the last straw that broke the camel's back' has no scientific evidence to back it up. To use another cliché, the defense was just 'grasping for straws.'"

The jurors appeared impressed by Kenneth Hamilton's assertions.

"I believe that you must find Dr. Artie Rosner guilty of negligence because he gave a toxic amount of nitrous oxide to Freddie Glaser that resulted in an intractable brain coma. You also must find Dr. Artie Rosner liable for punitive damages for these three reasons. He used an outdated machine when a modern 'fail-safe' unit was available. He had Freddie physically restrained because he was not vigilant enough to realize he was, at first, giving insufficient nitrous oxide to get the child into a deep enough state to have him numbed in order to have definitive dental treatment performed. He later spoke on the telephone to a travel agent while he was still working on the child who, by then, was receiving an overdose of nitrous oxide."

This again evoked a sigh from the audience.

Once it was quiet again, Hamilton said, "Although Freddie Glaser had been guilty of sadistic behavior toward small animals and insects, and the fact that he did not take good care of his teeth, should in no way have any relevance to the finding that this child is now in a probably permanent comatose state. In rendering an award, you should take into consideration the cost of daily medical care, the loss of earning power, a lifetime without any enjoyment for Freddie Glaser, and the loss of normal contact between him and his parents. Thank you for your time. I know that you will render a fair and deserving verdict."

Kenneth Hamilton walked away from the jury and sat down in the plaintiff section. His colleagues and the Glasers gave him a look of assent.

Judge Warrington pounded his gavel and said, "We'll take a fifteen-minute recess."

Artie asked Ernest Coniglia if there was an out-of-the-way room where he could take a quiet break. The defense attorney guided him to a small anteroom that could be locked from the inside. Artie could now have his privacy. The pain in his right hand reinforced his knowledge that he was stressed. He went inside, locked the door, sat on a chair, closed his eyes and began to meditate. Artie had taken a meditation course twenty years earlier, and he meditated regularly up to the time his wife Marlene died. After that he gave up meditation along with the belief in God. Psychiatric medication helped him that time. Following this current event, with the failure of alcohol, he returned to the use of Prozac® and Ativan® He also took Mark's advice and began to pray. This morning, he decided he needed another form of help and began to meditate again. Ten minutes later, he arose, feeling more relaxed and better prepared to face the next event in this horrendous nightmare. That would be Ernest Coniglia's defense.

Ernest Coniglia strolled casually to the front of the jury box. He, too, had changed his clothes, wearing a dark blue suit and black shoes. He addressed the jurors in his usual quiet, calm voice. "Good day, ladies and gentlemen of the jury. I, too, will not burden you with a long speech. What I have to say will only take a few minutes. As has been stated here repeatedly, Dr. Rosner is a good dentist and a highly moral person. He would never intentionally harm anyone. With respect to his continued use of the converted general anesthesia unit, Dr. Rosner believed that one should never throw out something that is still functioning perfectly. He could have purchased another 'fail-safe' unit, but he was comfortable with his old unit. It had worked perfectly for him for over forty years and is still working perfectly."

Coniglia first looked at Dr. Rosner, then focused on the jurors and continued. "It takes vigilance on the part of the dentist to both keep an eye on the dials and the patient to ensure that an overdose does not occur. Dr. Rosner had always been a vigilant dentist. He was vigilant on the morning of May 27th of this year. He set the dials for the correct mixture of nitrous oxide and oxygen, and his dental assistant Julie Parsons verified those settings. At first, with the normal dosage of nitrous oxide/oxygen, Freddie Glaser was uncooperative. Dr. Rosner realized that if he did not get Freddie numb, he would never be able to stop his pain, and Freddie would have remained in agony for the rest of the day. Dr. Rosner didn't want to use physical restraint, but it was the only way he could take care of Freddie's complaint."

The jurors appeared to be indifferent to this line of reasoning.

The defense attorney tried to ignore their bland appearance and said, "Dr. Rosner answered the telephone while he was working on Freddie. However at the time he was taking the call, he had just about completed the procedure. All indications were that Freddie Glaser had been extremely calm even with a very low dose of nitrous oxide. Julie Parsons has attested to this. Dr. Rosner knew that the call would be brief, and he kept his eye on the child while speaking on the phone. Julie Parsons also verified this. The moment Dr. Rosner saw that Freddie Glaser was beginning to turn cyanotic, he immediately ripped off the mask and gave the child pure oxygen under high pressure. This saved Freddie's life."

This seemed to have a somewhat positive effect on the jurors as could be judged by their calm facial features and lack of physical movement.

Conglia continued, "Mr. Hamilton stated that it is unusual that a single episode of an epileptic-like seizure can cause brain damage, but that does not mean that it did not happen with Freddie Glaser. A child with brain damage could go through four episodes of nitrous oxide/oxygen administration without any untoward effects and then on the fifth administration go into a coma. As Dr. Daniels stated, the four previous administrations of nitrous oxide/oxygen could have caused further brain damage that helped precipitate the coma on May 27th. There could be another reason that Freddie Glaser had such a horrendous result on that morning. It has been shown by the clinical psychologist, Dr. Melvin Kamfer, that stress can make a person more susceptible to drugs. Freddie Glaser was under tremendous stress that morning. He had a terrible toothache that began the day before. The combination of pain and fear could have resulted in the stress that led to the abnormal result with a routine administration of nitrous oxide and oxygen."

Ernest Coniglia paused and looked at the jury to see if they were "buying" his reasoning. He couldn't tell. Everyone had on a poker face. Coniglia rubbed his hands and continued. "Mr. Hamilton argued that Dr. Rosner should not have answered the telephone while working on Freddie Glaser. Still, the call was short, and the evidence indicates that Dr. Rosner was watching Freddie and was attentive at all times — even during that short telephone incident. The telephone call was certainly not the reason Freddie Glaser went into a coma. The child went into a coma because of preexisting brain damage, aggravated by stress, and initially caused by an epileptic-like seizure when he was six months old. I ask you to find Dr. Rosner not guilty of medical malpractice. I thank you for your time and courtesy."

Ernest Coniglia left the vicinity of the jury box and returned to the defendant's section.

Judge Warrington then spoke to Attorney Kenneth Hamilton. "Do you have any final statements?"

"Just a few, your Honor."

"Keep to that, counsel."

Kenneth Hamilton strolled to the front of the jury box and began. "Ladies and gentlemen, I will only take a few more minutes of your time. On the morning of May 27th of this year, Dr. Artie Rosner gave an incorrect mixture of nitrous oxide and oxygen that caused Freddie Glaser to go into an intractable coma. He used an outdated machine to deliver the gases. He had the child physically restrained while he forcibly gave him a local anesthetic injection and cleaned out and filled his cavity. He also received a personal telephone call from a travel agent while the child was deeply sedated with the gas mixture. No amount of words can obviate these facts."

Hamilton paused to let the jury consider these statements. He then continued. "No preexisting brain damage was present because on four previous occasions, nitrous oxide and oxygen were used successfully on Freddie Glaser. He did not have an undue amount of stress on May 27th. Everyone admits that Freddie only went to the dentist when he was suffering from pain or a swollen jaw. Everyone admits that he was apprehensive each time he went to the dentist. There was nothing different in Freddie Glaser's condition on May 27th that was not present on the four previous times he was treated by Dr. Rosner. Ladies and gentlemen, Dr. Rosner is guilty of medical negligence and punitive damages should be assessed. Thank you for your patience."

Appearing pleased, Kenneth Hamilton returned to his seat.

The demeanor of the defense attorneys was anything but encouraging.

Judge Warrington spoke to the assemblage. "We will take our lunch break now. Everyone, please return at 1:00 P.M. when I will give my instructions to the jury.

Artie and Burt walked to the First Street Diner. It was a short walk, but Burt had to slow down and wait for his brother. Artie had difficulty putting one foot in front of the other.

"Why are you such a slow poke?" Burt inquired.

"I'm sorry. It must be my nerves." Artie answered.

"I'm sorry for you, but we gotta get back by one. Get a move on it."

"All right," Artie said quietly.

At the diner, Burt had a hot pastrami sandwich and a Coke. Artie couldn't eat. He sipped a cup of tea with lemon.

"You gotta eat something, Artie."

"I'm not hungry."

"Get it through your thick skull. No matter what happens, I'll take care of you. I got more money than I need. So cut it out already."

"I'm sorry, Burt. I'm so empty inside."

"I can understand that, but this will pass over. Here, at least take a bite out of my sandwich."

"Thanks," Artie answered as he bit slowly into the sandwich.

At 1:05 P.M, Judge Warrington turned toward the jurors and spoke. "Ladies and gentlemen, you have an important responsibility to render a carefully considered verdict in this case. Take your time. If you do not finish today, return to the jury room at 9:00 A.M. tomorrow and deliberate until you reach a verdict. Remember, this is a civil case and five out of six of you must agree to render a verdict."

The judge wiped his brow with his right hand and continued. "There are several things for you to consider. You have to determine if Dr. Artie Rosner acted negligently in his treatment of Freddie Glaser. Was what he did within reasonable medical practice or was it outside the bounds of reasonable medical practice? If you find that what he did was within acceptable medical practice, then no matter what the consequences of his action, you cannot find him guilty of negligence."

Judge Warrington paused and said emphatically, "However, if you find him guilty of negligence, then you have a second duty. You must level a monetary assessment. You can consider the twelve million dollars that the plaintiffs are suing for, but you are not bound by that amount. You can assess more or less. First you award a certain amount for negligence. If you believe that punitive damages are required, you will award an additional amount for punitive damages."

The judge took a sip of water and continued. "In this case, punitive damages could be assessed if you answer any of the following questions in the affirmative. Was the use of an outdated, converted general anesthesia machine for nitrous oxide/oxygen conscious sedation so grossly negligent that it caused excessive physical harm to the child? Was the use of physical restraint to hold back Freddie Glaser during the dental procedures so damaging that it involved gross negligence? Was the taking of the telephone call while working on the child, considering all the facts of this case, so disruptive that it could be considered gross negligence?"

The judge further advised the jury about the standards of the burden of proof and other technical matters. He then concluded. "That's it. Good luck. Thank you, everyone. The jury is dismissed. We will remain in session until 5:00 P.M. If the jury has not reached a decision by that time, we will reconvene on Monday morning at 9:00 A.M."

After the judge had dismissed the jury, Ernie Coniglia told Artie to go out for a walk while the jury was considering the case. At 1:10 P.M., Dr. Artie Rosner left the courthouse accompanied by his brother, Burt. Having no destination in mind, they wandered aimlessly for about forty-five minutes. Artie didn't want to talk about the case, so they just chatted about the world situation and the President's problems. At 1:55 P.M., they returned to the courthouse and Artie called his office.

"Hello, Phyllis. Is Dr. Procter almost finished with his one o'clock patient?"

"Yes, he just finished. His patient is walking out of his room right now."

"Good. Will you transfer me to his extension?"

"Yes, Doctor."

"Hi, Mark. The jury's got it."

"How did it go today?"

"To tell you the truth, my so-called friend, Kenneth Hamilton, did a better job than my team's attorney, Coniglia."

"Coniglia had a harder job."

"That's for sure. I don't know how long the jury will be out, but there's a chance that they can come up with a verdict today. How many more patients do you have?"

"I should be through by four."

"Any chance that you could come to the court house for moral support?"

"Of course. I'll see if Ginny can come too."

"Thanks, Mark. I'll see you later."

At 5:05 P.M, the bailiff escorted the jurors to their seats. He then announced, "All rise for the Honorable, Judge Joseph Warrington."

The judge entered and said, "Everyone sit down please. Mr. foreman, please arise."

Henry Mayfield, the semi-retired accountant who had been elected the jury foreman, arose.

"Have you reached a verdict?"

"We have, your Honor."

Dr. Artie Rosner was at the defense council's table sitting next to attorneys Ernest Coniglia and Warren Wilkins. In the first row of the audience directly behind Artie were Artie's brother, Burt, his associate, Mark Procter, his assistant, Julie Parsons, and Mark's assistant, Ginny Walker.

"Please read it," the judge said.

"We the jury find the defendant, Dr. Artie Rosner, guilty of negligence with respect to the treatment of Freddie Glaser."

Artie appeared shocked. He got up and staggered.

Mayfield looked at the floundering Dr. Rosner for a moment and continued. "We also found the defendant liable for punitive damages. We award Mr. and Mrs. Bernie Glaser, on behalf of their son Freddie, six million dollars for negligence and an additional two million dollars for punitive damages. That makes a total of eight million dollars."

Artie reached the front of the defendant's box and fell down. Mark and Burt rushed to his side. Artie appeared to have fainted. Mark slapped him on the face and called for a glass of water. A few seconds later, he received the glass and gave sips to the reviving Artie.

Artie cried out, "What am I gonna do?"

"Don't worry," Burt said, "I'll be there for you."

Mark and Burt held Artie as they left the building. Ginny and Julie accompanied them. It would be a long and arduous night.

13

According to their original contract, the malpractice award of eight million dollars was to be evenly divided between the Glasers and the law firm of Hamilton, Burgess and Pettersen. Artie continued to work unenthusiastically for a little more than a month. He only had a small amount of money saved. His wife's prolonged illness set him back financially. He had been able to recover somewhat, but he made some foolish investments. Currently, aside from his car, apartment furnishings, dental equipment, supplies, furnishings and the good will from his practice, he had practically nothing. The little money he had, Artie had to use to pay for his private attorney, Warren Wilkins.

Artie's retired brother, Burt had a comfortable nest egg that he would never be able to spend. Accordingly, he gave his brother six hundred thousand dollars. Mark helped Artie out somewhat by purchasing the office equipment, supplies and furnishings for two hundred thousand dollars. He gave him another one hundred fifty thousand dollars for the good will of the practice, although he felt that many of Artie's patients would go to other offices. Since Mark lived in the same building as Artie, he decided he'd purchase Artie's elegant furniture and furnishings for another fifty thousand dollars. For all of these purchases, Mark didn't have that kind of money available. However, he knew that Artie needed the money immediately. Therefore, Mark took out a loan for the four hundred thousand dollars that was due to be paid back within a six-year period.

Artie had been fortunate in one respect. His malpractice policy coverage was the maximum — six million dollars. The money he received from Burt and Mark totaled another million. Artie still had five hundred thousand dollars in his retirement plan that could not be attached. Artie was one million short of the money needed, and he had nowhere to get it. Visibly stressed, he declared bankruptcy. One month after the trial ended, appearing disgraced and downhearted, Artie Rosner left town to live with his retired brother, Burt, in Delray Beach, Florida.

Once Artie left, Mark Procter took over the dental practice. For a while, he was under a great deal of stress. After a couple of months, the stress became manageable. The burden of maintaining the practice and his ongoing romance with Ginny, temporarily, got his mind off the recent tragedy.

It was now mid-April, about three months after Artie had gone to Florida. In spite of Mark's fears, very few of Artie's ex-patients left the practice. Last month, Mark had hired a dentist, who had recently graduated from Temple University, to carry the load left by Artie's departure. The new dentist's name was Willie Chow. Willie's work was exemplary. He got along well with both the patients and the dental staff. Julie, who had been retained as a roving assistant after Dr. Rosner's departure, was now back to being a full-time chairside assistant.

Since today was a Wednesday — Mark's day off — and the weather was delightful, Mark decided to play golf with his dentist friend, Jim Auclair. They were to meet at Mt. Laurel Golf Course at 8:00 A.M. Although they had announced their wedding engagement two months ago, Ginny still gave Mark free reign, but only as far as golf was concerned. Ginny spent the day at the Philadelphia Art Museum. They had a special impressionist exhibit. Ginny was thrilled. The impressionists were her favorites.

Both Mark and Jim were having one of their better days on the picturesque course with its rolling hills, large, stately oak and willow trees, curved fairways, two large water holes and numerous sand traps. The rough was particularly rugged. Today, there was practically no wind, the temperature was in the upper 60s with low humidity, and the sky was perfectly blue. They were about to enter the back nine. Mark shot a forty on the front nine, and Jim was only two strokes behind. There was a foursome hovering around the short, par three ninth hole. Mark and Jim had to wait a few minutes. They passed the time sitting on the low wooden bench near the tee off point.

"Mark, guess who came into my office for emergency treatment of a toothache?"

"Don't keep me in suspense."

"It was Kenneth Hamilton, the guy who used to be Artie Rosner's buddy and the lead attorney on the malpractice case that destroyed him."

"Incredible!"

"He told me that he had gone to Artie for years, but going back to that office was out of the question."

"I can understand that. What kind of a patient was he?"

"Don't you know about patient-doctor confidentiality?"

"In this case, you can make an exception."

"Why not, the guy was a bastard to Artie. At any rate, he's a lousy patient. He was extremely apprehensive and get this, he insisted on having 'nitrous.'"

"Yeah, I remember he took 'nitrous' in our office. I never treated him since he was Artie's so-called friend."

"He had other requirements. First he had to be certain that my unit was 'fail-safe,' and then all during the treatment, he kept asking what percentages he was getting. I tell you, I was tempted to give him one hundred percent nitrous oxide."

"You know you couldn't do that with a 'fail safe' unit. If you could, you'd be facing an attempted murder rap."

"I know. I'm just kidding. At any rate, I finished the filling. When it was all over, he told me that I should give him a full mouth examination and do all the work he needs as soon as possible."

"That's strange."

"I thought so too, until he told me he was retiring next month. He said he was in his sixties and had it with tough judges, and lying plaintiffs, defendants and witnesses. He also said that he had bad asthma and had enough of the cold winters. In addition, Hamilton told me he had all the money he'd ever need."

"When he said that, did you raise the fee?"

"Mark, I'm not that kind of guy."

"I was only joking. What happened next?"

"I asked him when would he be leaving. He said he'd be gone by the middle of May."

"Did he say where he was going?"

"He said he was heading for Florida."

"I hope he doesn't go anywhere near Delray Beach. If he does, Artie might kill him."

"For the sake of both of them, I hope he goes far from there. Maybe he'll head for Florida's west coast."

"That would work out fine."

The foursome in front of them just left the tenth hole. The hole was one hundred-fifty yards away. It was practically a straight line from tee to hole.

There was a tear-shape pond fronting the green and two large sand traps on the sides.

Mark took a No. eight iron and teed off. It was a high arching shot. The ball landed six feet from the pin.

With a smile on his face, Jim said, "I should give you surprises all the time if you're going to drive like that."

Mark laughed and remarked, "Maybe you should."

The same day, it was lovely in South Florida. The hot, humid weather had not yet arrived. During the three months since he had arrived in Delray Beach to live with his brother, Burt, Artie had not been too happy. He did the usual things that are done by Florida retirees. He sunned himself at the beach, read paperback novels, played golf and poker, ate out at a variety of restaurants, went to the movies and watched a lot of TV. Still, most of the time, he was bored. To give some excitement to Artie's life, Burt Rosner and his lady friend, Goldie Abrams, decided to take Artie to a dog race. Burt had gone to a lot of dog races and had become quite an expert about the sport.

Although Artie had previously shown little enthusiasm about anything that Burt had proposed to do, he was mildly interested in going to the dog track. Consequently, at 4:00 P.M., Artie and Burt got into the front and Goldie sat in the rear of Burt's late model, gray Dodge Ram.

While driving, Burt said to Artie, "I've chosen the Palm Beach Kennel Club for a few reasons. It's the closest, located on Congress Avenue in West Palm Beach, which is only a short ride north on Route I-95. It's one of the finest dog racing tracks in the country. It has an excellent eating establishment, The Paddock Restaurant. To cap it off, it has a special room — the Poker Room — where there are thirty poker tables with plenty of action."

"You know, Burt, except for poker, I'm not much of a gambler. Back home in Jersey, before it was closed down, I went to Garden State Park a few times and bet on the trotters. I only won once — a hundred bucks. Dog races are something else. I know nothing about them. On the way, why don't you clue me in?"

"Sure, Artie." He paused a moment and then began his explanation. "The only dogs that race are greyhounds."

"I know that greyhounds are fast. I also remember reading that greyhounds were ancient and had been revered." Artie wanted to display some of his own knowledge.

"Excellent. There were murals and paintings of greyhounds over four thousand years ago. Greyhounds were held in high esteem in ancient Egypt. Their pictures were etched on the walls of Egyptian tombs, and pharaohs rated them highest among all animals. The ancient Arabs were enamored with the speed and physical attributes of greyhounds. They were the only dogs permitted to share their tents and ride atop their camels. In early Arabian culture, the birth of a greyhound ranked second only in importance to the birth of a son."

"You mean girls didn't count?"

"I suppose so. It wasn't only the Greeks and the Arabs, though. In ancient Persia, Greece, Rome and Palestine, the greyhound was given similar high status. It's also the only canine mentioned in the Bible."

"I never knew that."

"It's true. Over three thousand five hundred years ago, the greyhound arrived in Great Britain. Around the year 1000, King Canute enacted the Forest Laws, which stated that only noblemen were permitted to own and hunt with greyhounds."

"That's typical male chauvinism."

"That changed completely. In the 1500s, Queen Elizabeth I abolished the Forest Laws and initiated the first formal rules of greyhound coursing, the pursuit of hares. This was the official inauguration of the 'Sport of Queens.'"

"That was a change into female chauvinism."

"At least for a time. Greyhounds were imported into the U.S. in the late 1800s in order to help Midwestern farmers control crop-destroying jackrabbits. Soon after, greyhound coursing events followed."

"Look out!" Goldie screamed from the back. "You almost hit that white Chevy."

"I'm sorry, Goldie. I'll keep my eye on the road. Where was I, Artie?"

"You were talking about greyhound coursing. I suppose that means to hunt for game."

"Yeah."

"When did the races start?"

"They started around 1910 when Owen Patrick Smith invented a mechanical lure. That made racing around a circular track possible. Close to 1920, the first circular track opened in Emeryville, California. That track was not too successful, but it paved the way for the development of the greyhound racing industry in the U.S."

"One thing still puzzles me. Why were greyhounds the only dogs picked to race?" Artie asked.

"For thousands of years, because of their extreme speed, greyhounds had been hunting dogs. With their long, sleek body, greyhounds are genetically programmed to run. Another part of their genetic nature is their gentleness. Greyhounds have always had a favorable relationship with humans. This continued with their breeding and raising."

"Are certain types of greyhounds picked to race?" Artie was getting quite interested.

"Yes. Only purebred greyhounds are selected to race. The gestation period of a racing greyhound is about sixty days. Litters usually range from five to nine pups. At birth, a greyhound weighs from three-quarters to one and three-quarter pounds. At the age of two months, a greyhound pup is placed in a run to begin exercising its legs. At three months, a pup is given an identifying tattoo. The pup's home for its first year is a breeding farm."

"How long is it before they're ready to race?"

"It takes about one year for greyhounds to grow to their normal size with body weights ranging between sixty-five and seventy-five pounds. They are then transferred to a training kennel. Training starts on a small track where the pups are handheld so that the lure, a mechanical device, is always in sight. Later, the greyhound graduates to a starting box, long distances and increased competition fields."

"Are there different types of racing greyhounds? You know pacers, trotters, things like that."

"Absolutely. During the first few schooling sessions on the training track, a greyhound establishes a running pattern, such as pacesetter, closer inside, outside, slow-breaker and fast-breaker. Some dogs become front-runners, others become back-runners, and still others are variable runners. These patterns and styles are often used for the rest of the dog's running life."

"What do they eat?"

"The normal meal for a racing greyhound consists of two to two and one-half pounds of ground meat, vegetables and roughage along with vitamin supplements."

"If I ate that, I'd become a horse."

"Undoubtedly, you would gain weight. Between fourteen and sixteen months of age, a greyhound is placed in a racing kennel. Each kennel has a trainer who is responsible for up to forty racing greyhounds. Every greyhound is extremely well cared for by its trainer."

All of a sudden, the car came to a jerk.

"What was that?" Goldie screamed.

"The guy in front of me slowed down without warning," Burt answered.

All three of them peered outside. On the shoulder of the road were two cars that obviously had rammed into each other. The accident didn't appear to be serious.

"Continue," Artie said.

"A greyhound owner must register its dog with the National Greyhound Association. With the registration papers, a name — a maximum of sixteen characters — is submitted. Each kennel only contains registered greyhounds, and the kennel itself must be registered. Every kennel enters into a contract with a track to race a certain number of greyhounds during the season."

"What happens on the day of a race?"

"Two hours before post time, the greyhounds are weighed. Track personnel then take them to the lock-up area, where the public can view the dogs. Greyhounds are kept under strict security and are blanketed before track personnel parade them to the starting box."

At 4:25 P.M., Burt pulled off I-95 and entered the West Palm Beach exit ramp.

"Tell me about the betting."

"Sure, Artie. A lot of the betting is like at the horses. The simplest betting is for either Win, Place, or Show. If you bet on Win, you only collect if the dog wins. With a Place bet, you win if the dog comes in first or second. With a Show bet, you win if the dog comes in first, second or third. For the Daily Double, you have to select the winner of two consecutive races. For Pick-3 or Bet-3, you have to correctly select the winners of three consecutive races."

"I've heard of those. What's a Perfecta and a Trifecta?"

"A Perfecta is when you select the first two greyhounds in a race, and they have to finish in the order you pick. For a Trifecta, you select three greyhounds in a race. If they finish first, second and third in the order you selected, you win big. A Twin Trifecta is when the three dogs you select finish in the order you selected in each of two races. The Superfecta is when you select four greyhounds in a race. If these four dogs finish first, second, third and fourth in the order you selected, you get a huge payoff."

"Good. How about a Quiniela?"

"You select two dogs in a race. If they finish first and second in either order, you win. There's also a Quiniela Double. With that, the dogs you select have to finish first or second in either order in two races."

"Are there any others?"

"There's the Pic Six. You have to pick the greyhound that finishes first in six consecutive designated races."

"I'm sure that one's not for me."

"Me neither."

"I suppose the odds on the dogs are developed in the same way as they are with horses."

"That's true. The odds are based on past performances, weather conditions — wet or dry track — age of the dog, stuff like that."

"How do you bet? Do you have any particular strategy?"

"I use the one I picked up a while ago on the Internet. So far, I've come out ahead whenever I've gone to the races. Right, Goldie."

"That's for sure, honey."

"This is the strategy I use. Let's say that you have a hundred bucks to spend. You should place four to six bucks on Win, Place, Show bets, two to five bucks on Quiniela and one to three bucks on Trifecta and Superfecta."

"Sounds simple. I'll try it later."

"One other thing, Artie. Simply watching the greyhounds is enjoyable. You know, dog racing is the number one spectator sport in Florida."

"I never knew that."

"It's true. So, let's watch the dog races, bet some, maybe play a little poker, and have a great meal at the Paddock Restaurant."

"That's for sure. The food is wonderful," Goldie added.

Burt now pulled the car to 1111 North Congress Avenue and entered the parking lot of the Palm Beach Kennel Club. The two men and the woman walked to the large clubhouse. Since it was Burt's suggestion, he paid both the parking lot fee and the entrance fees.

"This is the plan, Artie. We start off by spending a couple of hours in the Poker Room. You and I gamble our own money. Goldie's not into poker. Win or lose, I'll make reservations for the three of us at 6:30 at the Paddock Restaurant. Dinner's my treat. Then at about 7:30, we'll go out into the grandstand and watch the races and gamble until about ten. Like poker, we gamble using our own money."

"Sounds good to me."

"Burt, do I have to gamble with my own money, too?" Goldie asked.

"Of course not. Here's fifty bucks. Use it wisely."

"Thanks."

The afternoon and early evening went as planned. Artie lost fifty bucks at poker. Burt won twenty-five, and Goldie just watched. Dinner was wonderful. Artie and Goldie had filet mignon. Burt had the catch of the day.

Artie was impressed with the beautiful track and grandstand. He especially enjoyed the parading of the greyhounds before the start of each race.

For the first race, which was a sprint, Artie went up to the pari-mutuel window and bet five bucks on Hounddog for Place. The odds on the greyhound were ten to one. After Burt and Goldie placed their bets, the three of them went back to their grandstand seats to watch the race.

"What's that over the dogs' mouths?" Artie asked.

"Those are muzzles. They're either a wire, leather or plastic device with a white tip. They're fitted over the dog's mouth and jaws to be used as an aid in a close photo finish."

The greyhounds were all in their starting box. Hounddog was number six.

"What's that thing the man is holding ahead of the dogs?" Artie asked.

"That's a lure. It's a mechanical device attached to an arm and electrically driven around the racing strip. The operator keeps it at a uniform distance ahead of the greyhounds. The lure is the attraction that sparks the dogs to run."

"I see," Artie said.

They were off. It was a quick race and Hounddog came in next to last. Burt and Goldie also lost their wagers.

For the next couple of hours, everyone used Burt's strategy. By 9:50, Goldie was winning ten bucks, Burt was twenty-five dollars ahead and Artie was losing fifty dollars. They decided the next race would be the last one for them. Knowing that, they all were going to try a Trifecta. Each put two bucks on the race.

The race began. Artie had chosen Top Dog, Underdog and Hot Dog. The race was coming to a close. Burt and Goldie's dogs were way behind. Top Dog was in first, Underdog was second, and Dog-tired was third. Fourth was Sea Dog followed closely by Hot Dog.

Artie was standing and screaming at the top of his lungs, "Move up Hot Dog. You can do it. Make your move."

It seemed that the dog had heard Artie's pleading, because Hot Dog moved into fourth place. Approaching the finish line, Hot Dog closed in on Dog-tired, but it was too close to call. It was a photo finish.

"Did I win?" Artie screamed.

"Can't tell yet. Look at the board. It shows Top Dog, Win, Underdog, Place and a photo finish for Show between Dog-tired and Hot Dog," Burt replied.

"When will I know?" Artie asked with great excitement.

"Look at the board. You'll see in a minute."

To Artie, it felt like the longest minute in his life. It reminded him of the wait for the jury's verdict.

The sign then flashed, "Show to Hot Dog."

Artie leaped in the air and screamed, "I won! I won!"

He came crashing down on the back of the metal seat in front of him. He heard something snap. It was his left foot.

Burt took Artie's ticket and collected three hundred dollars. He and Goldie had to carry Artie, writhing in pain, to the car. They drove to the Emergency Room of West Palm Beach General Hopital. Artie's foot had been shattered and a cast was placed. It was to be worn for six weeks. The doctor told him that he wasn't certain, but because of the severity of the injury, he might have a permanent limp. It had been quite a day.

14

It was the first week of August. Almost four months had passed. Nothing eventful had happened. The only interesting bit of news was from Mark's dental golf partner, Jim Auclair. He had called Mark in the beginning of May. Jim mentioned that his patient, the attorney Kenneth Hamilton, told him that he was retiring to St. Petersberg, Florida. Jim wanted Mark to know that in order to reassure him that now there would be no chance that Artie Rosner, who lived on the East coast of Florida, would be tempted to kill Kenneth Hamilton, who would be living on Florida's West coast.

With the practice now stabilized and their romance in full bloom, Mark and Ginny had decided to get married in mid-September. It was 1:00 P.M. and Ginny was making up her list for the wedding invitations. They definitely wanted to invite Artie. Mark had said to drop a line in addition to the invitation stating that they would take care of the round-trip plane fare from Florida and a motel stay here. This evening they were invited to have dinner and a tour at the home of Dr. Merrick Bass. Mark told her that Merrick had the most fantastic collection of Japanese dolls found anywhere in America. Ginny had her own collection of dolls from around the world, but so far she had no Japanese dolls. She had seen a few of them in museums. Soon she would see a fabulous display. Ginny couldn't wait. While she was preparing the list, Mark was playing tennis at their local club, Pinedale Swim and Tennis Club. Ginny wasn't envious because she had her own match, scheduled at 4:00 P.M.

Mark and Ginny had good workouts although they both lost in close matches. They went home, showered, got dressed and at seven o'clock, they entered the Bass' Lindenwold, New Jersey home. It was a low stucco ranch corner home. Merrick was the first to greet Mark and Ginny. He was a large man in his late 60s with an imposing barrel chest. Many considered him to be handsome with his deep-set brown eyes and a well-groomed dark beard sprinkled with gray. With a strong, resonant voice, Merrick said, "Please come in, friends."

At his side was Franny, a petite, attractive brunette in her mid-fifties. "I'm so happy you could come," she added.

Walking in, Mark and Ginny had the feeling that they had been transported to another country and another time. This was a Japanese home in every way imaginable. It was filled with ningyo, human figure antique Japanese dolls. In the hallway, they were greeted by the ningyo Empress Jingu.

Franny gave them some background about the Empress. "She is the only female doll in the Boy's Day collection. In Japan, the Boy's Day festival occurs on May 5th. It is the celebration of the Samurai heroes and warriors."

Stepping down into the living room, white-faced ningyo either smiled or scorned at them. Shoki, the fabled demon queller, guarded the piano. Resting comfortably on the piano was Taketa, a theater ningyo, striking a dramatic action pose. To the left was the ningyo, Bo Musha, happily trapped inside a Chinese birdcage. Next to Bo was a storybook group of ningyo in the middle of a performance.

On a small table at the left sat the major attraction. It was a small ship containing seven ningyo known as the Seven Lucky Gods of Japan.

Merrick pointed to each god as he gave the name and purpose. "The first is *Benten*, the goddess of music and the arts and the patroness of the performing arts. Over here is *Ebisu*, the god of candor, wealth and good fortune and the patron of fishermen and sailors. This is *Hotei*, the god of fortune, and the patron of fortunetellers. Next is *Bishamon*, the god of dignity, and the patron of doctors."

Mark interrupted, "He's the god for both of us. Am I right? Aren't dentists considered to be doctors?"

"That's for sure. *Bishamon* is for all kinds of doctors. You know, osteopaths, podiatrists, optometrists, even chiropractors. He's already brought me plenty of good fortune. Let's look at the others. Here is *Daikoku*, the god of war and fortune and the patron of business people and farmers. This is *Fukurokuju*, the god of happiness, riches and longevity and patron of athletes, jewelers and magicians. The last god is *Jurojin*, the god of wisdom and the patron of accountants, airmen, journalists, politicians, scientists and teachers."

"*Jurojin* handles a weird combination of occupations," Mark said.

"It sure seems like that," Merrick replied.

"Can you be protected by more than one god?" Ginny asked.

"Yes. For example, I am a practicing physician, a teacher and a painter. In addition to *Bishamon*, I owe allegiance to *Jurojin*, as a teacher and *Benten,* as a painter."

"Interesting," Ginny said.

"It is. The magic ship that the seven gods are sitting in is known as the *takarabune*, meaning the treasure ship. The legend is that during the first three days of the new year, the Seven Lucky Gods of Japan become sailors and command the *takarabune*. The trip begins on New Year's Eve, when the gods steer the treasure ship from heaven into human ports. The cargo inside the ship is known as *takara-mono* or treasure things."

He cleared his throat and continued, "I'll point out each item and then describe it. This hat is *kakuregasa*, which is the hat of invisibility. These are *orimono*, meaning rolls of brocade. Over here we have *kanebukuro*, the inexhaustible purse. This item is *kagi*, which is the sacred keys of the treasure shed of the gods. Here we have *makimono*, translated as the scrolls of books of wisdom and life. This is *kozuchi* or Daikoku's magic mallet. This outfit is known as *kakuremino*, the lucky raincoat. This garment is called *hagoromo*, meaning the robe of fairy feathers. This last bag is known as *nunobukuro*, which is Hotei's bag of fortune."

Mark asked, "How long did it take you memorize all of this?"

"About seven years."

"That explains it. For now, I only have to know one, *Bishamon*, the patron of doctors." Mark said.

"You're right."

"I'm sure *Bishamon* would consider me, a potential dentist, as being eligible for his aid," Ginny added.

"I'm sure he will," Merrick replied sporting a grin.

Facing the living room and up the steps on the other side of the entrance hallway was a room lined with a variety of ningyo. Most were made from Paulonia wood, straw, silk and linen. Almost every doll's face looked as white as pure ivory. However, they were crafted out of wood and covered with Gofun, which is pulverized, powdered oyster shells, mixed with rice paste or animal glues. The outer coverings and accessories of some of the ningyo were colored to look like metal. Because the ningyo were so delicate, extreme care had to be exercised in touching them.

After the tour of the three hundred dolls, Japanese paintings and other antiques, Mark and Ginny were escorted into the small kitchen. They sat down and admired the Japanese screen next to the kitchen door outside exit. Dinner was Japanese of course with sushi, noodles and various delicacies. For dessert, they had Japanese cookies and Japanese green tea.

During the conversation, Ginny told her hosts about her own modest collection of worldwide dolls and then added, "To date, I have no Japanese dolls. Maybe, Mark will add one or two to my collection."

Mark smiled. "Could be," he responded.

It was an evening Mark and Ginny would never forget. The couple was on their way out when Mark noticed an opened newspaper on a small Japanese-style table. He glanced downward and saw that the paper was turned to the obituary page. Mark asked Merrick, "Do you have a specific reason for having the obituary page open?"

"At my age, colleagues and friends are dropping off like flies. I like to see if anyone I knew had passed on."

"Did you find anyone?"

"There's no one I know, but you might know the guy that's headlined. He was a Marlton dentist. Don't you practice in Marlton?"

"Yes. Let me see that paper."

Ginny heard a Marlton dentist mentioned and came over to Mark. She leaned over his shoulder as he read the paper. The newspaper was the *Courier Post*. Mark saw the headline Merrick was referring to. "Prominent Marlton Dentist Dies of a Heart Attack in Florida." The next line shocked him to the core.

"Dr. Artie Rosner, who had practiced here for over forty years and because of a malpractice verdict had to retire to Delray Beach, Florida, apparently had a heart attack and drowned. He had been fishing in the rough waters of the Atlantic Ocean on Thursday, August 5th. Dr. Rosner was reported missing at 7:30 P.M. by his brother, Burt. He had not been seen for eight hours. The body has not yet been found. Dr. Rosner was sixty-five-years old at the time of his disappearance."

Mark and Ginny were amazed.

Merrick and Franny noticed their concerned looks. "Did you know him?" Merrick asked.

"Know him?" Mark replied. "I worked for him. What a horrible tragedy!" Mark paused for a few seconds to collect himself and added, "Thanks for everything, folks. We'll have to be leaving now."

"We are sorry this lovely evening had to end this way," Franny said.

Merrick added, "It's unfortunate, Mark, but drive carefully. You don't want another tragedy,"

"Don't worry. I'll be careful. Good night and thanks again."

On the way to the car, Mark said, "I was looking forward to seeing Artie at our wedding. I knew he liked fishing, but I wasn't aware that he had a heart condition. I suppose we all live on borrowed time."

"Yes, Mark, but our time is just starting."

The previous month, Ginny moved out of her Cherry Hill apartment and into Mark's Marlton apartment. Mark lived in the same building in which Artie formerly had a place. When Artie was forced to leave, Mark exchanged his one-bedroom apartment for Artie's substantially larger three-bedroom apartment. It boasted thick, beige carpeting, a fireplace and a balcony. With her feminine touch, Ginny was able to blend her plush furniture with Mark and Artie's more masculine furnishings. The furniture they couldn't use was sold. One room was set aside for Ginny's dolls. Another room was their joint study, and the largest room was their bedroom.

It was nine o'clock, one hour after Mark and Ginny had left the surreal world of the Bass' home. Mark decided he would call Burt and find out the details. He dialed the number and signaled Ginny to pick up the extension.

"Hello, Burt, this is Mark Procter. I saw you at the trial. I was your brother's associate."

"Of course, Mark. Do you know that my brother has passed on?"

"Yes. I read about it in the *Courier Post*. Please accept our condolences."

"Thank you."

"Would you mind telling us what happened?"

"It's not a pleasant memory, but I'll do it this one time. It was eight o'clock in the morning last Thursday when Artie told me he wanted to go fishing. He had gone fishing a few times before without any problems. I'm not a fisherman. Artie always went alone. He told me it helped him relax and clear his mind."

Burt paused. The recollection was getting to him. He sniffed and continued. "After breakfast, I drove Artie down to the fishing place, Pushes, at the Pompano Beach dock. He had packed a lunch and had all of his fishing paraphernalia. He seemed to be in a good frame of mind. He rented the same small boat that he had done on the previous occasions from Pushes, and by 9:15 in the morning, he was on his way."

Burt coughed out loud.

"Are you all right?" Mark asked.

"Yeah. I got a frog in my throat. That was the last time I saw Artie. The weather had been good, but by late afternoon, a typical Florida electrical storm kicked up. The Atlantic waters must have gotten rough. At 7:30 Friday morning, the police found the capsized boat. They picked up some of his supplies and even Artie's wallet. The items had been locked in a bag. His shoes and pants were also found, but there was no sign of Artie. He must've been carried out into the middle of the ocean." Burt started to cry at this point. "I'm sorry. I can't go on."

"We're sorry we bothered you. If there is anything I can do, please give me a call. Good night, Burt."

"Thank you. Good night," Burt said tearfully.

Five weeks later, on a Saturday evening, Dr. Mark Procter and Miss Ginny Walker were married by a justice of peace at the Cherry Hill Hilton. About one hundred people were in attendance. On Mark's side, there were his mother, father, and a few cousins, aunts and uncles. For Ginny, there were her mother and a few of her close relatives. Marks friends who attended were Dr. Jim Auclair and Dr. Jake Daniels, with their wives. A few of Mark's colleagues came including Dr. Ed Cahn and Dr. Bill Irving and their wives. From the dental office came Julie, Kathy, Phyllis and Dr. Willie Chow and his wife. Dr. Merrick Bass and his wife Franny were also present. In reverence to Artie Rosner, Mark invited his brother, Burt. Burt agreed to take the trip. As he had promised for Artie, Mark took care of all the expenses for Burt's round trip from Florida. He also paid for Goldie.

The ceremony was non-denominational and was over quickly. The dinner was excellent, and a superb six-piece band played until two in the morning. The Procters received money and a variety of typical wedding gifts including trays, pitchers, dishes, tables, nightgowns and appliances. The gifts that Ginny cherished the most were two Japanese dolls. They were two versions of the same Japanese ningyo that the Bass' purchased especially for them.

Franny told Ginny, "The larger one is *Bishamon*, the one made-to-order for both of you. As you might recall, he is the patron of all kinds of doctors. Of special interest as you journey through life is the fact that *Bishamon* is a defender of evil and the bringer of good fortune. You never know when you might need him. Since I expect the two of you will do a lot of traveling, I also purchased a smaller version of *Bishamon*. This one is made of bronze. When you travel, you can keep him in your handbag."

Ginny thanked Franny profusely.

While Ginny was talking to Franny, Mark spoke to Burt. He wanted to find out some more details about Artie's death.

"I'm sorry to burden you with a question about Artie while you're enjoying yourself, but something has been bothering me."

"It's okay. What's on your mind?"

"Do you think that Artie was depressed?"

"I'm not sure, but he wasn't too happy. The only time he seemed to enjoy himself was the day we took him to the dog races."

"What I'm getting at is this. Do you think he committed suicide? Is it possible that the drowning was not an accident? Could it have been intentional?"

"That's a tough one. I never thought Artie was a quitter. But hell, I was never in a situation like his. I suppose it is possible."

"Thanks, Burt. Sorry to have bothered you. Enjoy the rest of the evening."

The following Thursday was Mark's last working day before the honeymoon trip that would begin on Saturday. Friday was set aside for preparation. The time was 4:00 P.M., and Mark's last patient of the day was Harvey Anderson, a ten-year old apprehensive boy.

Harvey was seated and draped. Ginny spoke to him, "Harvey, we're going to put these space age goggles and magical headphones on you. You've probably heard of virtual reality."

"Yeah, when I went to Universal Studios in Florida, I put on goggles and went 'Back to the Future.'"

"This is something like that. You're going to close your eyes and magically, even with your eyes closed, you'll 'see' flashing lights. They're all different colors. They might be red, purple, blue, orange or yellow. While the lights are flashing, you'll hear musical sounds — sort of like the waves coming in on a beach. You've been to the beach. Haven't you?"

"Sure. I went to the beach in Atlantic City. The waves were super."

"These waves will be even better. In a while, the lights will change to white and then you won't see them at all. Once that happens, Dr. Procter will put your tooth to sleep. You know about that, don't you?"

"Yeah. Everything gets numb."

"Good, but this time you won't even feel the tooth getting numb. After the tooth gets numb, and the lights stop flashing, you'll take a magical trip. You can go anywhere that you would like to. You can be an astronaut and fly to the moon. You can go to Disney World or back to Universal Studios. You can go to the zoo or the aquarium. Won't that be fun?"

"I can't wait to start."

"While you're on your trip, Dr. Procter will drill out that bad tooth decay and put in a nice new silver filling. Would you like that?"

"Yeah."

"Good, we're going to begin now."

While Ginny was setting up young Harvey Anderson, Mark recalled the time when he first got involved with these goggles and headphones.

Artie Rosner had retired to Florida in the middle of January. On the following Wednesday, Mark closed the office early and rented a truck. Instead of playing golf with his friend Jim, the two of them carried Artie's outdated, converted general anesthesia unit into the rear of the truck. Mark had previously called up the Dental History department at Temple University School of Dentistry. The department chairperson agreed to take and display the outmoded piece of equipment. When Mark and Jim arrived at Temple, they carried the unit to the display section of the Dental History Museum. Mark was pleased. The unit could never again harm another human being.

One month before — again on a Wednesday — Mark and Jim took a continuing education course entitled, "Brain Wave Synchronizers: A New, Safe, Non-invasive Method to Deeply Relax Patients." Dr. Melvin Kamfer, the same researcher who had testified at Artie's trial on the effects of stress, gave the course. Dr. Kamfer was the world's leading researcher on this relatively new modality.

Dr. Kamfer was discussing the technique. "These brain wave synchronizers or BWS are photostimulating white goggles with simultaneously flashing of right and left lights at variable frequencies. The BWS unit contains portable battery-powdered stroboscopes that emit simultaneously bilateral flashing lights and rhythmic sounds. The unit is designed for the patient to close his or her eyes, and when the alpha frequency is chosen, the patient rapidly enters the alpha state of deep relaxation. The flashing lights and the rhythmic sounds entrain the patient's own brain waves to come into the alpha state throughout the entire brain. Deep relaxation is a by-product of this synchronized alpha state."

Mark raised his hand.

"Yes, Doctor."

"Is the sensation similar to what one feels with profound meditation and hypnosis?"

"Absolutely. It is also similar to what can be achieved with nitrous oxide/ oxygen conscious sedation. The dentist and dental staff do not require any extensive training as is the case with 'nitrous,' intravenous sedation with drugs such as Valium® and hypnosis and meditation. Unlike drugs, with the BWS, there are no dangerous side effects. The only people who shouldn't use BWS goggles are epileptics, with whom there is the rare possibility that the flashing lights could induce an epileptic attack, and claustrophobics, who might be afraid to have anything over their eyes. With the BWS technique, the patient merely has to sit in the chair, close the eyes, and flow with the deep relaxation."

After the impressive talk, both Mark and Jim purchased a brain wave synchronizer unit. Mark had used the BWS unit with the relaxation sounds for about a dozen patients. The results were excellent. For a couple of patients who were terrified of dentistry, Mark used his 'fail-safe' nitrous oxide/oxygen conscious sedation along with the BWS unit. Those patients could "see no evil, hear no evil, and smell no evil." However for most patients, Mark was able to use the BWS unit rather than the "nitrous." In fact, Mark only had to use the nitrous oxide/oxygen conscious sedation with two other patients. This new modality was proving excellent, and most important, it appeared to be completely safe.

This September morning was the first time Mark was going to use BWS and the relaxation sounds with a child.

Ginny placed the goggles with the alpha setting and the headphones with the alpha sounds running on Harvey.

After a couple of minutes, Mark asked, "Where are you, Harvey?"

"I'm on a spaceship and you know what?"

"What, Harvey?"

"I'm not going to the moon. I'm going to Mars."

"That's wonderful, Harvey."

Mark then proceeded to give a local anesthetic injection in the upper right first molar region. Upper molar injections take effect rapidly and within a minute Mark was able to begin drilling. Harvey didn't flinch throughout the entire injection, drilling and filling procedures.

After thirty minutes, the flashing lights and the sounds stopped automatically. Ginny, then spoke to Harvey. "You can now land the spaceship back on Earth, Harvey. The mission is over."

Ginny waited a few seconds and then removed the goggles and headphones.

Harvey opened his eyes and said, "That was great. When can we do it again?"

"It'll have to wait until next month, Harvey," Mark replied. "Ginny and I first have to take a trip of our own."

With that, the happy child was dismissed.

"I hope our honeymoon will be just as joyous as Harvey's trip."

"I'm sure it will be," Ginny said.

Artie had given them such a glowing report about Costa Rica, and especially the B & B in San José, that Mark and Ginny decided that even though it was still the rainy season, they would take their three-week honeymoon in Costa Rica. They were even going to the very same B & B about which Artie had raved.

The Procters loaded the car Friday evening, and at the ungodly time of 4:30 A.M. on Saturday, they entered Mark's Corvette and began the drive to Philadelphia International Airport. They planned on getting there at 4:50 A.M, which would have given them more than enough time for the necessary, prolonged check-in for the 7.00 A.M. shuttle to JFK International in New York where at 9:30 A.M., they were scheduled to board Costa Rica's international airline, LACSA, for the seven-hour trip to San José airport in Costa Rica. The shuttle was scheduled to arrive at the JFK International gate at 7:30 A.M, which would have given the Procters two hours before the departure to Costa Rica. But the first part of the journey to the Philadelphia airport didn't go as planned.

While still in New Jersey, driving south on Route 295, Ginny said, "I'm glad you're driving. I'm still half asleep."

"No problem. Before you know it, we'll be there. We'll have plenty of time to sleep on the flight to Costa Rica."

Mark was alert, and he happened to notice a late model, gray sedan that had been driving behind them since they got on 295 at the Woodcrest entrance.

"Ginny, don't make it obvious, but look through your rearview mirror. There is a gray sedan that's been following us. I'm going into the right lane. See if it follows us."

Ginny did as she was told. Mark decreased the car's speed and stayed in the right lane. Ginny looked through the mirror. Sure enough, the gray sedan followed them.

"Mark, " she cried out, "it's on our tail."

"Turn around as if you're getting something out of the back seat. Try to see the make of the car. See if you can make out the license. Maybe you can see what the driver looks like."

Feeling slightly apprehensive, Ginny said, "Sure, Mark."

After she turned back, Ginny reported, "It looks like a late model Infiniti with a Jersey plate. I couldn't make out the whole license number. I think it had SNR in it. There's only one person in the car. He's a man and he had a scowl on his face."

"Could you tell anything about his features?"

"It was hard to tell from that distance, but he has black hair and is dark-complexioned, sort of a greasy-looking guy."

Mark slowed down as he pulled the car into Route 676 and soon he approached the entrance to the Walt Whitman Bridge. The gray sedan didn't stay in Mark's lane, but it also went on 676 and got on the Walt Whitman Bridge.

Mark noticed the sedan's movements and said, "Maybe it was our imagination. That driver's car is two cars back now and is in the middle lane."

Ginny again looked through the rearview mirror and said, "He's looking to his left, not at us." She seemed relieved.

Now they were at the bridge exit in Philadelphia. Mark drove into the exact change lane and pulled into the far right-hand lane to get onto the ramp for I-95 South. After he paid the toll, Ginny said, "That guy is getting change. He doesn't seemed to be in a rush now."

"Good. Let's forget about him. We've only got about ten minutes more on the highway and we'll be at the airport."

"Great," Ginny said.

Mark was driving in the middle lane, going about sixty-five miles an hour. His mind was on the upcoming honeymoon in Costa Rica. Ginny had her eyes closed envisioning the Costa Rican rain forests.

Without warning, the gray Infiniti crashed into the driver's side of Mark's Corvette. The Corvette spun around and landed on the side of the highway narrowly missing a convertible in the right lane.

Both Mark and Ginny had their seat belts on, and the air bags activated. Mark lost consciousness from the impact. Ginny was shocked but saw everything as if in slow motion. She could see the dark-haired man's face.

He displayed a vicious smirk as his car sped away.

A few minutes later, a Pennsylvania state police patrol car pulled over.

The trooper called inside, "Are you guys all right?"

By this time, Mark had awakened and was able to move his limbs. Aside from a slight headache, he felt fine physically. Ginny had a few bruises, but her head was clear. Both of them were anxious and concerned. Mark said, "I was out for a bit, but I think I'm okay."

"How about you, ma'am?"

"I think I'm all right, but what happened?"

"It looks like someone was in a rush, gave your car a pounding and took off."

Mark said, "The guy had been tailing me since I got on 295 back at Woodcrest in Jersey."

"Have you any idea who he was? Did you happen to see the make of car? Did you get his license?"

Ginny answered, "He was a dark-haired, dark-complexioned, greasy-looking guy. We never saw him before. The car was a late model, gray Infiniti sedan with a Jersey plate. I could only make out the letters SNR on the license."

"We'll do the best we can to trace him, folks. Meanwhile, do you want me to take you to a hospital? the trooper asked.

"No!" exclaimed Mark and Ginny simultaneously. Mark added, "We're on our honeymoon, and if we don't hurry we'll miss our plane."

"Sorry you had such a bad start. I'll stay here to make sure your car starts."

"Thanks," Mark said.

Mark started the engine, and it turned over smoothly.

"Since your car is quite banged up, I'll lead you into the airport to be certain you get there safely."

Mark and Ginny thanked the trooper. The ride to the airport went smoothly, and they were able to park in long-term parking. Because it was so early in the morning, they still had enough time to make the shuttle.

Once they were comfortably seated, Ginny said to Mark, "Have you any idea who was that crazy driver?"

"Beats me. Let's just forgot about it for now and enjoy this wonderful honeymoon." He then leaned over and kissed Ginny passionately.

15

After that disastrous start, the remainder of the trip to San José was smooth. The Procters spent most of the flight in gentle sleep.

At the Costa Rica airport, Ginny took her first breath of the warm, humid air. "It's wonderful," she said. "This is my first trip to a tropical country." A waft of a warm, tropical breeze crossed her face. To her, the breeze was a harbinger of tranquility and pleasure. To make sure, she reached into her handbag. Ginny then looked inside and saw *Bishamon* staring back at her. She knew it would be a great trip.

"Don't get too used to this wonderful weather, Ginny. Let's not forget that our permanent home is still in New Jersey. For now, we better get a cab to take us out to the B & B."

They hailed a small yellow cab with a diminutive native Costa Rican driver. Mark told him where they wanted to go in San José. When the cabbie answered, they realized that he knew a smattering of English.

While driving along the road leading into the city, Ginny noticed several large banners that seemed to have proclaimed a holiday. She spoke to the cabbie. "Excuse me, can you tell me what are those signs?"

The cabbie answered in broken English, "You peoples shoulda been here three days ago. Those signs are for our national holiday. Our day of independence, the day we got freed from Spain. It was September 15, 1821. Big celebrations here three days ago. You missed lots of excitement."

"We're sorry we missed the celebrations, but we couldn't leave before today. I'm sure we'll see many other things in your beautiful country," Mark said.

"Oh, yeah. Lots to see."

159

It was 5:00 P.M. when the cab driver arrived in the historic Barrco Otoya district of San José. Ginny was impressed with the architecture of Old Spain that graced the quiet streets of San José. A couple of minutes later, the cab pulled up in front of Sieta Hormingas Negras. Artie had told them that the name means Seven Black Ants. Mark carried the bulk of the luggage inside the small B & B. The architect owner, Paula Rodriguez, was there to greet them. Artie had informed them about her magnificent exotic decorations throughout the building. After the couple had unpacked their belongings, Paula gave them a tour of the small facility. Mark's Nikon recorded the B & B for posterity.

On the way back to their room, Ginny said, "Mark, isn't it wonderful. This place is a little piece of heaven. Let's look at the tour book. I want to do everything."

"That's fine, but first, I'd like to take a nap. Afterward, maybe we can have a pre-trip romantic interlude."

Ginny merely smiled.

Mark and Ginny had been so impressed with Artie's vivid descriptions of the places he and his brother went to in Costa Rica that they decided on duplicating the itinerary. One of the places the Rosners hadn't gone to, they were definitely going to visit, that is, a rain forest.

On Sunday, they woke up to a downpour. After having a delicious breakfast in the B & B, they visited a few of the numerous small Catholic and Protestant churches. They even checked out one of Costa Rica's impressive synagogues. On Monday, which was another rainy day, they visited the Museo de Oro, the Gold Museum.

After seeing the fabulous collection of antique jewelry, Ginny remarked, "You better start saving your money, Mark. There are at least ten of those gold masterpieces that I'd love to wear."

"It'll take a few years, honey. Right now, I can't afford one of them."

Tuesday, the sun shone brightly and the honeymooners spent the day at the Jardín Lankester, the Lankester Botanical Gardens.

Ginny was overwhelmed by the magnificent species of orchids. That sparked a memory. "Mark, do you remember when we were in New Jersey's Pine Barrens and saw those lovely orchids, you promised that you'd buy me some? You must've forgot. I'm not complaining, you bought me those beautiful roses."

"I'm not going to forget now."

With that, Mark went into the flower gift shop and bought Ginny a half-dozen magnificent, exotic violet orchids. Afterward, they spent several magical hours viewing and photographing the splendid gardens.

Ginny remarked, "I now know what the Garden of Eden must have looked like."

"Except there's no apple trees here," Mark quipped.

While walking back to the B & B, Mark remarked, "Ginny, I have a slight headache."

"Is this the first one you've had since that accident on Route 1-95?"

"To tell you the truth, I've felt a little woozy at times since then, but the feelings passed. This is the first headache."

Ginny, being concerned, said, "Mark, we should have gone to the hospital."

Mark stated emphatically, "You know we couldn't. We would've missed the plane."

"We've no excuses now. Let's go to the nearest hospital. Maybe you had a concussion."

Mark agreed, and they took a cab to the nearest hospital in San José.

Ginny waited nervously as the neurologist examined Mark. One-half hour after he entered, Mark walked out with Dr. Pedro Kolossen. The neurologist, speaking in Spanish-tinged English said, "Your husband tested normally. However, if the headache returns or gets worse, we'll send him in for a MRI. For the time being, enjoy yourselves."

Relieved, the Procters had a leisurely dinner and went to bed early.

Wednesday was another beautiful day. Mark awakened at 7:30 A.M. and said, "I feel great. My head's perfectly clear."

Ginny hugged him. They spent the day visiting the Jardín de Mariposas Spipogyra, the Butterfly Garden. Ginny was thrilled with the splendid colors of the numerous species. Mark photographed two particularly beautiful specimens. One had black-and-white wings and a brilliant orange body. The other had a tan body with bright red wings that were interlaced with stark white markings. They were both fascinated with the several types of hummingbirds. Mark photographed two outstanding varieties. The first had a brown body, a pink throat and a dark green head. The other tiny creature was pale green all over.

Thursday, the rain was torrential. The Procters spent it at the Museo de Jade, the Jade Museum. They were enthralled at the wonderful display of ancient jade. They saw a diversified collection of jade pieces — everything from vases to fertility symbols. Ginny laughed at the large penis on one of the fertility symbols. Marked smiled as if in recognition.

When they saw the table with jade, Mark said, "All right, Ginny. Even though I can't afford the solid gold jewelry, I think I can bear the cost of a nice piece of jade."

True to his word, Mark took Ginny to the gift shop and bought her a small jade ring.

"It's lovely, Mark." She then gave him an enthusiastic hug and kiss in front of all the curious onlookers.

Like a tease, the sun returned on Friday. Mark and Ginny decided to stay local. They walked to the Plaza de la Cultura, the Cultural Plaza. They spent the entire day there and had a wonderful time. There were shows from early in the morning until right before sunset. They saw a South American play, which was like a silent movie to them. Mark remarked facetiously, "Look, no English subtitles."

Ginny gave him a look of playful scorn.

They also listened to a delightful and colorful marimba band. Between numbers, clowns and jugglers entertained. After this, they heard stimulating musical performances, known as Andean music, which originated with natives living in the Andes, the great mountain chain of South America.

Between shows, the Procters bought inexpensive souvenirs for themselves, their parents, friends and the dental office staff. They had their meals in inexpensive restaurants. The honeymooners also purchased all the paraphernalia they would require for the planned rain forest trip next Friday, weather permitting.

Later, after applying a heavy dose of sunscreen, they rested on the grass in a small park and soaked up the Vitamin D and ultraviolet rays. It had been a great day.

Saturday remained bright and sunny. They took a cab to Tapantí National Park.

"Artie was right," Mark remarked, "it's a bird-watcher and photographer's paradise."

They had previously purchased a guide to the native animals. Examining the bird section, they were able to identify a number of the species. Ginny spotted a scarlet macaw, which Mark immediately photographed.

Mark then had a fleeting glance at a blue-throated, goldentail hummingbird. He called Ginny over and said, "Look what it's doing."

The blue bird was sitting on eggs and at the same time caring for its two tiny offspring perched on a nest in a thin branch. Mark moved several feet away and then captured the scene using his zoom lens.

They also observed a variety of insects, small mammals, amphibians and reptiles. The guidebook was a great help in identification.

Sunday was another rainy day. They used it to visit the Museo Nacional (the National Museum). Ginny was fascinated with the pre-Columbian artifacts, period costumes, colonial furniture and photographs of Costa Rican life throughout the ages. Mark was slightly bored but he feigned enthusiasm.

Monday was again warm and sunny. They took a cab to the Orosi Valley, which is a region of breathtaking views of luscious landscapes. The tropical forest was filled with a variety of trees and all sorts of exotic birds and small mammals. Again, the guidebook and camera came in handy.

"Each vista is more beautiful than the one before," Ginny said.

"Wait 'till we see the rain forest."

"I'm really looking forward to that."

Tuesday was a cloudy day with intermittent showers. Mark and Ginny used it to explore Mercado Central, the Central Market. It was as Artie had described, a loud area filled with foul odors. There were numerous dark, narrow passages on the sides of which the vendors were selling fruits, vegetables, fish, exotic spices, and wood and leather handicrafts. Mark bought an embossed leather wallet, and Ginny purchased a fine leather handbag. They spent the rest of the day reading in the small garden of their B & B.

Wednesday's weather was a replica of Tuesday's. They lounged around most of the day doing what honeymooners are supposed to do. For dinner, they followed Artie's advice again. So far, he hadn't been wrong. They ate at La Cocina de Léna in the lovely El Pueblo Shopping Centre. The center resembled a colonial village.

"It's sort of like Batsto in the Pine Barrens," Ginny said.

"It is somewhat like it, but with a Spanish twist."

They watched the native dances and listened to the folk music. Mark even remembered Artie's dining suggestions. They both had black bean soup and shared tamales and ox tail with yucca. The food was fine.

At night, they went to Teatro Nacional, the National Theater. They saw a native musical show. The music and actions of the dancers were enough for them to understand the thin plot and enjoy the wonderful performances.

A brilliant sun greeted them on Thursday morning. They took a cab to Parque Nacional Volcán Poás, Poás Volcanic National Park. The volcano was as magnificent as Artie had described it. Mark took photos from every conceivable angle.

Ginny looked down intently at the banded, gray-brown crater with its hot water lake at the bottom. Unbeknown to her, there was a jagged rock beneath her right foot. She leaned over the rail for a better look. Her foot entangled the rock, and she fell over.

"EEEh!" she screamed as she fell. Her life flashed before her. *I'm going to die. God, please. My life with Mark is just beginning.*

Mark heard the piercing cry. He ran over and tried to catch her. It was too late. She was already in a downward flight. "No! No! No!" he screamed from the top of his lungs.

No one knows if our deaths are predetermined or if we have free will? If we have free will, is it tempered by a certain degree of determinism? There is also synchronicity. Are certain events, things, or people placed in our paths for a beneficial purpose. Whatever, something happened at that moment when Ginny was in free fall.

Ginny fell rapidly, but to herself it was as if she were falling in slow motion. When people are under stress, their senses are heightened, and they can gain incredible strength.

For some unknown reason, on a ledge about fifty feet below the edge, a scraggly tree jutted out over the cliff. While falling, out of the corner of her eye, Ginny saw it and caught a branch with her left hand. She quickly grabbed the branch with her other hand.

Mark watched. His emotions ran from hopelessness and anxiety to hope and possibility. He called out, "Ginny, you can do it. Climb up the branch to the trunk. Take your time. I love you so much."

Mustering her adrenaline-induced strength, Ginny reached the trunk of the tree. However, she was not home safe. Although she was holding onto the trunk, her body was still on the branch. The trunk was narrow, and it hung precariously over the cliff.

Ginny examined her present position. *If I stay still, maybe, the branch won't break. Be calm, Mark will get some help. Thank you, God. Thank you, so much.* The self-talk helped a little, but Ginny was still frightened.

When Mark saw that Ginny had reached the trunk, he called down to her, "Stay where you are, Ginny. I'll get some help. We'll get you out of there safely."

Mark then ran to the main road about one hundred yards until he found the ranger station.

He approached Ranger Arturo Riviera and said loudly, "My wife fell into the volcano. Fortunately, she caught a tree limb about fifty feet below and managed to reach the narrow trunk. Please get some men and a rope or something to help her out."

Tall and bulky, Ranger Riviera answered in good English. "Calm down. We'll rescue your wife. If we can't do it by rope from the ground, we have a helicopter that can get real close. She'll be all right. Show me where she is, and I'll get everything started."

Mark brought the ranger to the site.

"There's no way we can climb down there or get a rope to her from here. I'll call up to get the helicopter. It'll take about fifteen minutes." Ranger Arturo then called out to Ginny. "Young lady, I know you're in an awful predicament, but in about fifteen minutes, we'll have a helicopter reach you and set you free. For now, the best you can do is to try and stay calm. I know it's tough but hang in there."

Ginny responded in a low, weak voice, "Thank you." She closed her eyes and thought about her wonderful day with Mark at the Pine Barrens in New Jersey.

The helicopter was low in gas. It had to be refueled, but all systems were in good working order. Ranger Arturo Riviera got into the co-pilot seat, and lanky Ranger Gina Torres entered the pilot's seat. The chopper took off.

About twenty minutes later, the chopper was close to the dangling tree with frightened Ginny holding on for dear life.

Mark was watching intently from above along with about twenty-five onlookers.

"Get ready, young lady," Rivera said. "I will toss this rope with a loop at its end. Put the loop around your waist, and snap the clasp. Okay?"

"Yes," said Ginny quietly. She was still extremely frightened.

Rivera tossed the rope, but Ginny missed it.

Mark looked down and moaned. A collective groan came from the onlookers.

After retrieving the rope, the pilot Torres brought the chopper closer, about five feet from the tree. Rivera again threw the rope. This time, Ginny caught it, placed it around her waist and snapped the clasp. "It's done," she said.

Mark and the onlookers held their collective breath.

Rivera pulled in the rope slowly as Ginny let go of the trunk. The moment Ginny was freed from the tree the branch broke. In a few minutes, Ginny was inside the helicopter. The chopper took off. The vibrations and wind from the takeoff impacted on the tree, and it broke off the edge and plunged into the volcano.

Mark and the onlookers first cheered and then screamed.

Ginny cried and hugged Ranger Arturo Riviera. "Thank you! Thank you! Thank you!" she uttered.

"That's quite all right," he replied.

Once they were safely on land, Ginny hugged Pilot Gina Torres and thanked him repeatedly.

Torres replied, "I am only happy that we were able to save your life. Do us one favor, though. From now on, hold on to the rail and look where you're walking."

"I will! I will!" Ginny exclaimed while running into Mark's arms. The onlookers cheered joyously. Mark hugged her dearly and then thanked Ranger Riviera and Pilot Gina Torres. They said they were merely doing their duty. Torres then left with the helicopter, and Rivera walked back to the station.

Mark said to Ginny, while still holding the tight embrace, "That volcano could've eaten you up alive." He spoke softly. "I love you so much. Please, be careful."

"I love you, too. I'm sorry. I'll watch my every move from now on."

"Please do, the best part of our vacation is still ahead of us. If the weather is good, tomorrow we start our rain forest excursion."

"That's right. Let's go home, Mark. We've got packing to do. I don't want to take any more chances."

A week before, Mark and Ginny booked the tour for the rain forest expedition at the new Piedras Blancas National Park. It was to be a three-day adventure. They packed last night and awoke at 6:30 A.M to a glorious day. The newlyweds were all decked out in their rain forest outfits with rubber boots, along with Mark's camera and *Bishamon* inside Ginny's handbag. They had an early outdoor breakfast sitting, delighting in the colorful garden at their B & B. At 7:45 A.M., Mark and Ginny entered a cab that took them to the intersection of Avenida 7 and Calle 10 where they picked up the charter bus.

The bus looked as if it had gone through the wars, but Carlos, the bilingual tour guide, assured the sixteen tourists that the bus was completely dependable. While Carlos was speaking, José, the walrus-mustached native driver, smiled broadly. At 8:00 A.M., José turned the ignition key four times before the engine caught on. It sputtered for a few seconds, but José revved it up and soon it was purring like a kitten.

The bus drove through San José with its grid-plan streets. Looking out the window, Ginny could see the conglomeration of mirrored high-rises and decorated bungalows. Soon they were out of the city heading in a southeasterly direction. Their first destination was to be the picturesque old Pacific Ocean banana port of Golfito, but it would be a while before they would get there.

Throughout the trip, Carlos gave the travelers a great deal of information about the country. He started off with the history. "The first Westerner to land in this country was Christopher Columbus. In the early morning of September 18, 1502, he was in the vicinity of a small island in the Caribbean Sea. Several boats needed repairing, and the admiral was sick. Columbus decided to stay a few days. Some of his crewmembers went to the mainland and found gold in the rivers. When they returned to Columbus' ship and told him the news, he decided to call the region, Costa Rica. The name means 'rich-coast.' Columbus' first impression was erroneous. Little silver and gold was found, and throughout the colonial era, the colony remained poor."

"I never knew that Columbus discovered Costa Rica," Ginny said.

"I didn't either," Mark added.

Carlos continued, "A brief period of comparative prosperity occurred in the years 1638-1639, when Captain General Sandoval constructed a new port at Matina and opened a road to the interior of the country. Near the road, the value of cacao plantations increased. Subsequently, the eastern coast and the Gulf of Nicoya were visited by trading ships. However, buccaneers swooped down upon the coast and seized anything of value. Indians completed the work of destruction. These chaotic conditions lasted throughout the eighteenth century. On September 15, 1821, Costa Rica and the other four Central American republics declared independence from Spain and formed a Central American Union."

Ginny whispered to Mark. "Isn't it interesting that three major events occurred in September."

"I just heard two of them: Columbus' discovery of the country and independence from Spain. What's the third?"

"How could you forget? Our wedding."

"Of course. I'm so, sorry. Let's listen to Carlos now."

"After independence was declared in 1821, a progressive government was formed. In 1830, President Juan Rafael Mora inaugurated reforms. Promoted was the production of coffee and bananas along with railroad construction. The first schools were organized, and in 1832 the law provided that education should be obligatory and free. The government of Braulio

Carillo was overthrown in 1842, and the new leader was General Francisco Morazán. He tried to restore the Central American Union. In 1844, the educational principles were incorporated into the first constitution. However, during Morazán's reign, Costa Rica entered a period of anarchy that was similar to that found in her sister republics."

Ginny spoke quietly to Mark. "I'm glad we decided to go to Costa Rica during peaceful times."

"That's for sure," Mark added.

The tour guide went on. "In 1849, the former president, Juan Rafael Mora, returned to office. He restored order, initiated reforms, and helped overthrow the North American filibuster, William Walker. Between 1859 and 1870, six presidents ruled, but their governments were weak. Soon after 1870, under the leadership of President Tomas Guardia, a new constitution was written that assured presidential succession. Guardia died in office in 1882. Liberals and clericals then alternated in power until 1886, when Bernardo Soto became president. In 1894, Rafael Iglesias y Castro became president, and the country entered its modern period. The constitution remained in force until a serious revolution took place in 1948."

Ginny raised her hand.

"Yes?"

"I'm sorry for interrupting, and I don't want to hurt your feelings." She paused for a moment.

Mark wondered what Ginny was going to say.

"Do you think there's something in Latin American blood that makes for so much fighting?"

"That's a theory that has been put forth by non-Latin Americans. The Nazis, the Japanese, the Serbs, and the Islamic Fundamentalists have shown us that it's not just Spanish blood that's warlike. It also seems to me that your country has been engaged in a lot of bloodshed that started with the American Indians."

Ginny felt so embarrassed. She wanted to crawl into a corner and hide.

Mark consoled her. "It's all right, honey. I heard that theory, too. Let's just listen from now on."

Carlos continued, "For the next thirty-four years, there were alternating periods of hostility and stability. In 1982, Luis Alberto Monge Alvarez was elected President, and he instituted a program of economic austerity. Oscar Arias Sanchez, of the ruling National Liberation party, was elected president in 1986. He worked toward a settlement of the area's violent disputes. In

1987, Sanchez initiated a peace plan calling for a cease-fire in Central America. For his efforts, Arias won the 1987 Nobel Peace Prize. Rafael Angel Calderon Fournier, of the Social Christian Unity Party, was elected president in 1990. He was opposed to Arias' peace plan, but Fournier promised to maintain close ties to the United States and to fight drug trafficking, poverty and crime. Tourism is now one of Costa Rica's largest industries, and as compared to most Central and South American countries, it is relatively safe for tourists."

Ginny whispered to Mark. "That's most important."

"Artie told us that he walked in the streets day and night without any problem."Carlos then concluded his talk with a brief discussion of geography, economy, historical sites, museums, restaurants, lodging, educational system and the ecology of the rain forest.

José took the creaky vehicle through the country's central valley and then took a curvy road along the rugged mountains. Looking down at the rocky terrain, Ginny remarked, "I hope he goes slowly. I wouldn't want to wind up being buried among those rocks."

"Don't worry, Ginny. I checked this tour out with the travel agent, and she assured me that the drivers are experienced in handling the mountainous roads."

"That might be true but this is a new national park we're going to. José might never have driven this way before." Ginny remained apprehensive.

"Costa Rica is a small country and José is no youngster. I'm sure he knows where he's going."

"I'll take your word for it."

Mark's word was not enough. As soon as they went around a sharp turn and the bus leveled out, a loud thump was heard. The vehicle tilted to one side, and José jammed on the brakes.

Carlos spoke to the anxious travelers, "I'm sure it's nothing serious. Please stay seated. José and I will check it out."

The tour guide and the driver got out of the bus and looked around. One minute later, they returned and Carlos spoke, "Like I said before, it was nothing major, folks. The bus hit a large pothole; we just had a flat tire. We'll change the flat quickly, and in no time we'll be on our way. Everyone, please get out. This will give all of you a chance to stretch or exercise your legs. Be careful getting off."

The "no time" turned out to be over an hour, but no one complained. Most of the tourists neither stretched nor walked. They just stood and chatted.

Mark wanted the folks back home to partake in this aspect of their adventure so he photographed the leaning bus with its flat tire. In the background, visible was the curving mountain road with its steep rocky descent into the valley below.

While the bus was pulling away, Ginny, who had regained her courage, exclaimed, "Thank God, we're on our way!"

The rest of the group applauded in assent. In appreciation, José said, "Gracias."

The next segment of the drive went without complications. They drove past the Cerro de la Muerte and descended into the lush lowland regions of southern Costa Rica. The Pacific Ocean was on the right as the bus pulled into the old port of Golfito. Mark and Ginny got out with their gear and had lunch sitting on a bench under a picnic table. They admired, and Mark photographed, the ocean and the picturesque old town.

Carlos addressed the tourists. "Folks, it is here that we say goodbye to José. He will stay with friends in Golfito and will meet us here about 1:00 P.M on Sunday. Let's thank José for the fine driving."

Everyone applauded and gap-toothed José smiled in appreciation. He quickly left the group.

Carlos pointed at the dock and said, "See that large, odd-looking canoe."

All eyes turned toward the long, wide, hollowed-out boat. "Are we going in there?" Ginny asked Mark anxiously.

"I suppose so," he replied.

"That," stated Carlos, "is known as a dugout canoe. It took several workmen a few days to chisel that beautiful boat out of a single giant wild chestnut tree."

A thin, nervous-looking American asked, "Is that for us?"

"Of course. And I've even arranged for each of you to have a bag of chestnuts from the tree it came from. That wonderful canoe is going to take us to the magnificent Piedras Blancas National Park. Don't worry. It's perfectly safe, or I wouldn't be going with you. We have two excellent oarsmen, Jaimé and Alfredo."

He pointed to the smiling men sitting on a rim of the boat. "There's plenty of room for all of you including all of your belongings. To make sure that the boat remains balanced, I'll give you seats according to your weight. There will be three in a row. Everyone now stand in two rows of eight each. I'll try to keep couples together. Let's get started. The boat ride should take us about an hour to get to Piedras Blancas National Park."

Before anyone got in, Mark photographed the amazing canoe. The travelers then entered in an orderly fashion. Mark and Ginny sat next to each other in the middle of the boat. Ginny had the outside seat. Mark was in the center, and the nervous young American was on Mark's right.

An outsider gave the canoe a good shove and it was on its way. They were canoeing down an inlet of the Pacific Ocean, and hence the waters were calmer than would be the case for the oceanic currents. The canoe swayed from side to side as it slowly moved.

Ginny asked Mark, "Do you think it would have been calmer than this if we took a canoe ride in the Pine Barrens?"

"I think this is safer. In the Pine Barrens, the water is choppy with lots of large rock obstructions, and branches of overhanging trees can get into your way and knock you for a loop. Once my canoe capsized, and I was drenched for an hour. This is less hazardous."

No sooner did the words come out of Mark's mouth than the boat hit a rough current and nearly capsized. Fortunately, Jaimé and Alfredo — the two expert oarsmen — quickly righted it. All the passengers suffered was a hefty dose of salt water.

"That was scary," Ginny said. *But not as scary as dangling over that volcano,* she thought

"I'm not talking any more," Mark said. "Every time I say anything about the bus or the boat, something bad happens. I'm going to keep my big mouth shut."

"Good idea, Mark."

Carlos was true to his word and one hour later — it was now 3:00 P.M. — the wet and weary tourists were on dry land at the entrance to the Piedras Blancas National Park. Mark saw deeply sculptured ridges that were covered with a heavily forested region of young trees. This was part of the mountains of the Osa Peninsula. His eyes descended from the forests and the terrain changed to smaller shrubs and pristine beaches alongside the inlet. This lower region was known as the Golfo Dulce buffer zone because the inlet is a buffer between the mighty Pacific and the rain forests of southern Costa Rica.

On the beach closest to Mark, known as Playa San Josecito, were two buildings. One was the El Lado Lejano Biological Research Station. The other was the group's dining facility, a thatched roof wooden building nestled amongst numerous trees and shrubs. Mark took several photographs. Afterward, he and Ginny went on a short walk from the dining facility to the group's living quarters. These were rustic, comfortable palm-thatched cabins located in a lush botanical garden at the edge of the rain forest. Each couple was assigned one cabin. As luck would have it, Mark and Ginny were in cabin Uno, the nearest one to the rain forest.

"I'm ecstatic," Ginny declared.

Mark picked her up in his arms, swung her around and held her tightly to him. "So am I," he added. Used to double locks on his apartment back in New Jersey, Mark couldn't help but ask Ginny, "Do you think it's safe being in a cabin that can't be locked?"

"I'm going to take a page from your book. These are experienced tour guide leaders. They would not expose us to anything dangerous." *Except volcanoes*, she thought.

"Thanks, Ginny. You're right."

"Ask me that same question at two o'clock in the morning. I hope I can give you the same answer."

Crossing his fingers, Mark replied, "You will."

The lovers unpacked and for the rest of the day, they swam, read, and relaxed at the quiet and clean beach. After dinner, Mark and Ginny headed for the fresh water lagoon where they, and the rest of the tourists, were accompanied by Enrico, a native guide. The goal was to study the biology of the shallow waters of the lagoon. The first thing Enrico pointed out was the "Jesus Christ" lizards.

"Have you ever seen anything like that, Ginny? Those little critters are running on top of the water."

Ginny replied to Mark's question with a look of amazement. Mark then photographed the incredible lizards.

Enrico said, "The true name for these reptiles is Basilicus basilicus, but as you can see they get their nickname because of their amazing ability on the surface of water. However, unlike Jesus, they run rather than walk."

Enrico next showed the awe-inspired group a slowly moving creature heading their way from the depths of the lagoon.

"My God!" screamed the nervous young American, "it's a crocodile."

"No, it's an alligator!" his portly wife cried out.

"You are both partly right and partly wrong," Enrico stated. "That tropical reptile is known as a caiman. It is usually spelled c a i m a n, but around here we spell it c a y m a n. A caiman is structurally related to the alligator, but superficially it resembles the crocodile. Does anyone know of a country with cayman in its name?"

Ginny, proud of her geographic knowledge, quickly blurted out, "Grand Cayman Island."

"Perfect," Enrico said. He added, "Of course, I must warn all of you not to get too close to the water. Caimans love human meat."

The caiman swam toward the group. Ginny was fascinated by its eyes. The caiman had red eyes that glowed in the reflected light of the surrounding lamps. "Spooky," she said quietly as she quickly backed away from the dangerous reptile.

"Folks, to your right is a most fascinating sight," Enrico said with enthusiasm.

The people's eyes were drawn to trees overlooking the lagoon with the branches loaded with hundreds of small, squawking creatures.

Enrico continued, "Look at them as they go about their frantic activity."

Mark and Ginny watched the small tree frogs crawling all over each other. They appeared to be mating on every branch overlooking the water. The unceasing activity caused the leaves to sway.

"Mark," Ginny said, "Look at their eyes, they're red, just like the caiman."

Mark was more interested in their behavior. "Have you ever seen such an orgy?"

"Mark!"

"Do you remember when we went to the Pine Barrens we only saw a couple of tree frogs?"

"Right, Mark. They were ventriloquists."

"They were great, but here there are hundreds of tree frogs in one spot. Incredible."

At that moment, a tree frog fell out of a branch. Mark happened to be watching at the time and had his camera cocked. With uncanny speed, the caiman swam to the site, opened its huge jaws and clamped down on the helpless amphibian. While Mark's Nikon captured the frightening scene, a loud simultaneous groan emanated from the other human onlookers.

Enrico said, "Unfortunately folks, that's an aspect of the predator-prey relationship. However, it's a good lesson for all of you. Never get too close to a caiman or an alligator or a crocodile for that manner. In case you're interested, we should see a crocodile later on in our trip. Be cautious. Crocodiles are even larger and more ferocious than caimans."

After listening to a few more sights and sounds of the lagoon, Mark and Ginny returned to their cabin. They found it difficult falling asleep listening to the sounds of the myriad of forest creatures, but around midnight, they fell asleep in each other's arms. Ginny awoke at 2:00 A.M. The forest noises had quieted, and Ginny had no need to reassure Mark about their safety.

They awoke the next morning to brilliant sunlight and the renewed sounds of the forest. After breakfast, Mark, Ginny, and the other tourists started off with a tour of the forest floor.

Enrico spoke to the assembled group. "Down here, we have fierce little marauders of the rain forest. We call them army ants. Let's get down on our all fours and watch them in action. I must warn you not to get too close. Unlike most ants that you are used to back in the States, these little creatures bite."

Except for their hands, Mark and Ginny were completely covered. They felt safe. Watching one group of ants and having his close-up lens attached and cocked, Mark said to Ginny, "Look at those small ants carrying large dead beetles on their backs. You would think they'd be crushed by the weight. For their size, they're incredibly strong."

Ginny noticed other ants carrying pieces of the bodies of other dead insects on their backs. "Looks like they're going to have a feast real soon," she said.

"Watch the way they march," Mark said. "It is like an army. Look, they're branching off into two rows. Up further, they've made a temporary encampment for soldiers in the field. In the army, that's known as a bivouac"

"Interesting, but see what they're doing now, Mark. They're linking their legs together."

"That's how they make the bivouac. Look inside. You can see the pupae. It is inside the pupa that the developing insect changes from its larval structures into those of the adult. Once the pupa is severed, the insect comes out as an adult. With their bivouac, the ants are watching over the pupae until they come out as adults."

"Great job, Mark. You should've been a teacher."

At that moment, they heard a loud scream. They turned and saw the nervous young American throwing ants off his arms and fingers. He had been wearing a short-sleeved shirt. From a discreet distance, Mark attached his zoom lens and photographed the frenetic man. The young American had not heeded Enrico's advice and was crying out in pain from the bites. Although army ant bites are acutely painful, they are not serious unless a person is allergic to them. After being given first aid, the young man quieted down. For several days, he would have visible swellings to remind him and everyone else about the danger of army ants.

Enrico then led the group through the forest where they marveled at the inhabitants. They saw small squirrel monkeys scurrying around. All of a sudden, missiles were being hurled at the tourists. A variety of fruit and nuts came flying out of the trees. The monkeys were having a ball.

"Hurry, folks, let's move on," Enrico yelled. "The monkeys are in a playful mood today, and I don't want any of you to get hurt."

"That was a scare," Ginny said. *How many scares do I need*, she thought.

"It sure was," Mark added.

Later, the group watched a chestnut-mandibled toucan feeding at a papaya tree.

Ginny whispered to Mark, "It looks like a flying banana."

"That's an apt description," Mark said as he photographed the bird lifting its large beak in the air and engulfing the fruit.

Ginny spotted a bird with long, brilliant plumage. She was about to ask Mark to check it out in their guidebook when Enrico announced to the group, "That beautiful bird, my friends, is known as a quetzal. It is native to these parts, but is especially prevalent in Guatemala. In fact, a quetzal is both the monetary unit of Guatemala and its national symbol."

After a picnic lunch, various reptiles were seen. One was an orange brown, basilisk lizard with an erectile crest on the head. Then the tourists saw three snakes. The first was a cat-eyed snake with an orange-colored head and a spotted body. The next that crossed their path was a reddish-orange boa constrictor — everyone kept their distance from that one. The last was a coral snake with red, yellow and black markings.

From a discreet vantage point, they saw a large crocodile. They also examined several frogs and toads. Of special interest was a smokey frog — with its brownish-black body and bulging red eyes — and a spotted brown, black-eyed marine toad. Also pointed out were two invertebrates. One was a creature known as a walking worm. The other was a multi-colored caterpillar.

A highlight of the trip was an encounter with a group of white-lipped peccaries that were mating in a muddy trail. They looked like a cross between a pig or hog and a boar.

Along with the animal life, various trees and shrubs were seen. The travelers marveled at stately palms and tiny orange-colored shelf fungi.

After a long day in the forest, everyone returned for dinner. It was a tropical special. The travelers were served green papaya slaw, creamed palm heart, quiche crust made from cooked bananas and araca nectar.

At night, another treat was in store. Those willing and able — which included Mark and Ginny and excluded the nervous American and his wife — went on a Tarzan-like expedition to the treetops. They sat in a hammock, and the view was magnificent. The treetops were connected in the form of a canopy by their intertwining branches.

Huge moss mats firmly knitted the trees together. There were hanging gardens of exotic plants and flowers. Special air plants, known as epiphytes, were everywhere. Beautiful orchids abounded.

Mark remarked, "It's like a corral reef in the sky."

Mark, Ginny and the other fearless tourists observed Howler and Capuchin monkeys. These monkeys were not in a playful mood, which made everyone happy. Mark captured on film a white-faced monkey choosing a yellow fruit the size of a tennis ball from a tree that he later learned was a monkey fruit tree. The monkey sucked the sweet pulp from the seeds of the monkey fruit.

Enrico pointed out a green iguana climbing to the top of an old papaya tree. It looked like a miniature dinosaur. Mark photographed it gulping down the newly formed leaves. The tourists heard buzzing noises coming from flying creatures. Enrico told them the winged animals were bats. Everyone shuddered.

After the bats left, they heard the deafening shrill drone of cicadae. The guide informed them that cicadae are often confused with locusts, and their sound is somewhat similar to crickets. It is the male's vibrating membranes that produces the loud, piercing sound. He added a bit of historical interest. "Ancient Greeks and Romans considered the cicadae to be sacred and the spirit of music. They come out in great numbers every thirteen or seventeen years. When they appeared, it was believed to be a sign of war. Don't worry, folks, we're years away from another cycle."

Reassured, the treetop adventurers descended and joined the other tourists. The tree toppers had a fabulous escapade, but by this time, they had enough of the nighttime sights and sounds.

Once on terra firma, Mark remarked, "It's good to be back on Mother Earth again."

"That's for sure," Ginny countered.

After the full day, they returned to their cottage, flopped down in bed and slept soundly the entire night.

They awoke on Sunday morning and looked out at a cloudy sky. After breakfast of freshly picked pineapple and papaya along with cold cereal and coffee, the group spent the rest of the morning feasting on the delights of the botanical garden. Of special interest were the various orchids, the orange, red and green-colored passionflowers and the multi-colored heliconias. By twelve noon, the group was back in the canoe. This time, Jaimé and Alfredo gave them a calm and smooth ride.

At one o'clock. José was at the dock to greet them. The ride home went without incident, and by six o'clock, Mark and Ginny were back at Sieta Hormingas Negras, their enchanting B & B. They had eaten enough local food for a while and ate dinner at a Chinese restaurant in town. The Procters were back in bed by nine. They soon drifted off to a peaceful sleep uninterrupted by the sounds of the rain forest.

16

Mark and Ginny awoke at 8:00 A.M. They were greeted by another cloudy sky. Following her usual strategy whenever they went out for the day, Ginny placed *Bishamon* in her handbag. Similarly, Mark had his camera with him. After a leisurely breakfast, they decided to walk around town, window-shop and maybe revisit some museums. At the intersection of Avenida 1 and Calle 8, they spotted a photo store. The sign in the window said, in both Spanish and English, "One-hour Developing."

"Mark, isn't that great, we can develop the pictures here. When we get home, we won't have to wait to show them off to everyone."

"Sounds good. There's only one thing. The shop I have my pictures developed back home is reliable. How can we be sure that they'll do a good job here? Let's wait. I'll be taking more pictures. Toward the end of the week, I can bring in a roll and see what kind of job they do."

"Fine."

At 10:30, Mark and Ginny were across the street from the Museo de Oro, the Gold Museum. Although they had visited it before, Mark hadn't taken pictures of the outside of the building, which was an architectural masterpiece. To get a good view of the entire complex, the Procters crossed the street. Mark then took a few shots of the building. There was a magnificent emblem on it of which he wanted a close-up view. Mark put on his zoom lens and was all set to photograph the emblem when Ginny called out, "That man, the man getting into the red Porsche, he looks just like Dr. Rosner."

Looking through the zoom lens, Mark remarked, "Incredible! He does look like Artie." Mark quickly took several pictures as the man entered the car. He caught a brief partial front view as the man opened the car door. He then photographed side and back views.

After taking a deep breath, Mark said to Ginny, "We must be mistaken. There's no way that can be Artie Rosner. The man is dead. At least every indication is that he died." He paused, reflected and added, "To be certain, let's get a cab and follow the guy."

The moment Mark hailed a cab, the red Porsche pulled away. Ginny had taken Spanish in high school, and she knew enough to tell the cabbie in Spanish to follow the red car without it being obvious. While they were driving through the streets of San José, an intense discussion was going on in the back of the cab.

"If he's not dead, why would he be here?" Ginny asked.

"I don't know except he might've had some money."

"I thought he was bankrupt."

"He was, but my attorney told me that if you have money in a retirement fund, it can't be touched in a bankruptcy proceeding."

"I understand, Mark, but why would he fake his own death? Once he withdrew the money he could've left the country on his own."

"That's right. If that's Artie ahead of us, something strange happened."

"I wonder what it could be and why?"

"Ginny, I never did tell you all of what happened with Artie Rosner and the Glaser kid. The reason was that the three of us, Artie, Julie and myself, were present when Artie discovered that the nitrous oxide and oxygen tanks had been switched."

"Switched? I never knew that gas tanks could be switched."

"Yes. With Artie's old converted general anesthesia unit, that could happen. We vowed that we would never tell anyone, because even if the tanks had been switched by Rudy Kennedy — the tech from Mohlner Equipment Service — Artie would have had the ultimate responsibility. When we found out that Freddie Glaser had a prior epileptic seizure and possible brain damage, we thought that would be sufficient defense for Artie."

Mark paused and added, "If that's Artie out there, possibly it wasn't Rudy Kennedy who switched the tanks. Maybe, just maybe, it was Artie himself who switched the tanks."

"Why would he do such a horrible thing?" Ginny asked.

"I have no idea. As despicable as Freddie Glaser was, he was still the son of one of Artie's best friends, Bernie Glaser. I don't get it, but if it ever came out that Artie Rosner deliberately switched the gas tanks, he wouldn't have been up for malpractice. It would have been a criminal trial, and he would have been up for attempted murder."

"Why would he put himself in that predicament?"

"I have no idea. Wait a minute. We're jumping to conclusions." Mark paused momentarily and continued, "Let's go on the assumption that it is Artie in front of us. When he found out that Rudy Kennedy was going to be deposed, wasn't it a coincidence that the tech died? I know Rudy was a lush and everything indicated that he died from an alcoholic-induced heart attack. Maybe, there was more to it than that."

"Are you saying that..?" Ginny couldn't finish the sentence.

"Yes. Maybe Artie had something to do with Rudy Kennedy's death. I forgot to tell you, someone else knew about the possible switching of the tanks. When Rudy Kennedy was in the office to do that repair job, after you went home, I asked him if he could have possibly switched the tanks. He denied it, but since he was a lush, both Artie and I thought he might've switched the tanks while under the influence of alcohol."

Ginny added enthusiastically, "I got it! If Rudy Kennedy was dead, he could never answer a deposition, discuss the tank incident, and claim that he had not switched the tanks."

"Right! With Kennedy out of the picture and Julie and me sworn to secrecy, there was no way that Artie could have been brought up on murder charges. The only charge could be malpractice."

"Why would he want to be sued for malpractice?"

"That's what we have to find out. For now, it look's like we're leaving town. Let's watch where we're going in case we have to return to wherever that Porsche is heading."

"Mark, I recognize some of the views from our rain forest trip. We're going south."

The cab temporarily lost the trail of the red Porsche, but since the Porsche was not driving at an excessive speed, soon the cabbie was able to reconnect. Ginny noticed that the route was now diverging from the rain forest itinerary. The Porsche was heading in the direction of the Pacific coast but more in the middle of the country. When they went to the rain forest, they went to the southern tip of Costa Rica.

"Mark, the Porsche is slowing down, and there's a sign ahead. It says, 'Approaching Quepos.'"

The red Porsche entered the port city. The next sign said, "Puerto Quepos." The cab followed at a discreet distance. The Porsche headed south along a paved road with a magnificent view of the Pacific Ocean.

After driving about four miles, the Porsche passed a lovely small hotel.

181

The sign on the outside of the building said, "Columbia Hotel." Shortly after, the cab drove into a region known as El Colibri. The cabbie said to the couple, "In English, means hummingbird." The Porsche then pulled into a small parking lot across the street from a large sign displaying the name,"Flamingo Condos."

The cab slowed down, and following Ginny's instructions to the cabbie, it remained on the main road passing the parking lot. From a distance of about a hundred feet, Mark looked out the window and cocked his camera. He watched the man lock his car and get out. Mark took some more pictures, but he still did not have a good front-face shot. The man then descended a series of steps down a steep hill until he came to the entrance of Flamingo Condos. He was limping.

In Spanish, Ginny told the cabbie to pull into the parking lot and wait for them. The couple got out of the cab and walked down the steps while keeping the man in their view.

"He looks like Artie, but Artie never had a limp when I knew him," Mark remarked. "Let's try and see which condo he enters."

They didn't have to wait long. They saw the man go to the closest condo, numero uno, take out his key, unlock the door and go inside.

"What should we do now?" Ginny asked.

"There's no rush. Today is Monday. We don't fly home until Saturday. If it's not Artie, we'll be making fools out of ourselves if we try to go inside now."

"You're right, Mark. We know where he lives. Let's take the cab back to San José." Ginny had a sudden insight. "Remember that quick development photo store in the center of town. We can bring them this roll of film. That will give us a better idea if that man is Dr. Rosner."

"Right! Unfortunately, we're going to have to test the shop out with our most important roll."

"We have no choice," Ginny said emphatically.

The cabbie was waiting for them as they reached the top of the stairs.

In forty-five minutes, they were back in the center of San José. Ginny directed the cabbie to the photo store. Mark then thanked the cabbie, paid him and added a good tip. They walked into the store and realized that they were the only customers.

"Perfect," Mark said.

To be certain the pictures would be ready, Mark and Ginny waited for two hours until they returned to the photo store. To spend the time, they took a leisurely stroll. Fortunately when they came back to the shop, there was an English-speaking clerk behind the counter. Before they examined the photos of the man, they glanced at the other pictures from the roll. Although there were two that were either poorly shot or underdeveloped, the rest came out fine. Satisfied, Mark asked the salesman if he could borrow a magnifying glass. The salesman readily agreed and allowed the Procters to sit at a counter where they would be more comfortable.

With trepidation, Mark began the examination of the photos of the would-be Artie Rosner. He looked at the first photo, the one with the partial front view.

"What do you think?" Ginny asked.

The first picture was sharp, and Mark had a quick response. "I won't say anything definite. Look for yourself."

Ginny examined it carefully and exclaimed, "That's him! That's Dr. Rosner!"

"That's what I thought, but I didn't want to influence you before you looked. To be sure, let's see the other shots."

After several minutes of careful examination, they were convinced.

"We know it's Artie. What should we do?" Mark asked.

"I'm not sure," Ginny replied, "but maybe we should call his brother, Burt, in Florida."

"That's reasonable but I don't think we should upset Burt right now. Maybe, there's a logical explanation. Before we act rashly, let's have lunch, go back to our place and devise a plan of action."

"Good idea, Mark."

Mark and Ginny had decided that the best chance of encountering Artie would be early in the morning — before he would go anywhere for the day. To do that, they planned on being in his neighborhood tonight. First Mark called up Flamingo Condos. The friendly woman, answering him in English, told Mark that they only rent out by the week or month. She recommended the adjacent, Columbia Hotel.

"I'm am sure you'll be able to get a room for the night there. You see, we're not filled up. This is the rainy season."

"I know," Mark said. Mark decided he'd ask about Artie. "By the way, I have an American friend that I think is staying at your place. He's about sixty-five years old, slightly bald, average build."

"We do have an American man who fits that description. What's your friend's name?"

"Artie Rosner."

Looking up the register, the woman said, "There's no one that goes by that name. The person who closely resembles your description is a very nice gentleman. His name is Noah Siegel."

"Thank you. I must be mistaken."

Mark was about to hang up when Ginny said, "Get the number."

Mark responded, "Can I please have the telephone number of the Columbia Hotel?"

"Of course. Welcome to our little section of Costa Rica. I hope you enjoy your brief stay. When you have more time available, we would love to have you come visit us."

"Thank you. We will."

The woman gave Mark the telephone number of the Columbia Hotel. Mark immediately made a one-night reservation for himself and Ginny. They packed the needed essentials for a one-night stand and by 5:00 P.M, they had hailed a taxi. By six o'clock, they had already unpacked and were eating dinner while admiring the beautiful Pacific Ocean. After dinner, they looked around the magnificent hotel grounds. Since tomorrow was going to be a potentially exciting day, they went to bed early. Their minds were filled with all sorts of intriguing possibilities.

At 6:30 A.M., they were awake and had finished breakfast by 7:45. At 8:00 A.M., they were across the way from condo numero uno at Flamingo Condos. Their only weapons were Mark's camera and *Bishamon*, hidden in Ginny's handbag. Both Mark and Ginny had their eyes peered at the entrance. They didn't have to wait long. Artie Rosner, or an incredible duplicate of his, opened the door. Mark and Ginny crossed the road. Mark called out, "Artie."

Startled, Artie Rosner responded in a quivering voice, "What are you two doing here?" *Damn hand.* He tried to shake off the pain.

"No," Mark replied, "the question is, what are you doing here?"

"I was just going to have breakfast with a friend, but that can wait. Come inside and I'll explain everything."

They followed Artie into a well-appointed, one bedroom condo. Inside were two beds, a double and a single. There was a standard refrigerator, a hot plate with two burners and a microwave. There was a three-piece bathroom with a shower. The unit was small but charming. From the picture window, there was a great view of the Pacific Ocean.

"Sit down," Artie said.

Mark examined him. His appearance was the same except for a healthy-looking tan.

The couple sat next to each other on the small lounge.

Artie sat on the upholstered chair, facing them.

"You've got a nice place," Ginny said.

"I like it," Artie replied.

"How long have you been here?" Mark asked.

"Almost two months."

"You came here just about the time you 'died,'" Mark said sarcastically.

"I can explain that."

"I'm sure you can," Mark added with more emphatic sarcasm.

"Before I do, I'd better call my friend. I'm sure he's been at the restaurant a while and is probably worried about me. I'll be back shortly."

Artie went to a small table. His limp was evident. He picked up the phone, dialed an extension and said, "Could you please page Ronald Wallace?"

Less than a minute later, from the dining room, a man answered the phone, "Wallace, here."

"Hi, Ron. I'm sorry I'm late. I have unexpected visitors. The man was a former associate of mine, and he's here with his assistant. You better have breakfast alone. I'll see you in about an hour by our usual spot on the beach."

Artie walked back to the chair, sat down, turned toward Mark and Ginny and said, "We now have plenty of time for me to explain what happened and why."

"Please do, but first could you tell us how you got the limp?" Mark asked.

"That was really stupid. I went to the dog races with my brother, Burt and his lady friend, Goldie. I had just won the Trifecta and leaped with excitement. I fell down and crushed my left foot. The result was this limp."

"That's too bad," Ginny said with a touch of sarcasm.

"It's all right. Let me now get back to what happened. My brother, Burt, is a great guy. He's got a nice apartment, but he's always with Goldie. I was out of place there. Aside from that racetrack excitement, I was bored. I'd been there about seven months and had to get away. Burt thought I had no money. You probably thought so, too."

"It crossed my mind," Mark said cynically.

"I found out about a catch in the bankruptcy laws. Any money in a retirement fund can't be attached. I decided that I would take out the five hundred thousand dollars that I had in my Keogh plan in one lump sum, pay the necessary taxes and get the hell out of there."

"That's logical, but why did you fake your own death?" Mark interjected.

"I thought the Glasers would get some resolution that way. You know, me paying the ultimate price for my stupid action. Besides, the way my dental career ended, I wanted to make a clean break. I knew it would sadden Burt, temporarily, but I concluded he'd get over it. When everything would blow over in a year or two, I figured I'd call him and let him know what I did."

"What about me and Ginny? How about Julie, Kathy and Phyllis? Don't we have feelings, too?"

"I considered that, and I'm sorry. The bottom line is that it's my life and death. I knew you'd all get over me."

"Why did you choose Costa Rica?" Ginny asked.

"Since I was officially dead in the States, I wanted to start over in a foreign country. From my previous trip, I knew that Costa Rica would be great. I suppose that's why you're here. Am I right?"

"Yes, Artie. When you raved so much about Costa Rica, Ginny and I decided to come here for our honeymoon."

"You guys are married? Congratulations."

Ginny said, "Thanks."

Changing the subject, Mark asked, "Why did you take the name Noah Siegel."

Acting surprised, Artie said, "You found that out, too. I figured if I was making a clean break, I ought to change my name as well. In college, I had two good friends. One guy was Noah Clements. The other was Jack Siegel. I combined half of each name, giving me Noah Siegel."

"That's the whole thing. It has nothing to do with Freddie Glaser and the malpractice case?" Mark said.

With a look of consternation, Artie said, "Why should it have anything to do with the kid and the case?"

Mark thought for a moment and replied, "Never mind."

Artie stood up, "How are things back home? How is the office?"

"Things are fine. The practice is doing well. I have a new associate. His name is Willie Chow, and he's working out well so far."

Artie sat down again. "Wonderful. Tell me, what do you like best about Costa Rica?"

Ginny answered, "Without a doubt, the rain forest." She looked at Mark and said, "Right?"

"You've got it," Mark added. He then turned to Artie and said, "On your first trip, from what you told us, you didn't go to any rain forests. Am I right? If so, have you gone to any since?"

"You're right. The last time, we didn't have time to go to a rain forest. I've been to several since. Which one did you folks go to?"

"We went to 'Piedras Blancas National Park' and it was wonderful," Ginny answered.

"You picked the newest and the best. I went there last week."

Mark stretched. He was getting restless. Placing his arms down by his side, he asked, "Artie, how long are you intending to stay in this condo? Have you any other plans?"

"For the time being, Mark, I'm staying here. I'm renting on a monthly basis, but I expect to either buy a larger condo or have a home of my own built. For now, I'm just enjoying the place."

"That's great, Artie. You've answered our questions. We'll be on our way."

With that, Mark and Ginny got off the lounge and started toward the front door.

Artie rose from the chair and said, "Hold on a minute. How long are the two of you staying in Costa Rica?"

"We'll be here until Saturday," Ginny replied.

"That leaves three full days after today. Right now, money is no problem for me. Let me take you honeymooners on a nice adventure. Have you been to the Monteverde Cloud Forest?"

"No," Mark answered.

"It's a great place. Let me pick you up tomorrow, and we'll spend Wednesday and Thursday there. I bought myself a new, red Porsche, and I can pick you folks up early tomorrow."

"We know about your red Porsche," Mark said.

"You do? Hey, that reminds me. How did you ever track me down here?"

"I'll answer you, but first I need some fresh air," Mark said.

"No problem. Let's sit on the outside porch."

With that, the three went outside and seated themselves on the wicker chairs.

Mark began. "I was photographing the outside of the Gold museum, and Ginny saw you getting into your Porsche. At first, we weren't sure it was you. I used my zoom lens and took some photos of you."

Ginny continued, "We then got a cab, and I used my broken Spanish to tell the cabbie to follow your car at a discrete distance. We saw you go into your condo."

"The one thing that threw us was the limp. You've cleared that up for us," Mark added.

Ginny took over again. "When we got into San José, we had the photos developed quickly. After we saw the pictures, we were convinced the man we followed was Artie Rosner."

"Last night," Mark added, "we slept over at the Columbia Hotel and met up with you this morning."

"How about that! You guys were spying on me. You're a couple of real sleuths. It should be apparent to you now, though. The mystery is solved. By the way, I forgot to ask you. Where are you're staying in San José?"

"Artie, you raved so much about your B & B that we checked into the same place" Mark said.

"And?" Artie deliberately paused while displaying a broad smile.

"We love it," Ginny said.

"What do you say, Mark, Ginny? Are you ready for a great adventure, tomorrow?"

Mark looked at Ginny. She nodded her head up and down.

"We're in," Mark said.

"Great, I'll pick you guys up at 8:00 A.M. Bring your camera and lots of film. Pack the same as you did for Piedras Blancas."

"See you tomorrow. Thanks, Artie," Mark said.

While walking back to the Columbia Hotel to check out, Mark said, "I told you that there could be a logical explanation."

Ginny replied, "I suppose you're right, Mark." Her voice lacked conviction.

Wednesday morning was glorious with a brilliant sun and a cloudless sky. After Mark went to the window and looked outside, he remarked, "This weather's an omen for a perfect day."

It started out that way as the honeymoon couple had an early morning lovemaking session. After a shower, they felt happy and refreshed. Breakfast at the B & B was delicious and satisfying. They were outside with their overnight bag, camera and *Bishamon* resting comfortably inside Ginny's handbag, when the red Porsche pulled up. It was exactly 8:00 A.M.

"Artie was always on schedule in the office, and he still keeps on time" Mark said.

"That's a good trait," Ginny added.

After greeting them, Artie put the overnight bag in the trunk. Mark held on to his camera. Ginny did the same with her handbag.

Ginny said, "Mark, why don't you sit in the front with Doctor." She paused out of embarrassment and continued. "I mean Artie? You guys have a lot of catching up to do."

"Are you sure?"

"Yes, Mark. It'll give me a chance to finish my book." Ginny had realized that most of the countryside surrounding the roads they had traveled was the same. If she encountered anything unusual, she'd put down her book. For now, she was content to read.

While driving the car out of town, Artie chatted with Mark. In the back, Ginny was immersed in her mystery novel. The men spent the two hour-long, bumpy drive to the Monteverde Cloud Forest Reserve talking about the office, dentistry, current events and what Artie had been doing since his forced retirement. Ginny was wrapped up in her book. Consequently, neither Mark nor Ginny had any idea of the route that Artie had taken.

A few minutes before they arrived at the cloud forest, Artie asked Ginny if she would like to stop reading and listen to some facts about their destination.

"I'd love to hear about this place," she replied.

"Good. First of all, Monteverde is located in the Tilaran Mountains. These mountains are a portion of the range that runs from Nicaragua to Panama. Surrounding the mountains on the east are the Caribbean lowlands and the Pacific lowlands are on the west."

"Is this a new preserve like Piedras Blancas or has it been around for a while?" Ginny questioned.

"This is the story I got the last time I was here. About twenty years ago, a young graduate student from the University of California at Davis was studying tropical birds in Costa Rica. He became interested in obtaining land to protect these birds. He enlisted the help of several people and some conservation organizations. After a number of years of politics and fund raising, the Monteverde Cloud Forest Reserve came into being."

"Does it only protect tropical birds?" Ginny asked.

"No. It also affords protection to monkeys, tapirs and the largest collection of hummingbirds in the Americas. It's a glorious rain forest."

"What exactly is a rain forest?" Mark questioned.

With pride in her voice, Ginny interjected, "I can answer that, Mark. A rain forest is a tropical woodland that has an annual rainfall of at least one hundred inches. The forest is marked by lofty broad-leafed evergreen trees that form a continuous canopy."

Mark faced Artie and added, "We were up on a hammock in the treetops our last night in Piedras Blancas."

"Have you ever been on a tree forest hammock, Artie?" Ginny asked.

"No. Because of my expanded beer barrel and lack of guts, I prefer staying on the ground." He looked directly ahead and added, "That's enough talking for now. We're here. You two get out and do some preliminary surveying. I'm going inside to register for the rooms. Remember, it's on me. I'll be back in a couple of minutes with your room key."

Artie entered the main house, and Mark and Ginny looked around at the edge of the beautiful forest and gardens.

Five minutes later, Artie returned with their keys. "The two of you have cabin numero dos, and I'm next door to you in cabin numero trais. Let's go into our rooms, unload our baggage and clean up. I'll meet you out front in." He looked at Ginny and said, "What do you say? Is twenty minutes enough?"

Ginny and Mark looked at each other and nodded affirmatively. "That will be fine," Ginny said.

Twenty minutes later, with the Nikon in Mark's hand and *Bishamon* in Ginny's handbag, they were ready to begin their great adventure.

In some ways, the Monteverde Cloud Forest was similar to Piedras Blancas, but in other aspects, it was different. Unlike Piedras Blancas, Monteverde was high in the mountains, close to the clouds. The sky was now packed with the cumulus variety. Here, there was an impressive variety of tropical birds and a myriad of hummingbirds. The three Americans spent the late morning captivated by these birds. Around noon, they temporarily left the forest for a leisurely lunch.

When they returned, they were thrilled by another difference from Piedras Blancas — the great variety of monkeys. The trio spent a few hours with mankind's closest relatives, and then were exposed to the last species the Procters hadn't previously encountered at Piedras Blancas. They caught a group of tapirs in action. Artie had seen these mammals before but knew little about them.

Ginny had some background knowledge. She said, "Tapirs are considered nocturnal ungulates. Possibly because it's so dark here, it's nighttime for them. Ungulates are hoofed mammals of which most are herbivorous and many-horned. Tapirs are found in tropical countries such as Central and South America. They are sort of like a cross between a horse and a rhino. Tapirs are smaller than both and, like a rhino, have one horn. How's that for a lesson?"

"Excellent. You should become a guide down here," Artie said.

"Thanks, but no thanks. I'm happy just seeing these interesting animals. By the way, I forgot one other thing. Unlike rhinos and wild horses, tapirs are friendly creatures."

"Whatever you've learned, Ginny, my advice is that we keep our distance," Artie said emphatically.

The remainder of the day, they spent looking at the trees, tropical plants and tropical flowers.

Before they came in for dinner, Mark spotted a pack of small mammals that looked like raccoons. "Are they raccoons?" Mark asked.

"This one, I know," Artie answered. "These animals are related to the raccoon but they have a longer body and tail and a long, flexible snout, somewhat like mine. They are known as coatimundi or coati for short. They're only found in tropical Central and South America." He paused for a few seconds. "It's time to eat. Tonight we go fishing."

"Don't worry. I really am an excellent fisherman, and we won't go too far out in the ocean. From the water, you can see wonderful phosphorescent life. Believe me, it will be the highlight of your trip."

Reluctantly, Mark and Ginny agreed.

At seven o'clock, the couple, with camera and *Bishamon as* their companions, reentered Artie's Porsche. He drove for about fifteen minutes until he reached a fishing dock overlooking the Pacific Ocean. Artie rented a fishing boat and fishing poles and gear for the three of them. He showed Mark and Ginny how to bait a hook with the use of a live worm. Ginny flinched but so did Mark.

"I'm a woman, but you're a big tough dental surgeon, and you winced at baiting a worm. I'm surprised at you, Mark."

"It's been a long time since I went fishing," Mark retorted.

"Don't argue my friends," Artie added. "I also had it rough the first time I had to bait a worm. If the two of you are ready, let's get in."

The three entered the fishing boat. In addition to the fishing gear, Artie carried a shopping bag containing several bottles.

"What's in there?" Mark asked.

"It's liquid refreshment for the ride. I'm gonna put it in the fridge. I'll be right back."

When Artie returned, he started the engine.

"There's one other thing, folks," Artie said. "This boat is fully equipped.

It has a bathroom, a small kitchen, a TV and a two-way radio. If the weather gets bad, I'll hear about it on the radio, and we'll be able to return in plenty of time. There's nothing to worry about. Sit back and enjoy the ride."

Soon, they were heading out to sea. They were in the water for about five minutes. Without saying a word, Artie then turned the boat toward the shore. In the distance, a late model, black Toyota Corolla was driving on the seaside road toward the place that Artie was bringing the boat.

Mark and Ginny were astonished, wondering what was happening.

Artie saw the bewildered look on their faces and said, "I'm sorry folks. I have to make a quick detour. It'll only take a couple of minutes."

As the boat was accelerating, he added, "I forgot to tell you. My best friend down here, Ron Wallace, had asked to join us. I thought he would be at the dock when we were ready to leave. When he wasn't there, I thought he changed his mind. That's when we took off. I thought I would take one last look before we got too far out. When I did, I spotted his car."

Ginny thought, *Is he telling the truth? It sounds a bit odd. We'll soon find out.*

"That's him down there in the Corolla," Artie added. "I'll pick him up, and we'll be on our way."

Mark looked at Ginny quizzically. Ginny reached inside her handbag and held on to *Bishamon*.

17

The fishing boat pulled in close to the shore. The black Corolla parked in a secluded spot nearby. A tall, out-of-shape man with white hair got out of the car and headed toward the approaching boat. His kept his hands in his jacket pocket as he walked.

From the distance, Mark had a faint recollection. *The last day of Artie's trial, the plaintiffs' attorney. Could that be him? Could that be Kenneth Hamilton? I must be going crazy. How could it be him?*

Ginny was also in the courtroom on the day the jury rendered their verdict. She also had seen the plaintiffs' attorney acting joyously after his victory. *That man looks like the plaintiffs' attorney in Dr. Rosner's malpractice case. What was his name? Forget it. I'd recognize that flabby body with the white hair. That must be him, but why in God's name would he be here?*

Kenneth Hamilton, in the guise of Ronald Wallace, was there and he was approaching fast.

Before Mark or Ginny could act on their assumptions, Kenneth Hamilton pulled out a Ruger 9 mm and aimed it at the couple. "Stay where you are!" he shouted.

Mark and Ginny remained seated and looked anxiously at Artie.

"Good evening, Ron or should I say, Kenneth," Artie said. "Come join us, friend. We were just going on a fishing expedition."

By now, Mark and Ginny were flabbergasted. They were clueless about what had happened.

"Don't look so stunned my friends. I will explain all of this to you in due time. Kenneth will now join us. We have some fishing to do."

With the gun still pointed at the couple, Kenneth Hamilton got in the boat and spoke, "Artie, get the rope." Artie went toward the back and opened a tackle box.

Hamilton turned toward Mark and Ginny and said, "Unfortunately, you folks are still around and know too much. For the time being, we'll have to tie you up. Later, we'll decide what to do with you."

Mark thought, *What did he mean by us being 'still around'?*

Ginny had a similar thought.

Mark started to advance toward Hamilton. The lawyer saw his movement. He didn't hesitate and shot Mark in the left foot.

Mark screamed, and Ginny cried as the blood poured out of his foot.

Hamilton called out to Artie and said, "Unfortunately your young dental friend did not cooperate. After you get the rope, bring out the first aid kit."

Artie returned, stopped the bleeding, placed a bandage, and opened two bottles of pills. "Why didn't you listen, Mark?" he said. "Here, swallow these."

"What are they?" Mark asked with hesitation.

"One's five-hundred milligrams of penicillin so the wound won't get infected. The other's eight-hundred milligrams of ibuprofin for the pain."

Mark nodded, took the pills and a cup of water from Artie, and downed them with the water.

With Hamilton still pointing the gun at them, Artie tied Mark and Ginny's hands and feet to seats on the side of the boat. The retired dentist paused for a couple of seconds, pointed to Mark's foot and said, "Now you'll know what it's like to have a limp."

"I'm not looking forward to that."

"Enough of that. If you cooperate and keep quiet unless I ask you a question, I won't gag you. Let's get out of here now. Afterward, I'll let you know what this is all about."

Artie revved the engine, and the fishing boat went out to sea. The night was calm and clear, but there was terror inside the hearts of Mark and Ginny Procter.

At 8:15 P.M., Artie shut off the engine and let the boat drift in the calm sea. Kenneth Hamilton sat and listened while Artie began his explanation. His gun remained pointed at the Procters.

"First of all, Mark, how's your foot?" Artie asked.

"The pain's almost tolerable."

"Good. You know, you guys screwed yourselves. Obviously, you survived back in New Jersey. Why did you have to come to Costa Rica?"

Mark and Ginny had the simultaneous thought, *What did he mean about surviving back in New Jersey?*

Mark answered, "We came to Costa Rica because you raved about the country. We also thought you were dead."

"I'm sorry about that."

"Can I ask you one question?"

"Make it quick," Artie responded.

"What did you mean about us surviving back in New Jersey?"

"I'll answer that in due time. At any rate, when you came to see me yesterday morning, I knew there was going to be a problem. You heard me call Ronald Wallace on the telephone. When I told him that my former associate and his assistant were here, that automatically put him on alert. He skipped breakfast and kept a watch on the condo. If anything had gone wrong, he would have burst in. Fortunately for all concerned, you guys 'bought' my story."

"I thought it was a little fishy," Mark said, "but you spoke with such honesty that I had to believe you."

"That comes from my acting lessons in college."

"I never knew you had acting lessons."

"You'll soon find out that there's a lot about me you never knew."

"I'm finding that out already."

"Don't be a wise guy. I told you to only speak when I ask you a question." He glared at Mark and continued. "After the two of you left, Kenneth and I had a long talk. We realized that our previous effort to get rid of you was unsuccessful."

Mark couldn't contain himself. He had now figured out the "surviving back in New Jersey" statement. Ginny also knew what it meant.

Mark exclaimed, "You mean that when that greasy-looking guy crashed into us on I-95 in Philly, it was no accident!"

"I'll tolerate that one outburst, Mark. Yes, Kenneth Hamilton hired that guy. We had already figured that you knew too much and might have uncovered our plot. With his underground connection, Kenneth hired the same thug, who had previously done a number for us on Rudy Kennedy, to get rid of you."

Mark screamed, "You had Rudy Kennedy killed!"

"Keep your damn mouth shut. When I get good and ready, I'll tell you what provoked that incident. Let me now get back to my conversation with Kenneth. We realized there was no way we could be certain you would be silent about my whereabouts and sooner or later, you would find out about Hamilton and his connection to me. Were we right about that?"

"We weren't going to say anything," Mark said.

"Things change, and we couldn't afford to take a chance."

"What are you going to do with us?" Ginny asked apprehensively.

Artie didn't answer her question. He said loudly, "I told you two to be quiet if you want to hear the story. If you don't keep your mouths shut, the gags go on."

Mark, fearing the worst, looked at Ginny and said, "All right, we'll just listen."

"Good. Yesterday afternoon, we hatched our plan. It started with you spending a couple of days at Monteverde Cloud Forest. After dinner, I invited you to go fishing in the Pacific. Kenneth was then to come here and meet us after I first took you out in the boat."

Ginny thought, *How could they have been so deceitful?*

Artie paused to let the latest deception sink in; then he continued, "You're now caught up with that part. However, that tells you nothing about how Kenneth and myself happen to be in Costa Rica together. You've gotta be asking yourselves, 'How could the plaintiffs' attorney, Kenneth Hamilton, who destroyed Artie Rosner so effectively in his malpractice case, be together with him?' You probably would have thought that if I ever saw him, I'd try to kill him."

That's just what I believed, Mark thought.

Gloating, Artie went on. "The truth is, Ken and I had been scheming this plot for six months before Freddie Glaser came into our office. That's a shocker. Isn't it? Don't answer that."

Kenneth Hamilton interjected, "Let them digest that for a few minutes. I could use a drink. I'll keep an eye on these two. Artie, I know you haven't been drinking since that so-called accident, but I think that tonight calls for a celebration. What do you say?"

"You're right, Ken. I'll make myself a small scotch. I'll get you a large one." Turning to the couple, Artie said, "You two can answer me now. Do you guys want anything to drink?"

"I'll just have a soft drink. A 7-up or Sprite or whatever you've got," Mark replied.

"How about you, Ginny?"

"I'll have whatever you bring Mark."

"Good. After our liquid refreshment, I'll let you two know that there were good reasons for what we did."

Ten minutes later, Artie and Kenneth had finished their drinks. Mark and Ginny had to take their sodas through a straw as Artie held each glass in turn.

Artie then resumed his story. "This goes back many years. Bernie Glaser, Ken Hamilton, and myself were buddies ever since our youth in New York. We stayed friendly all these years. Ken and I kept our friendship, but eight months before the incident with Freddie Glaser, Ken and I found out that our so-called friend Bernie, who is a speculative investor, had screwed us out of a million dollars each."

Ginny thought, *I hope I never have friends like that. On second thought, I pray I'm around to have any kind of friends.*

Artie continued, "It was supposed to be a can't lose deal. He promised us we would make millions. I took a big gamble. You see, my wife's prolonged illness several years before drained me financially. With sound stock market investments, I made a good recovery. Foolishly, Ken and I listened to Bernie. For Ken, a million bucks was a lot, but he still was left with plenty more. For me, it was almost all I had remaining."

Thinking about what happened made Artie frown as he went on. "Bernie's 'can't lose' deal was an investment in an offshore oil deal. He had the audacity to inform us by mail instead of in person, that the investment bottomed out. The drilling came up empty. We had lost everything. I was back to close to zero financially."

Artie then looked at Hamilton who nodded in response. Artie resumed the narrative. "Even though Ken was far from wiped out financially, he was as pissed off at Bernie as I was. We felt we had to do something to get even. It took us about two months to concoct a plan. Six months before Freddie came into the office, we finalized the details." He paused. "I think I'll have another drink. How about you, Ken?"

"I'll take a refill."

"Good. You two?"

Mark and Ginny shook their heads.

"Okay. I'll fill you in the details of our plot after we finish this round."

All the time Artie Rosner had been talking, Mark had been working on the knot tied around his hands. Using his fingernails, he had been able to slightly loosen the knot. While he and Ginny were being tied up, Mark realized that even if it hadn't been for the malpractice case, Artie would have had to retire in a few years because of the ever worsening arthritis in his hands, especially his right hand, the scarred, working one. Consequently, when Artie tied up the couple, the knots hadn't been that secure. Even had he completely loosened the knot, Mark didn't want to try anything until he untied his feet and caught Kenneth Hamilton off guard. He knew that the attorney had no hesitancy about firing a gun. The only possible weapon Mark possessed was the camera beneath his feet.

At the same time, Ginny had been having similar success in untying her hand knot. She also had decided that she would not try anything until she untied her feet and got some sort of signal from Mark. Ginny had no weapon, but then she remembered that *Bishamon* was still in her handbag that lay by her feet.

Artie put down his empty glass and resumed his talk. "We wanted to get our revenge, but we were uncertain about how to do it. You're the lawyer, Ken. Why don't you fill in the details about the legal ramifications?"

Kenneth Hamilton had been holding the cocked gun for quite a while, and his right hand was getting tired. "All right, Artie, but first you take the gun. My hand's getting stiff. Make sure you keep it on them."

Artie took the gun and remarked, "Sure thing, Ken."

"Good. I knew that we couldn't kill Bernie in cold blood. We thought about drugs, rigging his car, hiring a killer. Things like that. No matter what plan we came up with, I figured it would be too difficult to disguise as an accident."

Hamilton then smiled and said, "I then got the brilliant notion that we should get even with our 'friend' through his bratty kid. I mean, his kid was bad news. It was well known that Freddie Glaser destroyed insects and little animals. He had an obnoxious personality. Freddie was a child that only a mother could love. A father, too, I suppose. We knew for sure that Bernie Glaser loved his Freddie, even with all of his faults. The big question was, how should we do it? That's when Artie, with his dental knowledge came in. Tell them, Artie."

Happy to get rid of it, Artie handed the pistol back to Hamilton. Artie then picked up the story. "From the few times he had been in to see me and from his mother, Pauline's description, I knew that the kid was a chocoholic. I impressed upon her the necessity for him to cut down drastically on sweets and come in to see me every six months, but neither was done. The parents catered to the kid's every whim. Freddie continued to pack in the candy and cake, and he only came in the office when he had a toothache or swollen jaw.

I told Ken that undoubtedly the kid would need dental work in the near future. When that would happen, Ken and I decided to set up a malpractice scenario."

Mark was shocked. *I fell for that completely*, he thought. *I was a real jackass.*

Artie appeared to be really enjoying telling this part of the plan. He continued with the explanation. "Ken was a malpractice attorney. If I did something to Freddie Glaser substantially bad, undoubtedly there would be a malpractice suit. We figured Ken would get the case because Bernie, Ken and I had been best friends for years. Bernie would have to ask Ken — one of his closest buddies — for advice."

He smiled broadly and continued, "The plan was that Ken would at first hesitate because he was also my friend. Ken would finally relent because of the seriousness of the injury. Everything was set up. Freddie Glaser would become permanently injured. Kenneth Hamilton would be the plaintiffs' attorney, and the odds would be rigged heavily on the plaintiffs' side so that undoubtedly there would be a huge award."

Artie looked at Hamilton and then back at the Procters and said, "We figured the Glaser's would sue for about ten million. Instead, they sued for twelve. We realized that no matter what they sued for, the most the jury would give them would be seven or eight million. It turned out to be eight million. Six million would come from my policy, and I figured that I would be able to scrounge up another million. Since I was a million short, I had to declare bankruptcy."

Mark continued to mentally berate himself. *To think that I felt sorry for the bastard and didn't even haggle over the price for all his stuff.*

Artie appeared to be proud of himself as he expounded. "When the pot would be divided, Ken's firm would get three-and a-half million. Since Ken was the senior partner and the one pleading the case, his share would be three million. I took the major risks, and Ken had plenty to spare. Considering that, he would give me two-and a-half million. He would only keep a half-million for himself. That way, I would get back everything I lost — the one million Bernie swindled me out of and the one million I might be able to come up with toward the malpractice award. I also would come away with another half-million. With this scheme, we would kill three birds with one stone."

God, are they horrible, Ginny thought. *It's unbelievable how people can be so two-faced.*

Artie laughed at his own humor and elaborated. "First, we get even with our dastardly friend, Bernie. Second, we get a real horrible kid out of circulation. I knew about the evidence that children that start off in life by tormenting and killing insects and animals often wind up doing the same thing to adults. We had no qualms about permanently damaging the kid. The third bonus is that I would get back my money and a little extra for my effort. Ken would make a half-million. He was also tired of practice. The lawyer jokes and burden of trying cases were finally getting to him. Am I right about that?"

"Damn right!" Hamilton said.

Artie continued. "I had some money in my retirement plan, but I wanted to get revenge on Bernie. This act would give me revenge, and I'd now have more than enough money to retire in luxury. Ken and I always got along well. We thought you two were out of the way."

Mark thought, *The bastard, how could he plan to get rid of us after I had tried to help him win the malpractice case? We must get out of here before it's too late.*

Now Artie put on a serious face as he said, "When the two of you popped in unexpectedly, we had been living a life of leisure. That's why I took my vacation in Costa Rica. I had heard it was great, and I wanted to case the place. Costa Rica is a magnificent country as you both found out. Before I tell you how I decided to harm the kid, my throat's getting dry from all this talking. I'll need one last shot."

"You can bring me one, too, Artie," Hamilton said.

This time there was a fifteen-minute lull in the verbal action. It had given both Mark and Ginny enough time to completely untie the knots around their hands, but they kept their hands together. They then attempted loosening the knots on their feet by wiggling their toes and moving their feet. That took much longer because they couldn't let Kenneth Hamilton observe them, and his gun was still pointed in their direction.

Artie got up from his seat. He hobbled on his gimpy foot. The alcohol made his limp worse. Kenneth Hamilton remained relatively sober. From the many legal meetings he had attended in his lifetime, Kenneth had learned how to hold his liquor. He stood tall and immobile. The gun was steady as a rock in his right hand.

Artie began to speak. A slight amount of slurring could be heard in his voice. "The next major question was, how was I gonna disable Freddie Glaser? I knew from the previous visits the kid loved 'nitrous.' Considering that my unit was an old one without 'fail-safe' features, I could conveniently switch the gas lines — put the nitrous oxide into the slot for the oxygen and vice versa. Toward the end of the visit, when the kid would require one hundred percent oxygen, he would be getting one hundred percent nitrous oxide. I figured that should be enough to put him into a coma."

Ginny heard this and winced. *How could he do such a thing?* she thought.

Mark thought, *My guess that Artie, and not Rudy Kennedy, switched the tanks was right. What a bastard.*

Artie smiled again as he continued to describe his sadistic plot. "Earlier in the treatment, because of the rigged lines, the kid would be getting a high percentage of oxygen rather than nitrous oxide. That would make him uncooperative. Having the girls restrain him might possibly add a punitive aspect to the case. I wanted to make sure I lost the case."

After clearing his throat, Artie revealed more of the nefarious scheme. "I previously had asked my travel agent to call me about 8:15 A.M. I didn't know if the kid would be under treatment at that time, but I figured if the agent called and Freddie wasn't there, I would tell my receptionist that I couldn't take the call right then. Fortunately for me, the agent called at a perfect time. Me taking the call while he was 'under' might also add a punitive aspect to the case."

Artie rubbed his eyes and continued. "I knew that using an outdated general anesthesia machine to deliver nitrous oxide/oxygen conscious sedation might also be grounds for punitive damages. Our receptionist, Phyllis, knew nothing about the gas machine and how it was set up. So I didn't have to worry about her."

Hearing Phyllis' name mentioned, Mark wondered why Artie didn't mention her accidental encounter with the x-ray arm and its subsequent blow to the kid's head. *I suppose because it had nothing to do with the outcome. Even the attorneys didn't consider it*, he thought.

Ginny had loosened her feet, but she was getting anxious. *When is Mark going to give me some kind of signal for us to attack them? Please, God, don't let him wait too long.*

Artie looked directly at Ginny as if he realized something untoward was about to happen. But he shook his head as if it was just related to his eyes becoming blurry, and continued to reveal more details of the dastardly plot. "Julie was a different story. She's a sharp girl with a keen eye. I installed the lines backward early that morning, before anyone came into the office and long after the cleaning men had left. I then brought the unit to the back of the dental chair and had it placed in such a manner that the tanks would be partially hidden from Julie's view."

Mark thought, *He has a sharp mind. Too bad, he used it for such a macabre purpose. Artie's speech sounds a bit slurred. I better get ready.* Mark had also partially untied the knots on his feet.

Artie continued, "When we began to work on Freddie and he was understandably agitated, I immediately asked for the assistance of the two women. I figured they would be busy holding back the kid so Julie wouldn't notice the tank attachments. I was right."

Artie assumed a heroic pose as he said, "I also wanted to act in part as the hero. That's why I didn't let the kid die. We never planned to kill him — just cause enough damage for us to have our revenge. By immediately using oxygen under forced pressure from the portable unit, I saved Freddie's life. It appeared that I was sincerely concerned and did everything possible to save the child."

Some hero, thought Mark.

Artie was starting to get tired. He stretched a bit; then continued. "It was a lucky break when we found out that Freddie had a brain seizure as a kid. That at least gave us something plausible to use as a defense strategy."

Ginny thought, *It's unreal that none of us knew anything about this... Forget about that, we've got to get free.*

Artie was enthusiastic as he said, "I didn't want a reasonable defense. In that case, the parties might have settled out of court and the monetary award would have been much less. When I later 'found out,' with Julie present, that the tanks had been switched, I played along with everything you had suggested, Mark. The malpractice scenario was set up perfectly."

He stopped speaking and then said, "I've gotta rest a minute now. My throat's getting even drier. I'm gonna get some water. Anyone else want some?"

The other three shook their heads. Artie left to get a glass of water. Mark and Ginny remained ready for action when the opportunity would arise, but Hamilton's gun never wavered.

A couple of minutes later, Artie returned. His limp was even more pronounced. "Ken, tell them about the court case."

Handing Artie the gun, the lawyer grinned and said, "My pleasure. During the trial, as must have been obvious to you, I trashed my friend, Artie. It was easy. I was working with a loaded gun."

He smiled at that comparison to the present situation. "The malpractice insurance company's attorney, Ernest Coniglia, however, did a credible job with the little he had going for him. The staging was great. Everyone thought Artie was near tears, and I was a mean son-of-a-gun the way I laced into him. Not only was the jury sucked in, we had the judge and the defense attorneys convinced that I was sincere in my presentation. I was beginning to believe it myself."

He laughed and continued. "We got everything we asked for. After the verdict, Artie deliberately fainted. He wanted everyone to think he was extremely upset at the verdict. He then continued the fake scenario. Tell them, friend."

After almost slipping, Artie returned the gun to Hamilton.

Mark was about to leap at Artie during the exchange but stopped at the last second. Hamilton's grip on the gun was as steady as ever.

"Hey, buddy, did you have a little too much to drink?" Hamilton asked.

"No, I'm fine," Artie answered. "Let's get back to what happened." He continued, "I began to drink. I wanted everyone to think that I was so upset that I had to resort to alcohol to deal with my nerves. I then faked the car accident. I went to Reilly's Bar and Grill because I knew that Rudy Kennedy, the equipment company service tech, was a lush, and he frequented that place. The accident set up the premise that I was feeling so sorry for myself that I got drunk and crashed. I tried to make sure that the accident wouldn't be serious. I nearly screwed up. I almost got a concussion."

You should have, Mark thought.

Now Artie brought out some additional details. "When I found out, in spite of your assurances, Mark, that Rudy Kennedy would be deposed, I couldn't trust the guy. I knew that if Rudy realized that he didn't switch the gas tanks, then it would've had to be someone else. Kennedy might've figured that for some reason it had to be me. I considered that if Rudy testified, he'd spill the beans about the switched tanks."

Artie stopped talking. He felt a little woozy.

"Are you okay, Artie?" Hamilton asked.

"No problem."

"I should add," Hamilton said, "that I didn't want to depose Kennedy, but my partners insisted. I had to go along with it."

Artie drank some water and continued. "If Kennedy stated that he definitely didn't switch the tanks, then it might come out that I did it. The case could then become capital with the charge being attempted murder. I couldn't let that happen. When I found out that Kennedy would be deposed, I realized that the tech had to be killed."

After momentarily looked at the attorney, Artie added, "I talked it over with Ken. We knew Rudy was a lush and went to Reilly's every day after work. Ken had underground connections. He arranged to have a mobster go to Reilly's. The mobster slipped a non-detectable drug, chloral hydrate, into one of Rudy's drinks. Remember that one, Mark? It had been used for sedation before barbiturates and Valium® became popular."

Mark nodded his head.

Artie smiled again. He now had some startling information to reveal. "The thug did it without anyone seeing him. We figured that Kennedy's death would be attributed to an alcohol-induced coma. You know, mixing the two downers, alcohol and chloral hydrate. Kennedy didn't die from a coma. That's right. He died from a heart attack. How did I know? Wait 'till you hear this."

He paused for a few seconds, took another sip of water and continued. "A few days after the death, Ken had the thug call the medical examiner's office. What was that thug's name, Ken?"

"I don't know his full name. He went by the name of Tony."

"Right, Ken, I should have remembered that. Anyway, Tony pretended he was Rudy's brother and asked the pathologist for the autopsy result. Get this. Kennedy died from sudden cardiac arrest. He had atrial arrhythmia and fibrillation, and he keeled over dead in his tracks."

After saying that, Artie almost fell down.

"You better watch out, buddy or the same thing'll happen to you," Hamilton interjected.

Mark was watching the action, but Hamilton's gun remained pointed at him. He realized that he couldn't make a move yet.

Artie righted himself and said, "I'm okay, Ken, just a little woozy. Let me get back to this. The best stuff is comin' up. The medical examiner told Tony the thug that Rudy died from what they call 'Holiday Heart.' It seems that around holiday times like Christmas or New Year's, alcoholics really go overboard and drink themselves to death."

Kenneth Hamilton interjected, "We even found out what was making Rudy act out noisily. It seems that when he walked into the bar, he yelled out loud enough for Tony to hear that his girlfriend had just left him."

"Right," Artie added, "Rudy was getting drunk, but it wasn't for joy. He was drinking out of his mind because his girlfriend had deserted him. Isn't it ironical that in spite of our best intentions, the drug Tony slipped into Rudy

Kennedy's drink didn't kill him? He was dead before it could even take effect."

You unfeeling bastard, Ginny thought.

"Ain't that a kicker, Mark? Kennedy did it to himself. Technically, me and Ken aren't murderers."

"That don't matter," Hamilton said. "Us getting rid of Kennedy was a necessary evil," He paused and added, "By the way, just for the record, I found out from my sources that the thug, Tony, was gunned down during one of his other endeavors. Of course, that was after, he screwed up in getting rid of you two."

That last remark really riled Mark and Ginny, but Hamilton's steady hand deterred them from taking immediate action.

Hamilton then added, "Artie's not a bad person. He usually saves people's lives. Right, Artie"

"You mean that stroke of luck. That was definitely not planned, and it made everyone in the office think I was a great guy and didn't deserve the bad break from the malpractice case. I'm talking about my resuscitation of Herman Averill. I saved the guy's life, and I was proud of myself. After all, there's some good in all of us. You must realize, however, that none of this would have happened to Freddie if my so-called friend, Bernie Glaser, hadn't screwed us up."

"Tell them how we faked your death, Artie," Hamilton said. "That was a work of art."

Artie Rosner and Kenneth Hamilton were so involved in the discussion of their dastardly scheme that they didn't notice the thickening clouds enveloping the sky. However, Mark and Ginny were aware of nature's insidious change.

Artie picked up on Hamilton's suggestion. "I set that up with Burt by going fishing by myself a few times before. I had asked Burt to join me, but I knew that he's a lousy swimmer and is deathly afraid of drowning. Of course, he refused to go fishing. Unlike Burt, I'm a very good swimmer. In college, I had been the captain of the swimming team. I never told you, Mark, but many times I went swimming on my day off from the practice."

I often wondered where he went, Mark thought.

There was a gleam in Artie's eye as he expounded. "Thursday, August 5th was to be the day I died. I got a kick out of that. Not too many people can choose the day they're going to die. You know by now that Ken had underworld connections. About a week before, he got me a falsified ID, passport and credit card under the name of Noah Siegel. He also mailed me a black hairpiece, a fake mustache, a pair of thick eyeglasses and a round-trip ticket to Costa Rica. Even though, I had planned on staying in Costa Rica, we didn't want anyone to be suspicious so he got the round-trip ticket."

Artie paused again and drank some more water. "On that Thursday morning, I rented a car. I bought a valise and various items I'd need for a few days. I then drove to the Pompano Beach dock and parked the car in a secluded area, a block away from the pier. I walked to Pushes — the fishing rental shop —, and using my own ID, I rented the fishing boat. I spent the whole day fishing.

Artie was getting real enthusiastic as he continued, "When it got dark, I took off my pants, socks and shoes and left them in the boat. I put my wallet and some other items in a protected leather bag, locked it, and also left it in the boat. I then dumped the boat and swam to shore. I walked to the car, got out my fake ID and credit card, and put on clean clothes, the wig and mustache."

Hamilton interrupted Artie. "Hey, it's startin' to get cloudy. It look's like rain. You better finish it up."

"I'm almost done, Ken. I drove to a motel near the airport. I put on the thick glasses to complete my disguise and using the fake credit card, I rented a room for the night. The next morning, I parked the car in a cruddy area near the airport. After, I made sure that no one was watching, I took the jack from the trunk and smashed the windows and headlights. I also made a few dents in the car. I replaced the jack and abandoned the vehicle. I figured the cops would assume that someone had carjacked the vehicle at the fishing pier, drove it around for a while, wrecked it and then dumped it. That assumption proved to be correct. All that remained was for me to walk to the airport and get on the plane to Costa Rica."

Although he despised what Artie had done, Mark admired the resourcefulness of the plan.

Artie finished that aspect of the plot as he said, "After I disappeared, everything worked out exactly the way we thought it would. Burt thought that I died and sent a death notice to the *Delray News*. He figured that the people back in New Jersey would also want to be informed of my death. So Burt sent another obituary notice to the *Courier Post*. When I got to San José, I went to the selected bank and my share of the money was waiting for me."

Artie was feeling dizzy now, and his throat was extremely dry. He paused for a few seconds and said, "Ken, you can finish it off by telling them about the money and how you got here."

By now, the wind had picked up and a few raindrops were beginning to fall. Noticing this, Kenneth gave the gun to Artie and said, "It's starting to rain. We don't want to get caught in a storm, so I'll make this quick."

He turned to the couple and said, "I retired from my law firm in the middle of May and moved to St. Petersberg, Florida. Artie and I would periodically meet at some spot halfway between our two homes to finalize the future arrangements. After I took care of all the arrangements for Artie, I purchased a round-trip ticket to Costa Rica. I told the owners of my St. Petersberg apartment that I would be on an extended trip to Costa Rica. I then paid my rent six months in advance. I also put together a third-party arrangement involving a Caribbean bank for Artie to receive his money."

Hamilton rubbed his hands together and said, "Before I left, I had Tony the thug keep an eye on you two. When he reported to me that you had purchased tickets to Costa Rica, Artie and me figured you were on to something. Unfortunately, Tony failed to stop your trip. I trust nobody, except Artie. So, I didn't let Tony know we were in Costa Rica. But that wouldn't have mattered anyway as Tony was killed soon after. Now knowing that you guys were on your way to Costa Rica, Artie was able to concoct that story in case you found him. And as usual, he did a good job."

He sure did fool me, but I can't believe that ungrateful bastard, Artie, would try to harm us, Mark thought.

Hamilton felt the heavy raindrops and added, "It's starting to pour. It's time to take care of the final arrangements."

I wonder if that means what I think it means, Ginny thought.

The boat began to rock violently. Thunder roared and lightning flashed. Mark had untied his hands and his feet were loosely bound, but as of yet, he didn't make a move. Ginny was in a similar situation but looked to Mark for guidance.

"Give me the gun, Artie. We've got to get rid of them, now!"

Artie started to hand over the gun, but the combination of the torrential rain, violent wind, effects of the alcohol and his arthritic right hand caused him to lose a grip on the weapon. He had a sudden flashback. It was the last day of the "nitrous" course. He tripped. He fell. The flames were everywhere. His hand burned. He felt the horrible pain. "Aaaah," he screamed. The gun fell to the deck.

Mark saw what happened. He bent down and completed the untying of his legs. He was free. Ginny was less successful but was working her hands on the remainder of the rope. Kenneth leaped for the gun and slipped on the wet deck. Sliding, he reached the gun and from a sitting position, he pointed it at the advancing Mark.

"Stay right there!" he shouted.

Mark knew that Hamilton would shoot, but he had to do something. He quickly grabbed his camera and flung it toward Hamilton. The camera hit Kenneth's right hand just as he fired the pistol. The bullet nicked Mark in his left thigh. He tried to get up but the pain and bleeding were too much and Mark collapsed.

Kenneth advanced toward Mark and spoke, "Okay, we've stalled long enough."

Artie, still feeling woozy and in pain, got up and walked toward Ginny. By now, Ginny had dislodged all of the ropes. She reached to her side freeing *Bishamon* from her handbag.

"Overboard you go, young lady," Artie said.

Artie grabbed Ginny ready to throw her into the ocean. Ginny lifted the Japanese doll straight up, and using all of her adrenaline-enhanced strength, she smashed it on Artie's head. He crumbled to the ground, unconscious.

At that moment, a violent wind gust almost overturned the boat. Ginny was flung into Kenneth, and the gun flew overboard. Mark and Artie fell into the ocean.

The water partly revived Artie, but he had suffered a severe concussion from the encounter with *Bishamon*. The concussion added to his alcoholic intoxication and the stress-induced pain. He flailed aimlessly. "Mark, save me!" he cried out.

Mark was having troubles of his own. Although Mark was an excellent swimmer, he was in severe pain from the thigh wound and the previous foot injury. Still, he had a strong upper body and great willpower. Mark heard Artie's plea and thought, *They tried to kill us and now he wants me to save him. He's got to be crazy! But how can I let the poor guy die?*

Mark swam towards Artie. Artie's head was bobbing up and down in the violent ocean. The moment Mark reached out to grab his head, Artie was torn away by a vicious wave. He took his last breath, and as he was sinking to the bottom of the ocean, his dying thought was, *If I never took that damn "nitrous" course, none of this would have happened.*

Mark was also thinking of Artie's fate. *Poor guy. I bet if it wasn't for Hamilton's influence Artie would have never gotten involved in that horrendous scheme.* Mark quickly forgot about Artie. He needed to concentrate on saving his own life and that of Ginny. Mark forced himself to swim to the boat where he grabbed onto the edge. On the opposite side, he saw Kenneth Hamilton push Ginny overboard.

Ginny was in the best shape of them all, having suffering no injuries aside from rope burns. She swam underwater and saw Mark's legs on the opposite side. She surfaced next to him.

Mark whispered, "Keep hidden, Ginny. Hamilton probably thinks all three of us have drowned. He's opposite us now, but he'll have to get to the engine and steer the boat back to shore. Once he gets behind the wheel, I'll slip back in the boat and surprise him."

"Hurry, Mark," Ginny said quietly, "I'm cold and scared." She took a deep breath and added, "You can do it. I know it. Hamilton's had a few drinks and is probably a little drunk by now."

"I know I'm stronger than him, but my leg is killing me. If I only had a weapon. "

Ginny whispered, "See if *Bishamon* is still around. He did Artie in. Maybe, he'll be able to take care of Hamilton, too."

"I'll look. Hamilton's behind the wheel. I'll try to get up now." Mark acted heroically in Ginny's presence, but he, too, was cold and frightened. He couldn't stay in the water much longer.

The rain was pelting the boat mercilessly. The wind was rocking it from side to side. Dangerous amounts of water were pouring in.

Ginny gave Mark a slight shove, and he fell into the boat. Fortunately, the thunderous downpour blocked out the sound of Mark's entrance. Quietly, Mark crept toward Kenneth Hamilton. Kenneth was completely involved in keeping the boat level and getting it to shore. He didn't hear the advancing Mark.

With a quick thrust, using his right arm, Mark grabbed Kenneth around the throat. A violent confrontation ensued. First one man was on top, then the other. They threw punches wildly. Mark was hit in the jaw. He felt wobbly. Kenneth came up to him, and Mark kicked him with his good right leg. Kenneth fell, only to get up again. They flailed away at each other. Kenneth picked up Mark's camera and hit him in the head with it. Mark immediately lost consciousness. Kenneth then dragged him to side of the boat and flung him overboard.

While this was happening, Ginny raised herself aboard. She was freezing and felt queasy and dizzy. She wouldn't give up. The pouring rain made it difficult to see, but Ginny became dimly aware of the Japanese doll about five feet away. She mustered all her strength and crawled to the doll. Ginny quickly picked up *Bishamon* and slowly advanced until she was next to Kenneth. "Take this, you bastard!" she screamed while smashing *Bishamon* into his face. Taken by surprise, Hamilton fell into the water along with the Japanese ningyo.

The cold water revived Mark in time for him to see Ginny force Hamilton into the water. Mark felt groggy and remained in agonizing pain. Undaunted, he grabbed the floundering lawyer and gave him a knockout blow to the jaw. Kenneth Hamilton didn't have a chance to utter a word. He sank to the bottom where he joined his buddy, Artie. Although they had planned it for Mark and Ginny, the sea swallowed up the retired lawyer and the retired dentist.

Ginny helped Mark get back into the boat. It was still pouring. They shivered but held each other in a loving, tearful embrace. After a few tender moments, they bailed out some of the water. When the boat was no longer in danger of sinking, Mark started the engine. Soon, they were heading for shore. The worst day in the lives of Mark and Ginny Procter was coming to a close, and they were both grateful to the Bass' for their gift of *Bishamon*.

It had been a little after nine on that fateful Wednesday evening when Mark and Ginny banked the boat and entered the fishing boat rental place. Between Ginny's partial knowledge of Spanish and the attendant's having a smattering of English, the gist of their close encounter with death was revealed. After inspecting the boat to ascertain that no serious damage had occurred, the attendant called a cab. The couple was driven to a nearby hospital where Mark's wounds were managed. Because the wounds were gun-inflicted, before discharging Mark, the doctor in attendance realized that it was now a police matter and he was required to inform the police department.

"Look," he said, "you told me that you were shot by a man intent on killing you and that he and his associate were drowned in the struggle. It's not that I don't believe you, but your wounds are obviously gunshot. The police will have to check that out. I can see how tired and shook up you guys are. I'll hold off until morning before I call the station."

"Thank you. I appreciate this," Mark said.

The doctor then told the couple the location of the police department in San José. Mark and Ginny then took a cab back to their B & B in San José.

After a fitful night's sleep, the couple awoke at 7:00 A.M. Following breakfast, they took a cab to the police department and told the English-speaking inspector, Franciso Ortega, the entire story. They even told him about the thug named Tony who attempted to kill Rudy Kennedy and rammed into their car in New Jersey. Ginny gave him the partial license plate number and told him that she believed the car was a gray Infiniti.

The inspector commented, "Dr. and Mrs. Procter you sound like reasonable people, but the story you told me is difficult to believe. From an examination of your wounds, I want to have my forensic people try to identify the type of bullets used. We'll then determine if a person who used the name Ron Wallace purchased a gun in Costa Rica that uses bullets of that caliber. I'll check out if you or your wife purchased any guns here. I'll also call the New Jersey authorities and make inquiries about this man named Tony."

"Thank you, inspector, but we did not purchase any guns," Ginny stated emphatically.

"I still have to check it out."

A few minutes later, a forensic team took impressions of Mark's wounds. Unfortunately, they had to first remove the bandages, which caused Mark a great deal of pain. He rationalized silently, *At least I'm alive. The pain should eventually go away.*

"I realize how painful it is Mark, but isn't it interesting they are using an alginate impression material, the same way we do for dental impressions?" Ginny asked.

"Right, and their also going to make stone models, using the same dental technique. The only difference is we look for teeth or teeth marks, and they look for bullet wounds."

"I hope they can identify the bullets."

"I'm no gun expert, but I think Hamilton had a popular kind of pistol. Identification might not be too much of a problem."

While the forensic experts were pouring up the models, Inspector Ortega, made faxes and telephone calls. He determined that Ronald Wallace had purchased a pistol in San José, but he didn't want the forensic team to know the type until they identified the bullets. The inspector received information that no guns were legally purchased by the Procters.

After making several calls to New Jersey, he found out that with Ginny's limited identifying criteria, the New Jersey state police had been able to pick up Tony, the thug in his Infiniti. His real name was Anthony Maciotti, and he had a long-standing criminal record. He was jailed for reckless driving and attempted manslaughter. Unfortunately, he escaped, but a few weeks later, he was found dead, himself a victim of murder. Inspector Ortega also received information about the malpractice trial, Dr. Rosner's apparent drowning, Rudy Kennedy's apparent alcohol-related death, and Kenneth Hamilton's retirement in Florida.

Once the forensic team had been able to identify the bullets, Inspector Ortega called Mark and Ginny into his private office. He said, "I'm sorry to have detained you for so long, but we had to verify your story. I found out that a person using the name, Ronald Wallace, purchased a Ruger 9 mm in San José, and the bullets used to injure you were from a Ruger 9 mm. That means we can be sure that he or his friend — the person using the name Noah Siegel — shot you in two different places in your left leg."

The inspector paused to clear his throat; he then added, "Whether or not you shot them in return, we have no knowledge. But until their bodies surface, if they ever do, no determination can be made."

"What are you going to do?" Ginny asked somewhat apprehensively.

"Since neither of you had a gun, I can only assume that Ronald Wallace intended to kill you. I can also assume that in self-defense, you overcame him and his partner and in the ensuing struggle, they went overboard and drowned. I will let you return on your regularly scheduled flight on Saturday. However, I have your names, addresses and telephone numbers. If the bodies resurface, and I find gunshot wounds on them, we'll call you back for further questioning."

"I guarantee you we didn't shoot them," Mark said. He didn't mention the *Bishamon blows*.

"If that's true, I will be pleased," the inspector said. "At any rate, I'm very sorry for your misfortune. I hope it didn't detract from your impressions of Costa Rica."

"Absolutely not," Ginny said. "I'm in love with your country."

"That goes for me as well," Mark added. "We'll tell everyone back home how beautiful Costa Rica is and that the people are overly friendly."

"I almost forgot. You'll be pleased to hear that your identifying clues were enough, Mrs. Procter to have the New Jersey state police pick up Tony, the thug. His real name was Anthony Maciotti. He had a long-standing criminal record and was jailed for reckless driving and attempted manslaughter. Unfortunately, he escaped, but…"

Before, he could finish, Ginny exclaimed," He was killed during one of his murderous undertakings."

"How did you know?" asked the inspector.

"Hamilton told us that when he and Dr. Rosner were explaining their dastardly schemes."

"Good. Before you leave, a doctor is on his way. He will redress your wounds, Dr. Procter, and give you any medication that is required. Have a good trip."

"Thank you," Mark and Ginny said in unison.

18

When they returned to work Monday morning, the newlyweds told the staff their tale of horror. During the lunch break, Mark had the unenviable task of calling Burt Rosner in Florida. Artie's brother was severely disturbed, but he thanked Mark for telling him and wished Mark the best. Gradually, the rest of the South Jersey community, including Kenneth Hamilton's partners, learned the gruesome details of the scheme pulled off by Dr. Artie Rosner and Kenneth Hamilton.

After Bernie Glaser found out the reason behind his son's comatose state, he was so shook up that then and there, he quit his equivocal way of earning a living. The family had more than enough money, and he assured himself that it was time to make the most of what life had to offer.

At midnight of Saturday, January 1st, the New Year arrived. By the time the sun arose, it became evident that his was going to be an atypical January day. At 8:00 A.M., it was already 50 degrees. The June in January weather was welcome throughout South Jersey. However, weather was not on the mind of the occupants of the Glaser home in Medford Lakes. With the help of nurse Bobbie Wise, Freddie Glaser had finished eating breakfast. Two hours later, physical therapist Rhonda Fletcher was exercising Freddie's arms and legs. Bobbie was watching close by. They were in Freddie's bedroom. He was on his bed, propped up by two pillows. Although it had been almost sixteen months since Freddie had gone into a coma, Bernie and Pauline Glaser had not given up hope.

Taking advantage of the surprising mild weather, Bernie had been on the golf course since 7:30 A.M. Ever since his self-imposed retirement, he had decided to partake of life's more pleasurable activities. Golf was one of these.

Pauline was home, reading in the library. Freddie was still inside that Black Hole engulfed in nothingness.

The moment Rhonda brought Freddie's right arm down to his side, she noticed his eyes had closed. She lifted the lids. The pupils were fixed.

"Bobbie!" she shouted.

The nurse came running over.

"Check his vital signs."

Bobbie felt for Freddie's pulse. It was absent. She listened to his heart and heard nothing. His chest was immobile. No air was coming out of his lungs. "Quick," she screamed, "call 911!"

Rhonda made the call. Pauline came into the room. She was frantic.

Combining their talents, Bobbie and Rhonda started emergency resuscitative measures. After three minutes, there was still no response from Freddie. They were about to give up hope of achieving any success when they heard the ambulance siren screeching. The vehicle was a couple of blocks away.

Freddie came out of the nothingness. He was still inside the Black Hole, but in the distance he saw the faint glimmer of a light. The spaceship was gone. He was now moving by himself effortlessly. The air was warming up as he approached the light. The light was getting brighter and brighter. It soon changed into many beautiful colors of the rainbow. The light was a mixture of red, orange, yellow, blue and violet. It was the most beautiful light he had ever seen, and he was being drawn to it.

Freddie turned around. The Black Hole was gone. He was completely surrounded by the brilliant, multi-colored light. Freddie looked everywhere. From all sides, he saw figures approaching him. When they got closer, he could see that they were small children with wings and halos. They were smiling at him. With the sweetest sounding voices, they called out, "Freddie, Freddie."

Freddie was not afraid. He felt wonderful. He felt better than he had ever felt in his entire life. The angelic creatures parted, and from their midst came a large man with a white beard. He was completely engulfed in light. Freddie was in awe. *Is this God*, he thought. *Am I dead?* he wondered.

"Come here, Freddie," the white-bearded entity called softly.

Freddie moved slowly toward him.

The emergency medical technicians gave Freddie oxygen. No response.

They injected adrenaline directly into his heart. No response. The paddles were prepared.

Freddie now knew he was face-to-face with God. He was sure he was going straight to hell because he killed so many of God's little creatures. *Why was I so mean?* he thought. He spoke to God, "Am I going to hell?"

God answered him, "Do you want to go to hell?"

"No, God."

"Will you change, Freddie? Can you become a good little boy?"

"Yes I can, God. I will change. I'll never hurt another thing again, not even a fly."

"I think you mean it, Freddie. I'm going to give you another chance."

The shorter technician applied the paddles to Freddie's chest. No response. He tried it again. No response. "We're not getting anywhere," he said to his partner. "I'll try one more time and then we'll head for the Emergency Room, but I don't see any hope."

Freddie left God, and he could hear the little angels saying softly, "Goodbye, Freddie, have a wonderful life." He was soon moving quickly back to Earth — this time without a spaceship.

The technician applied the paddles for the last time.

Freddie saw two men near his body. One had just lifted up two paddles. Around the men, he saw two women and his mother. She was crying. *Don't cry, Mommy*, he told himself.

The taller technician said, "Let's get him into the stretcher."

At that moment, Freddie opened his eyes, "Don't cry, Mommy. I'm back and I'm gonna be the best little boy in the whole world."

The first miracle of the New Year had occurred.

Even though Freddie Glaser miraculously recovered, the ambulance was obliged to take him to Mt. Laurel General Hospital to check him out thoroughly. Pauline Glaser paged her husband at the golf course. He called home.

"Bernie, you won't believe it. Freddie came out of his coma."

"What!" he screamed.

"It's true. It's a miracle."

"My God. I'm so happy."

"The ambulance is taking him to Mt. Laurel General to check him out. I'm taking Bobbie and Rhonda with me."

"I'll meet you there. I can't believe it."

In ten minutes, the ambulance pulled in at the hospital. Pauline Glaser and her companions arrived two minutes later. Bernie Glaser entered the Emergency Room parking lot, five minutes after that. Because the ambulance driver had called ahead, a neurologist was there to evaluate Freddie. Considering that he was originally involved in the diagnosis, Dr. James Conover, Chief of Neurology, would have been expected to be present. However, he was in San Francisco with his wife welcoming in the New Year. Instead, Dr. Jake Daniels, Mark Procter's friend and the neurologist who testified at Dr. Artie Rosner's malpractice trial, was on call. He was there to greet the child as he was resting on a bed inside the Emergency Room.

After a thorough examination, Jake Daniels was simply amazed. Freddie Glaser was completely normal. There was no sign of brain damage. His answers to questions were those that would be expected of a child of his age. Not only that, he appeared to have a complete personality change. The technicians told him that Freddie Glaser had been clinically dead, and when they had given up all hope, he suddenly awoke.

Jake questioned Freddie.

"Tell me what you remember, Freddie."

"I saw a shiny light. It became a lot of colors of the rainbow. It was real beautiful."

This sounds like a near-death experience, Jake thought. "What happened next?"

"I saw little angels. They called my name. I wasn't scared. I felt great."

"Anything else?"

"I saw God. I talked to him."

This definitely was a near-death experience, I know the pediatrician Melvin Morse has seen a lot of them with children. This'll be my first. Getting back to Freddie, he asked, "How did you know it was God?"

"He had a long white beard and he was all shiny like."

"What did you say?"

"I asked Him if I was going to hell?"

"Did God answer you?"

"He said, 'Do you want to go to hell?' I told him, 'No.'"

"Tell me the rest."

"God asked me if I could be a good boy. I told him I'd never hurt another bug or animal. God said he would give me another chance."

"What happened then?"

"I left God and the angels. It got weird. I saw myself on my bed with two men lifting up paddles. Mommy and two ladies were there, too. Then, I woke up."

He had the whole works, an out-of-body experience, too. Returning to Freddie, he said, "Good boy, Freddie. One more question."

"Yeah."

"What's the last thing you remember before you saw the bright light?"

"I was in a spaceship and it went into a real dark hole. The next thing I saw was the light."

He remembered nothing for sixteen months. Amazing! Holding Freddie's hands, he said, "Great, Freddie. You're perfectly healthy. You can go home, now."

"Thanks, doc. I'm going to be a real good boy from now on."

Two days later, Mark and Ginny welcomed in the New Year with Burt Rosner and Goldie Abrams by having a relaxing stay at a Boca Raton resort.

Reality returned on Monday morning as the Procters went back to work. The office was in full swing with Mark, Willie Chow and Kathy Perrin having full schedules. At exactly twelve noon, Phyllis buzzed Mark in his private office. He had a telephone call from Dr. Jake Daniels.

"Hello, Mark. How did you welcome in the New Year?"

"Hi, Jake. It was great. We were in Florida."

"How lucky can you be? I had to work."

"Someone has to work," Mark added with a touch of sarcasm.

"The reason I'm calling you is related to my working. You'll never believe what happened on Saturday."

"Don't keep me in suspense."

"You remember Freddie Glaser?"

"How could I ever forget him?"

"Three unbelievable things happened. The first was he died."

Upon hearing that, Mark responded with a severe knot in his stomach. All he could say was, "That's terrible."

"No. He came back to life," Jake said matter-of-factly.

Mark was confused and exclaimed, "What!"

"Yes. He was clinically dead when the technicians arrived at his parents' home. When they gave up all hope, he came back to life."

"Was he still comatose?" Mark asked.

"No. That's the second unbelievable happening," Jake answered.

"There was no residual brain damage. He wasn't a vegetable?" Mark questioned.

"Not at all. He was completely normal and perfectly coherent."

"That's incredible, Jake. What was the third unbelievable event?"

"He had a full-blown near-death experience. He saw the brilliant light, angels, God, and he had an out-of-body experience, seeing people surrounding his body. Not only that, when he awoke, he had a complete personality change. He became the sweetest kid you'd ever want to meet."

"How did that happened?" Mark asked.

"He said he had to promise God that he would be a good boy."

"Whatever works."

"I still can't understand it, Mark. When a person is in a coma that is induced either by a drug like nitrous oxide or asphyxiation, the coma is irreversible. What happened to Freddie is not supposed to happen. Only if someone gets into a coma caused by trauma, is it possible to come out of it without permanent brain damage."

"Did you say trauma?"

"Yes, but what does that have to do with Freddie Glaser?"

"Maybe everything, Jake."

"Now you've got me in suspense. What is this all about?" Jake asked.

"There were a few things that happened that were never brought out in the trial. One of them, I told you already. That is, the fact that Artie switched the tanks so that he deliberately gave the kid one hundred percent nitrous oxide instead of oxygen toward the end of the dental procedure. Artie assumed that Freddie Glaser became comatose because of the high dose of nitrous oxide."

"What else could it have been?" Jake asked.

"The two women had been restraining Freddie. Since he started to get into deep relaxation, Artie told the receptionist, Phyllis, to go back to her desk. While leaving, her shoulder inadvertently hit the x-ray arm. It swung and hit Freddie in the head. Artie checked the kid's head and saw no evidence of a wound or swelling. Consequently, he ignored the event. Neither Phyllis nor his assistant, Julie, saw the incident."

"Interesting." Jake said.

"There's more. At the hospital, your chief, James Conover, checked

Freddie out. I believe he noticed a small wound and swelling on Freddie's head, but he attributed it to a minor encounter during the ambulance ride to the hospital. The attorneys on both sides also knew about it, but everyone thought that it was an overdose of nitrous oxide that caused the coma. The result was the incident never came up in the trial."

"What you're telling me is you think Freddie's coma was, at least, partially trauma-induced," Jake said emphatically.

"It could have been. From what Phyllis and Julie told me, Artie immediately ripped off the mask as soon as Freddie's skin showed the faintest tinge of blue. Artie then gave him one hundred percent oxygen under forced pressure. He probably thought he induced a permanent coma with the nitrous oxide. Now that you told me Freddie came out of the coma unscathed, I'd be willing to bet that it was the trauma that was mainly responsible for the coma."

"Mark, you should've been a neurologist. It was a miracle that Freddie recovered, but the miracle was caused by an accidental encounter with an x-ray arm put in motion by a dental receptionist."

"Whatever the reason, we have to thank God. He allowed this minor miracle to occur, and He talked Freddie Glaser into becoming a good boy," Mark said.

Jake interjected. "That is if you believe that near-death experiences or NDEs, are spiritual encounters giving a glimpse of the early stage of the afterlife rather than just some physiological changes brought on by a dying brain."

Mark asked, "What do you think?"

Jake answered, "At first, I thought NDEs were explainable scientifically, but later I did a great deal of reading about them. It has been estimated that fourteen million Americans have had a NDE. The similarities among them are leading me to believe that what Freddie experienced was real. Someday we'll all find out."

"Mark said, "Hopefully, later than sooner." He hesitated for a few seconds and then added, "I thought of something else."

"What is that?"

"The irony of the entire matter is that Kenneth Hamilton and Artie Rosner committed dastardly deeds in order to get revenge, get rid of a bratty kid and make some money. The truth is the dastardly deeds turned out completely different than they had anticipated."

"In what way?"

"Rudy Kennedy, the one person they thought they had killed by the hired thug, Tony, caused his own demise by drinking himself to death. Tony also tried to get rid of us by ramming into my car when we were on the way to the airport. Tony missed out on that one."

"Right" added Jake, "or you wouldn't be talking now."

"That's for sure. The other major outcome is Freddie Glaser's coma reversed, and he became a good child. When it was all over, they didn't get revenge, they didn't get rid of a bratty kid, they hardly used the money, and they wound up in the bottom of the ocean."

"It just shows that revenge is a dangerous motivator," Jake added.

"You're right about that." Mark paused, reflected a moment and added, "In an ironical twist, Kenneth Hamilton and Artie Rosner accomplished something beneficial."

"What's that, Mark?"

"Freddie became a nice kid, and since his father, Bernie, retired, he can no longer swindle any one else out of money. One other thing, thanks to Artie, Ginny and I discovered a great place for a vacation, Costa Rica."

Jake smiled and said, "This shows the old maxim is true. 'Sometimes good can come out of bad.'"

* * * * *

Author's Addendum

This book is a work of fiction. What occurred to Freddie Glaser could not happen now and in the foreseeable future. In October 1998, the American Dental Association's House of Delegates adopted a number of guidelines for the use of conscious sedation, deep sedation and general anesthesia for dentists. These guidelines were published and distributed to the American dental community in the January 11, 1999 issue of *ADA News*. Coincidentally, on January 20, 1999, the program, *60 Minutes II*, (9-10 P.M. East Coast) on CBS television focused on three young boys who died after being deeply sedated or anesthetized with a general anesthetic in three separate dental offices. Deep sedation involves the use of intravenous drugs. This was not used in the fictional account with Freddie Glaser. For him, inhalation conscious sedation was used. However, the new guidelines specifically prohibit the actions that the fictional Dr. Artie Rosner did. The pertinent guidelines that Dr. Rosner did not follow are these:

1. Equipment:

A. Must have a fail-safe system that is appropriately checked and calibrated.

B. If nitrous oxide and oxygen delivery equipment capable of delivering less than twenty five percent oxygen is used, an in-line oxygen analyzer must be used.

2. Preoperative Preparation:

A. Inhalation equipment used in conjunction with combined conscious sedation must be evaluated for proper operation and delivery of inhalation agents prior to use on each patient.

B. Determination of adequate oxygen supply must be completed prior to use with each patient.

3.Oxygenation:

A. Color of mucosa, skin or blood should be continually evaluated.

B. Oxygen saturation must be evaluated continuously by pulse oximetry.

4.Ventilation:

Must observe chest excursion and/or auscultation of breath sounds.

5.Emergency Management:

Regardless of procedure, a positive pressure oxygen system suitable for patients being treated must be available. (In the story, Dr. Rosner did follow this guideline; that is, proper emergency management.)

In conclusion, if you elect to have conscious sedation with nitrous oxide/oxygen used for yourself or your child, make sure you go to a dentist who follows the guidelines set up by the American Dental Association. In addition, be sure that you inform the dentist of any possible complicating factor, such as Freddie Glaser's prior epileptic-like seizure in the story.

When used properly by trained personnel, nitrous oxide/oxygen conscious sedation is an extremely safe and effective procedure.

It had been believed that nitrogen and oxygen only came together as one part nitrogen and two parts oxygen to form nitrous oxide. In the 1980s, it was discovered that another compound of nitrogen and oxygen existed. It was shown that when nitrogen and oxygen came together in the proportion of one to one, nitric oxide was formed. At first, it was believed that nitric oxide was only a toxin and a component of smog.

In the 1990s, it was shown by the renowned medical researcher, Dr. Sol Snyder of Johns Hopkins University, that nitric oxide is formed in the body and works in at least four regions. In the heart, it controls blood flow. In the brain and central nervous system, it acts as a neurotransmitter and is considered to be responsible for brain tissue death that comes from a stroke. In the gastrointestinal system, nitric oxide regulates stomach contractions that move food through the digestive tract.

The most well known use of nitric oxide is its action in the penis, where it stimulates an erection. This led to the development of the drug, Viagra,® which helps the body release nitric oxide. Hence, it can be seen that both nitric oxide and nitrous oxide are compounds of nitrogen and oxygen that can either be beneficial or toxic. Following the well-known song, let us try to "accentuate the positive and eliminate the negative."

In the story, Ginny Procter, fell into the volcano at Costa Rica's Poás Volcanic National Park. In reality, this would be extremely unlikely since adequate safeguards are present to prevent such a mishap. My wife and I have recently returned from a vacation in Costa Rica. The country is just as it is portrayed in this book. In these days when fear of war and terror, and anti-Americanism are widespread, it is wonderful that such a beautiful and relatively safe country as Costa Rica is so close by. The vast majority of Costa Ricans are warm and friendly and like and appreciate America and Americans.

The NDE that occurred to the fictional Freddie Glaser is based on similar types that have occurred to numerous children and adults throughout the world. The subject of NDEs is thoroughly covered in my latest book: Morse, Don, *Searching for Eternity: A Scientist's Spiritual Journey to Overcome Death Anxiety.* Eagle Wing Books, Memphis, TN, 2000, pp. 35-76. Dr. Melvin Morse has pioneered the study of NDEs in children. His book is: Morse, M. with Perry, P. *Closer to the Light: Learning From Children's Near-Death Experiences.* Villard Books, New York, 1990. In addition, Dr. P.M.H. Atwater has written an outstanding book on children's NDEs; her book is: *Children of the New Millennium.* Three Rivers Press, New York, 1999.

Although the malpractice case described in this book is fictional, the stress engendered, the courtroom proceedings, the financial settlements, and the type of outcomes for both plaintiffs and defendants are based on fact. In this book, the defendant was a dentist. However, aside from the details of the malpractice scenario, the manifestations are similar to those that occur with physicians. Malpractice is now a major problem in the United States. In at least 17 states, physicians are either going out on strike, moving to another state or country, or leaving the practice of Medicine. President Bush even made recent television pronouncements about the problem (February 2003). On CBS TV's program, *60 Minutes* of March 9, 2003, the medical malpractice crisis was highlighted. Malpractice is a problem that must be solved if the health of our nation's residents is to be preserved.